ABNORMAL STATISTICS

MAX BOOTH III

D1496324

Copyright © 2023 Max Booth III
Apocalypse Party
All Rights Reserved

ISBN: 978-1-954899-14-8

Cover Art: Matthew Revert

Interior Layout by Lori Michelle
   www.TheAuthorsAlley.com

This is a work of fiction. Names, characters, places, and incidents either are the product of the author's imagination or are used fictitiously. Any resemblance to actual persons, living or dead, events, or locales is entirely coincidental.

No part of this book may be reproduced or transmitted in any form or by any means, electronic or mechanical, including photocopying, recording, or by any information storage and retrieval system, without permission in writing from the copyright owner.

ALSO BY MAX BOOTH III

I don't know who this book is for.

STORIES

INDIANA DEATH SONG

SOMEHOW YOU MAKE it to another payday.

The hotel casino comps dried up last night, meaning the three of you were looking at sleeping in the car again if some cash didn't turn up quick. Call it good timing. Call it luck. Call it whatever helps you forget about the situation. Of course, you wouldn't mind stretching out in the back seat, feet pressed against the window, body wrapped in a blanket like a burrito. Your fifteen-year-old body is just short enough to fit without feeling uncomfortable. Car sleep is the best sleep you ever get. But your parents, though—they disagree. Homelessness embarrasses them.

There's no long-term plan here. That much is clear. The three of you are like wild dogs, worrying only about the present day. Where are you going to sleep? What are you going to eat? Anything beyond that seems incomprehensible.

You check out of the casino hotel a little after six in the morning. Jessica and Louis, your parents, barely manage to squeeze all of your guys' belongings into their brown Oldsmobile. One more bag and they'd have to start using the bungee cord again. Otherwise, the trunk would blow wide open, spraying the street behind them with dirty clothes and empty bottles of methadone.

The Oldsmobile's muffler roars to life as you drift down the long, windy road leading away from the casino. You've never heard a car as small as your father's get so loud. Back when you still had a house, you and your mom would know when Louis was almost home from work before he'd even pulled onto your street. Neighbors gave him death stares and threatened to call the cops for noise pollution, but now none of you have neighbors anymore—only each other. And whoever happens to be renting the hotel rooms next to you at any given time. But those aren't the kind of neighbors you're supposed to socialize with, anyway. People check into hotels because they want privacy. Because they're trying to escape from something. Because there's nowhere else to go.

Louis drives under the white archway sign welcoming patrons to the area, which consists of two gambling boats, several restaurants, and a hotel. You glance out the back window and grimace at the bright red letters spread out across the sky from one end of the archway to the other.

BUFFINGTON
HARBOR
CASINOS

Then, to the right of the archway, a smaller sign resides above a row of hedges:

Majestic
Star
CASINO

You tuck your hand under your chin so your parents can't see and stick out your middle finger at the signs. Every time you see them, you feel sick to your stomach. It doesn't matter which direction you're heading. The dread never goes away.

"What are you doing?" Jessica says from the passenger seat. Puffing on a Virginia Slim. The only kind of cigarette you've ever seen her smoke. "Would you sit down? You wanna get us a ticket?"

You turn around. You buckle your seatbelt. You don't say a word.

Sometimes cops hide by the casino exit hoping to catch drunk drivers. That's what your dad theorizes, anyway. You wonder what a cop would say if you did get pulled over. A car jampacked with grocery store bags of clothes. A man and a woman and their fifteen-year-old son. Not even seven in the morning. How would your dad explain the situation? Would he tell the cop they'd lost the house due to unexplainable reasons and now lived in various hotels around Northwest Indiana? That they'd pulled you out of school since it was too much of a hassle for Louis to drive the extra half hour to Lake Station, drop you off, drive another half hour to the steel mill, work eight-to-ten hours, drive back to Lake Station, pick you up, then drive all the way to the hotel, only to repeat the same process the next day, and the next? What would a cop think about all of that? Would they drag you into the back of their squad car and dump you in the nearest orphanage? Child Protective Services would have a field day interrogating you, that's what would happen. They'd write books about your situation. You'd be the new poster child for how not to be raised.

You double and triple check the seatbelt. You remain facing forward. If the car gets pulled over, it will not be your fault. You rub your jaw and moan. Yesterday, you lost a tooth while tossing and turning in your hotel room. It felt loose, so you reached into your mouth and it simply fell out of your gums. Which doesn't make any sense. It didn't look like a baby tooth—and, besides, aren't you a little old for baby teeth, anyway? You asked your mom and she shrugged, said sometimes that happens. You asked her what you were supposed to do with it. She said you were too old for the tooth fairy. You asked if you should throw it away. She looked at you like you were an idiot for asking the question, like you should already know. You slid open the hotel room window and flicked the tooth outside. It landed somewhere in the bushes below. The rest of the day you kept sticking your fingers in your mouth, expecting to find the tooth still attached to your gums. It *felt* like it was there. A phantom tooth. A ghost haunting the inside of your mouth.

Up front in the Oldsmobile, Jessica says, "You don't gotta couple dollars hidden somewhere?" Directing the question to your dad, but the cigarette smoke that she blows out her window hits only you.

"What're you talking about?" Louis asks, amused. "What dollars?"

"Like five or ten. There's a McDonald's across the street."

Your dad chuckles and says, "In what magical land do you think I'm hiding this money?"

"Sometimes you have a little bit stashed away."

"Yeah, and you already *found* that." He takes his eyes off the road and glares at her. "Wanna guess which slot machine you fed it down?"

"Oh, fuck you." She blows another cloud of smoke behind her. You try not to cough too loud. Nobody seems to notice. "All I was asking for was a lousy five dollars to feed your son some breakfast. No reason you gotta be an asshole about it."

Your dad laughs and bites down on his tobacco pipe. "Yes, dear."

The moment he lights it, the scent of stale vanilla fills the Oldsmobile. It's almost as bad as your mom's Virginia Slims.

✶✶✶

Louis drops you off at the Gary Public Library fifteen miles from the casino, then heads off to work. Ever since Mittal acquired Bethlehem, the steel mill's gotten trigger-happy with write-ups and layoffs. He can't afford a minute of tardiness.

The library doesn't open until nine, which gives you and your mom a couple hours still before you can go inside.

INDIANA DEATH SONG

The two of you huddle together on the front bench with a small blanket draped over your laps. Every time Jessica blows a cloud of cigarette smoke, you match it with your own breath. Early spring in Indiana can be just as miserable as winter. The snow is mostly melted but the cold's made no indication of leaving any time soon. Across the parking lot, there are several tents and shopping carts set up in a field. Bodies curl against bodies, desperate for warmth. There's not that much separating you from them, you think. Except of course there is, and you feel ashamed for comparing yourself to them. At least you aren't sleeping in a field. At least you have the hotels. At least you won't have to worry about dinner tonight. Any one of the people across the parking lot would kill to be in your position. You try to remind yourself of this. Inside your head you repeat the mantra, *Life is okay, life is okay, life is okay . . .*

"This is bullshit," Jessica says, half-moaning against a new gust of wind. It feels like tiny knives against your faces. "No reason at all they can't just let us in now."

You say you don't think anybody's here yet.

"I don't care. It's still bullshit."

Your mom describes most things as being bullshit. It's hard to argue with the harsh whisper of Lake Michigan gnawing away on your bones.

You rub your stomach under your blanket and groan. Last night all you'd eaten for dinner had been a stack of stale lobby bagels your mom smuggled back to your room in her purse. She'd forgotten the cream cheese cups, so you'd just had them plain. Your dad complained the entire meal. Kept making these loud sighs between each bite and chewing louder than necessary. His own way of reminding your mom that she'd made a mistake, and he wasn't going to let her forget it. You know how your parents argue. They're as predictable as housekeeping knocking every morning at eleven forty-five. Later than other rooms because you've been staying longer than most guests. Their primary concerns aren't the stayovers but the guests who have already checked out. Otherwise, how could new guests check in if there aren't any rooms clean? It makes sense, then, that the housekeepers wouldn't get to you until almost noon. Your mom often complains about how late they show up, but that's only because bitching is her favorite pastime, and she's damn good at it. In reality, she almost never allows hotel staff to enter your room. Instead, she blocks the doorway and swaps out used towels for new ones and stocks up on toiletries. Every five days, by Indiana state law, the hotel is required to send somebody from housekeeping to clean the room. You and your mom wait down in the lobby and the whole time she's whispering paranoid concerns about sneaky maids with quick fingers pocketing things that don't belong to them. But you know the truth, of course. Your mom is a day sleeper. Housekeepers knocking on your door means she has to get out of bed. Most nights are spent down on the boat, gambling away what little remains of your dad's paycheck.

9:00 A.M. arrives. Inside, the library is warm and safe. The computers here don't require the PIN from membership cards, otherwise your mom would be screwed, since you can't get a Gary library card without a Gary residence, and technically a person can't claim to "live" at a hotel. Hotels are not apartments. Hotels accept *guests,* not *tenants.* According to your parents' Indiana IDs, the three of you still live at the abandoned house in Lake Station, which doesn't do you much good at a library in Gary.

One neat thing about libraries, though, is you only need a card to *check out* books. There's nothing stopping you from plucking something off the shelves and finding a nice comfortable chair somewhere in the corner of the building. Which is exactly what you do the moment the doors open, parting ways with your mom as she searches for an unoccupied desktop.

You try to frequent two different libraries whenever possible: this one, and the library in Lake Station. At the latter, you still possess a card, allowing you to check out long-form narratives like novels without fear of not finishing before having to leave the premises. But at the Gary location, you only mess around with short story collections and anthologies. Things you can begin and finish in one sitting. After twenty minutes of vigorous internal debate, you finally settle on *Books of Blood* by Clive Barker. This early in the morning, the library is still empty, leaving every chair and sofa free for you to choose from. You decide on a little recliner away from the eyes of staff and hide behind the thick paperback. The more you can lose yourself in this book, the less energy you have to focus on how empty your stomach feels.

Somewhere on the other side of the library, your mom spends the rest of the day entering internet contests and stepping outside for cigarette breaks. Even before you'd lost the house, she had always obsessed over these contests. And why wouldn't she? It's an easy way to gamble and the only thing she has to pay upfront is an email address. So what? Takes like three seconds at most to delete an unwanted spam message, right? She also seems to have more luck with these than she ever has with the slot machines. Once she won a giant flatscreen TV, which sold for a pretty penny down at the pawnshop. Not soon after that, she also won a lifetime supply of Pop-Tarts, which had lasted all of one month. When nobody was home, you offered free boxes to all the kids in your neighborhood. You weren't sure why, but it felt good, the way people thanked you. The next day, after discovering what you'd done, your mom shouted until her throat got sore.

Weirdly enough, since moving into the hotel, she hasn't won a single contest.

✱✱✱

After his shift at the mill, your dad picks you up outside the library and books it to Lake Station. The check cashing store tends to close earlier on Fridays. If you guys miss this window, you'll be shit out of luck until Monday.

At one point, on the highway, your mom complains that Louis isn't driving fast enough, so he slams his foot on the gas and starts dipping in and out of lanes to cut people off. You and your mom jerk along with the car's sudden motions like you're aboard an unreliable rollercoaster.

"Would you stop driving like a goddamn lunatic?" Jessica says, voice high enough to make your teeth hurt.

"I thought I wasn't driving fast enough for you," your dad says, using his knees to control the steering wheel as he attempts to light his pipe.

"Jesus Christ! You're gonna end up killing us. Would you *pay attention* for once in your goddamn life?"

Instead of wincing at the sound of Jessica's howling, your dad smirks and drives faster. "Now," he says, "what would be so wrong with that?"

"What are you *talking* about?"

Louis gestures to the opposite lane of cars beyond the concrete traffic barrier. "All it'd take is one flick of the wrist in the wrong direction and *bam*, we'd all be toast."

Your mom shakes her head, mortified. "Why would you even say something like that?"

"Wouldn't that be nice, honey? To end it all, right here and now?"

"Shut up," she says. "Just shut the hell up. You're not funny. You're not even close to funny."

But it *is* kind of funny. At least you think so. From the back seat, you yell for him to do it. You beg him to kill all three of you. Family annihilation. Hell yes.

Jessica glances at you from the front passenger seat. "What's wrong with you? What're you egging him on for?"

You ignore what's she saying and tell your dad not to listen to her. You tap him on the shoulder and suggest he does a *Thelma & Louise*.

"Which one of us is Thelma?" Louis asks.

You shrug and say his name is already pretty close to Louise, so . . .

"No way," Jessica says, shaking her head. "Your dad is Brad Pitt's character."

You ask why. Is it because he's a thieving drifter?

She pats him on the thigh as he drives and says, "Because he's *sexy*."

∗∗∗

The check cashing place is located in a tiny strip mall, squeezed between a pawnshop and a liquor store. Your parents join the line inside, leaving you a couple minutes to explore your old town.

Since you've moved into the hotel, whenever you return to Lake Station everything feels strange and surreal. Like any time spent here is borrowed energy from a forgotten dream. Over a year has passed since your world collapsed, but standing out here in the middle of the strip mall parking lot, you aren't so sure anyone's actually noticed.

Traffic passes on Main Street. Are any of these cars watching you? Are any of them thinking, *Wait a second, isn't that the kid who vanished last year? Isn't his family the freaks who abandoned their house and skipped town without so much as a goodbye?*

Of course, nobody's thinking that. Nobody sees you at all. You are a ghost. You could stride out into the middle of traffic and scream for help and the best outcome you could hope for is an instant transformation into roadkill. Your corpse would rot in the gutter for days before local businesses complained about the smell. Then the town would issue out someone on community service to come hose away the decay and that would be that, once and for all.

It sounds kinda pleasant. Like how people in movies talk up beautiful sunrises.

The pawnshop door chimes when you enter. A man with a brown ponytail and numerous neck tattoos peeks his head over the glass counter and glares. Sauce drips down his chin. He sets down half a gyro still wrapped in foil and sighs.

"Did you need something?"

You tell him no, that you just want to look around.

The clerk considers this request, then reluctantly nods. "Just . . . don't touch anything."

You thank the clerk and tiptoe toward the back of the pawnshop toward the video games and samurai swords. Did the guy recognize you? Before the hotel happened, you and your best friend Ian used to come in here all the time. Most CDs are only a dollar and sometimes you'd find old punk stuff like Dead Kennedys and The Misfits. DVDs are only a dollar extra, too, which is how the two of you had discovered gems like *Repo Man* and *Suburbia*.

When you live in a small town like Lake Station, no place is as interesting as the pawnshop. It stores an entire community's worth of junk. The stuff available to purchase here hadn't been delivered on some truck from a big city. None of this crap had been manufactured to be sold within these four walls. Everything here was previously owned. Most of it holds some semblance of sentimental value, only surrendered during bouts of severe desperation.

Like the Xbox 360 displayed in the corner of the game system cabinet behind the glass counter. The one with a half-shredded *Gears of War* skin. It'd once belonged to someone. Someone like you, specifically. Already a year has passed since moving into the hotel and still nobody has bought it. You view this as a good sign. If the system is still available, then you can still get it back, and if you can get the Xbox 360 back, then you can get everything else back, too. Things can return to normal.

You wonder if anybody's ever bothered removing the disc you'd left in the game tray, or if it's still in there, waiting for your return. Not a game, but a movie you'd rented from Hollywood Video. *Kiss Kiss Bang Bang*. At this point, the late-fee must be outrageous. It's the last movie you watched before the hotel. You remember how proud you'd felt, asking your mom to rent it. Just a random DVD you stumbled upon in one of the aisles. You read the back and thought it sounded great. Your mom made fun of you for wanting a movie with the word "kiss" in the title. You told her so what and reminded her of *The Long Kiss Goodnight*, and she couldn't say shit after that. The best part of the whole thing? The movie turned out to be good. Your parents laughed their asses off and congratulated you on an excellent discovery.

Now it was stuck in the Xbox 360, possibly forever.

One day you'll get the system back, along with the DVD, and you and your parents will watch it again in a new house and things will be better.

The pawnshop door chimes. Behind you, out of breath, your mom shouts your name. "Come *on*," she says. "We've been *waiting* on you."

∗∗∗

"C'mon, let me see it," your mom keeps saying, as Louis maneuvers the Oldsmobile out of the strip mall parking lot.

"See what?" he says, idling at the exit, waiting for his chance to merge.

"You know what. Cut it out."

An opening in traffic presents itself. Louis guns it forward in a straight line across the street, skidding to a stop next to the Long John Silver's. Just fast enough to piss off your mom. After he parks, she asks him the same question she's been asking since leaving the check cashing place.

"See *what*?" he asks, unbuckling his seatbelt.

"Would you knock it off?" she says. "How else do you want me to pay for dinner?"

Your dad smiles. "I'm perfectly capable of paying, dear."

Jessica mutters a dozen different profanities as you all make your way into the Long John Silver's and place your order. They like to go here on paydays because it's more expensive than McDonald's. It feels like they're treating themselves to something special. Most of the time they just pick up a couple double cheeseburgers in the drive-thru and return to the hotel, except none of you have eaten anything since yesterday. At this point, food has taken priority over shelter.

Your dad makes a big show of pulling out his wallet and paying the cashier. Jessica glares at him like she's contemplating homicide. You find a booth and sip a glass of water as you wait for the food to finish frying. Your mom's death glare has not dimmed. Louis chuckles at her expression and asks, "What's wrong, honey?"

"You're being a real cocksucker," she says. "Do you know that?"

You edge against the booth's wall divider, wishing you were smaller. Suddenly you are no longer hungry.

"No, Jess," your dad says, "I guess I didn't know that. Thank you ever so much for enlightening me." He clears his throat. "Although, I guess, personally speaking, as far as cocksuckers go, you'd know how to spot them. Isn't that right?"

You want to vomit. Can other people in the restaurant hear them talking? You should've just done the drive-thru. This is stupid.

"Nice language," Jessica says, then points at you. "Right in front of your own son. How appropriate."

Your dad laughs and pushes up his glasses using only his middle finger.

"Are you really going to be this way?" she asks.

"*What* way?"

"You know what. Just let me see it."

"Why?"

"What does it matter?"

He chuckles louder.

"I want to count it," she says.

"You know how much it is."

"Louis, goddammit."

They stare each other down, challenging the other to blink first. You watch them with a terrible feeling in your stomach. You want to get up and leave the building, but your mom is sitting on the outer end of the booth, boxing you in against the wall. There is nowhere for you to go. If they start finally killing each other in this Long John Silver's, you will be left with little choice but to witness the violence in its entirety—or, alternatively, *participate*.

Your dad breaks first. He always does.

He sighs and tosses a thick wad of cash on the table. Jessica grins and scoops it up, then nods toward the front of the restaurant. "Our food's ready."

"So go get it," Louis says.

"Can't you see I'm busy? C'mon, it's all gonna get cold if you leave it sitting up there."

He eyes her again, perhaps considering rebellion, then gets up and retrieves the dinner tray. When he returns, the money is in her purse.

"Well?" he says. "You done counting it?"

"Louis. Stop it."

He laughs. "Stop *what*? You said you wanted to count it. I'm asking if you did."

Your mom grits her teeth. "I did."

"And?"

"And what?"

"Was it all there?"

"Yes."

"Great." He holds out his hand, palm up. "Now give it back to me."

You grab a hushpuppy from the tray and nibble on it like a mouse. You don't even like hushpuppies all that much. They're bland and forgetful. Balls of deep-fried cornmeal. But there's something about the consistency that comforts you. Every hushpuppy tastes exactly the same. No surprises.

Except this time, when you bite into the hushpuppy, the texture feels strange, and you're reminded of the tooth you recently lost.

"Well?" Louis says, still waiting.

Your mom hasn't budged. "Can we eat, please?"

"Sure. Just as soon as you give me back my money."

"It's in my purse, okay? What did you want me to do, leave it out on the table for everybody to see?"

"Jess."

"What do you think I'm going to do? Just wait until we get back in the car. Jesus Christ. Let's eat, okay? Can't we just eat?"

He stares at her for a few seconds longer, biting his tongue. You know what he's thinking. That it's useless continuing the argument. That he's never going to see his paycheck again. The money's already in her purse. She's won. She always wins. It's why you're living in a hotel. It's why you no longer go to school or get to see any of your friends. It's why your Xbox 360 is still in the pawnshop along with anything else of value you'd once owned.

Winning is what your mom does best, second only to losing.

✳✳✳

On the same morning you checked out of the hotel, a man plummeted off the casino parking garage roof and obliterated his body against the concrete walking trail below. A maintenance man discovered what remained of his corpse while picking up litter. Without the driver's license in his wallet, it would've been impossible to identify him. Some gambler from the boat who bet everything to his name and lost it all.

That's what Jessica is telling you and your dad as you carry luggage into the elevator. She'd overheard hotel employees gossiping about the suicide while paying for a new room at the front desk. It's late in the evening and the previous shift had been in the middle of passing the news on to their relief.

"Who was it?" Louis asks. "What was his name?"

"I don't know. They didn't say."

"Can you imagine that? Freefalling from that kinda height." He shakes his head, impressed. "Sometimes, you know, people don't really mean to off themselves. They're just looking for a little attention, so they slit their wrists the wrong way, or take a buncha pills, tie a noose to something flimsy. But leaping off a parking garage?" He blows air out of his mouth. "Nobody's surviving some shit like that."

Another man in the elevator with you looks like he is going to be sick. "I don't think that's very appropriate talk for a child." He gestures to you, and you smirk, then lean forward and press the third-floor button. The elevator kicks into gear and starts going up.

Louis laughs and says, "Why? Don't you think it's important for my boy to know the difference between real suicide and cries for attention?"

"It's not a guaranteed death," the man says, avoiding eye contact.

"What did you just say?"

"Jumping from a building. Sometimes people survive."

"It'd have to be a pretty short building then."

The man shakes his head. Tears streaming down his cheeks. "My brother survived."

"He jumped?"

"Yeah."

"Jesus Christ," your dad says. "What was his problem?"

The elevator is still in motion. Somehow it hasn't reached the third floor yet. You press the button again. Harder this time.

"His *problem*?" the man says, and chuckles. "I couldn't begin to unravel a question like that, sir."

"But he didn't die? He lived?"

He nods. "Leapt off the Empire State Building some fifteen years ago. Landed so hard his legs stabbed into his stomach and his feet poked out of his mouth, but still he lived, still he screamed and begged to be put out of his misery. Toes curling around his teeth like he'd sprouted new tongues."

"No he fucking didn't," Louis says.

"I saw him do it with my own eyes."

"Then you need glasses."

The man turns toward Louis, offended. "I'll have you know, sir, that every eye doctor I've ever visited has congratulated me on my superb twenty-twenty vision. Once I was even presented an award."

"An award for what? Seeing good?"

"That's right. What's so funny about that?"

You press the button and this time hold it in place. Jessica pinches your shoulder—her way of telling you you're being rude. You ignore the pain and keep your finger against the button. It doesn't make any sense why you haven't reached the third floor by now.

"I don't believe you even have a brother," your dad finally says, still on this impossible elevator.

The man gasps. "I oughta take you down to the nursing home they stuck him in. He can't even talk without biting his toes. See how tough you feel then."

Louis laughs again and tells him he's a nut job.

The elevator doors open on the third floor just as the man balls up his fists. Instead of fighting Louis, he runs out in front of them and sprints toward the stairway exit at the end of the hallway. You're pretty sure you can hear the man sobbing.

✶✶✶

Your mom doesn't waste any time once you make it to the room, which is the same room the casino always seems to give you: 333. She pees and brushes her hair, then starts gathering her purse and cigarettes from the table. Louis glances up from the bed he'd sprawled out on only seconds previously.

"And where do you think you're going?"

She gives him a *what-are-you-an-idiot?* kind of look. "What do you mean?"

"You know what I mean."

She sighs. "Really?"

"Really *what*?"

"You're really gonna give me a hard time right now?"

"You wanna go to the boat, be my guest," he says. "But not until you give me back what you took."

"I didn't *take* anything."

"Where's my paycheck, Jess?"

She crosses her arms over her chest and taps her foot against the carpet like a cartoon character. "I *got it*. It's *fine*."

"Yeah, it'll be fine once you give me back my fucking money."

You roll over in bed and face the wall, waiting for them to finish this well-rehearsed charade. This is what happens every two weeks, like clockwork, Jessica talking her way into taking his check down to the boat, Louis pretending like he's actually going to stop her, only to surrender after a couple minutes of arguing.

There isn't a soul in this world who can out-fight your mom. You've witnessed her go head-to-head with cops, fast food cashiers, Walmart managers . . . it doesn't matter who, the moment someone disagrees with her about something—*anything*—they become her mortal enemy, and she will do whatever it takes to break them down to nothing. In most areas, Jessica is not an intelligent person, but when it comes to being the loudest, the most irrational, the most *conniving*, she is a genius, a pro.

Several outbursts later, Louis finally says, "Okay, but if you think I'm letting you leave me in this room while you go down there without any supervision, you got another thing coming."

She grins with the kind of satisfaction one gets after witnessing a fortune cookie come true. "Well then get your shoes on already, for crying out loud."

Louis groans as he climbs back out of bed. These long shifts at the steel mill do things to a human. You often wonder how your dad has the energy to do anything besides sleep after work. Yet here he is, nearly seven at night, getting dressed again to accompany Jessica down to the boat to make sure she doesn't feed his entire paycheck into the slots.

"We'll be back in a little bit," Jessica tells you.

"One hour," Louis says. "That's it."

You say okay without looking at them.

The door opens and slams shut. You wait all of three seconds before jumping up and sliding the deadbolt in place. Then you unlock and re-lock it another two times in quick succession, just to make sure it's functioning properly. You never know. Maybe not all locks work the way they're supposed to work. When you're alone, the door *has* to be locked. This isn't a rule your parents gave you or anything. Sometimes you just get paranoid someone from the hotel staff will barge in, or maybe another guest will be checked into the wrong room by mistake. Anything can happen. Hotels have never felt safe. They're unknown territory. People from all over the world check in and out every day. Some of them have to be murderers. Most of them are definitely psychos. One of your favorite things to do is read the "Lists of people who disappeared" and "List of unsolved deaths" pages on Wikipedia. Nobody on this planet is safe—especially in a hotel.

Back when you were still in school, a couple of your friends started going through puberty at the end of sixth grade or the beginning of seventh. Here they were, with hair on their armpits, hints of mustaches, voices deepening, and then here you were—some pudgy boy who sounded like a little girl. Not a hair in sight. No evidence whatsoever that you'd transform into a man. You weren't even sure you *wanted* to become a man, truth be told, but you certainly didn't want to stick out among a classroom of people already Going Through the Change.

The change didn't start until after your parents withdrew you from school. They signed you out two months before graduating seventh grade and never returned—with the false promise that they would now be "homeschooling" you. Later that year, in the winter, things started developing. Biologically speaking, at least. When a person spent all of his time in a hotel room, often alone while his parents gambled at the casino, he had plenty of opportunities to explore his own body.

With the door locked, you gather the empty ice bucket from the bathroom and hurry back to your bed. In high school comedies, the characters always watch internet pornography. You can't bring yourself to try this, at least not yet. The internet is full of viruses, and you suspect they're in abundance on porn sites. One of your deepest fears is downloading a virus on your PlayStation Portable (PSP) and being forced to ask your dad for help fixing it. What if he's able to trace the source of the virus? What would that conversation be like? You never want to find out.

The casino hotel doesn't have many channels. Maybe twelve at the most, and one of those seems to consist entirely of previews of movies available to rent. Not once during your time here have you or your parents rented a movie. The price is outrageous, and besides—as Jessica often assures you—this time away from your house is merely temporary, and you will be able to rent movies again once you return home. You've watched this preview channel more than any other channel offered by the casino hotel. You like to study the previews and come up with the rest of the plots in your head. It isn't that difficult, really. Most movie trailers hit the same beats, and they *all* give too much of the plot away. That always bugged you before the hotel, but now you find the spoilers greatly appreciated.

Usually every month, the previews are swapped with new movies, except for one particular preview that has remained in rotation since you moved here. It also happens to be the longest preview of the channel's selection, lasting nearly seven minutes. Not exactly a movie, either, more of a . . . documentary? What is *Girls Gone Wild* supposed to be, exactly? You aren't one-hundred percent positive, but you desperately yearn to see it in its entirety someday. Until then, you will have to be content with the seven-minute informercial offered on the preview channel, which only seems to air late at night. Even if you want to, you won't be able to rent it on the hotel TV. The only option available is to order the official DVDs by calling a listed number or visiting their website, which you are terrified of googling. You know perfectly well how to erase your search history on the PSP, but what if there's still a way to track it down, somewhere secret where the deleted items are buried?

At this point, the *Girls Gone Wild* infomercial holds a bizarre nostalgia. Last winter, while initially going through puberty, this very clip had been the first thing you'd ever masturbated to. Since then, you've repeated the action so many times your mind has started building up the preview's *universe* in a similar fashion as you've done with the other movie trailers. Only this one is a little more personal. You've assigned first names to all the girls presented on the screen. You can recognize them by the way they smile at the camera. After a while, it stopped mattering that black censor bars block their exposed breasts. It got to a point where even the GIRLS GONE WILD logo flashing across their chests was enough to turn you on. You're pretty sure you no longer need it to be playing to experience the clip. You can visualize every second of it with your eyes closed. Still, if it's available, why not let it play, right? What harm does that do? Isn't like the hotel can keep track of what channels are playing. Or maybe they can? You've never considered that possibility before. You assume they can see what you search for online, which is another reason you hesitate to explore internet pornography, but can they also tap into the TV? Are all the televisions in the hotel hooked up to one central database down in the lobby?

You quickly change the channel, out of breath, sprawled out across the bed.

Almost a full minute of silence passes before you flick it back to the infomercial and finish yourself off into the empty ice bucket.

You start wondering how long this video has existed. Since you've moved into the casino hotel, it hasn't updated. It's always the same group of girls removing their shirts. You wonder how old they are now. You wonder if any of them are still alive.

After rinsing the ice bucket out in the sink, you return to bed and channel surf.

Out of the other eleven channels offered by the Majestic Star Hotel, USA is usually the best option for stumbling upon a decent movie or TV show. As fate would have it, you've timed your ejaculation perfectly: a new movie is still in its opening credits sequence. Something called *The Truman Show*. You've never heard of it before, but you recognize the lead actor as the guy from *Dumb and Dumber,* so how bad can it be?

You turn off all the lights and curl up under the blanket, wondering if you should unlock the deadbolt in case you fall asleep and your parents return. Unlocking the door and going to sleep is an open invitation for anything in this world to come inside and violate you in any number of ways. Not just sex. You don't think anybody—or anything— would ever want to do something like that to you. But still. There are other ways besides sex to violate a human being. You do not intend on experiencing any of them firsthand. The door remains locked. You'll force yourself to stay awake until they make it back to the room. Hopefully this movie is exciting enough and you don't drift off. You can picture it now. Waking up a few hours later to the sound of your mom banging her fists against the door and screaming at you for being so careless. Asking you why in the hell you would lock the door knowing they were still at the boat. Never once attempting to understand your own reasoning for keeping it locked, never considering that you might have more in your life to be afraid of than pissing off your mom.

As it turns out, the movie is more than exciting.

It is terrifying.

***

They pulled you out of school in early May, only a month and some change shy of graduating seventh grade. In July you would turn fourteen. At the time, the idea was exhilarating, and you were fully on board. You hated school. And, most of the time, you got the feeling school hated you. You spent more time picking scabs in ISS than you did in an actual classroom. All it'd take was one wrong smirk and any of your teachers would kick you out into the hallway. You were considered a troublemaker. You were considered bad news. Both you and your friend Ian. Lost causes, the both of you. So, no. You didn't care when your parents decided to withdraw your enrollment. You encouraged it.

The plan was simple. Until the situation returned to normal and things were under control again, your parents would homeschool you, at least for the rest of the semester. It'd be easier on everybody, especially your dad, who couldn't deal with the extra driving before and after work five days a week. Later on, you'd wonder if your mom was nervous you'd let something about the hotel slip in front of your teachers. But, in the moment, all you could focus on was the fact that you were starting summer vacation almost two months early. After school that day, both of your parents were waiting outside. Your dad waited in the car and your mom led you back inside to the main office. The whole process was over in less than half an hour. You thought it would have taken longer to remove a student from school. You thought maybe someone would have been sad to see you go. Nobody cared. As the two of you walked out of the building, not a single person batted an eye in your direction.

It never occurred to you that you wouldn't return for eighth grade.

Or ninth grade, for that matter, which is the grade you should be in now, but you're still in the hotel, aren't you?

Not once have your parents attempted to teach you anything.

You don't know where this is leading.

You don't know if you'll ever go to school again.

You don't know if there's a future for you beyond this hotel.

You don't know if you'll ever see Ian. You don't know if he even remembers you anymore.

You don't know anything.

Sometimes you ask your mom what the plan is. Sometimes you ask her why you still haven't gone home. Sometimes you ask her if you're ever returning to school.

Usually, she doesn't respond.

Other times, she gets pissed, tells you to stop being such a smartass, and if you try pressing the issue she just starts screaming until all the sound in the world is swallowed and drowned.

You don't bother asking your dad. He knows less than you do. Or, at least, that's what he pretends to be the case. True or not, you know you'll get nothing out of him.

✶✶✶

Your mom doesn't like it when you go outside alone, and most of the time you obey her wishes, but once in a while you muster up enough confidence to revolt. What's she going to do? *Ground* you? Most consequences exist only within the realm of your own paranoia. Sometimes it's difficult to remember this.

You slip your shoes on, wiggle into a hoodie, and tell her you're going for a walk, you'll be back in a few.

"Fine," she says, still half-asleep from the previous night's gambling expedition. "Just don't talk to anybody."

You ask her who you'd talk to, and you're genuinely curious to hear her response. Nobody your age stays here. Casinos don't exactly encourage children to loiter on the premises. It's never been advertised as a place for families. It just happens to be where *your* family ended up.

"I don't know," she says. "Anybody."

You echo that last word back at her.

She shakes her head, no patience for an interrogation.

"They don't need to know about our business," she says, and rolls over in bed, promptly falling back asleep.

You consider further questioning her about what exactly your *business* even is, but you know it's useless, a waste of time—which is funny, of course, since *all* you have is time. When a person lives in a small hotel room with their parents, time behaves erratically. Days melt at the pace of a glacier. You once watched a TV show about someone in prison who described the time they were serving as one really long day. The same can sometimes be said about living in a hotel.

At the door, you grip the knob and wiggle it up and down three times in quick succession, then slip out into the hallway. Fortunately, housekeeping has either already hit your floor or they haven't gotten there yet. The hallway is absent of all other life. Behind the elevator, there is a small enclave for the laundry chute and ice and vending machines. You get down on your stomach and feel around under them for dropped coins or any other forgotten treasures. Once you'd found an unopened condom here and kept it for all of three hours before getting paranoid someone would catch you, so you threw it away in a lobby trash can where it couldn't be traced back to your room. You still aren't sure why you'd bothered taking the condom in the first place. What the hell would you've done with it, anyway? The idea of anybody ever entertaining the thought of having sex with you seems like a cruel joke. You aren't delusional. You know exactly what you look like.

You scavenge five quarters from the dirty carpet and buy a pack of lemon Zingers, which you devour on the elevator ride down to the lobby. Some snappy pop song plays on the overhead Muzak station. You don't recognize it. At this point, you are completely out of touch with what is new anymore. Life did not stop and wait for your family to get their shit together.

Sometimes you wonder if any of your old friends still think about you, or if they've already moved on. You've tried messaging a couple of them through Myspace on your PSP but the conversations tend to dry out before ever really taking off. The moment your parents withdrew you from school, you had become a ghost. Maybe sometimes, at lunch or in class, someone would do or say something that reminded them of once having a friend with your name, and they would go, "Oh yeah, remember him?" And, as time passed, more and more the answer would be, "No."

After all, what is a ghost if not a forgotten memory?

✳✳✳

The casino sometimes seems endless. Like how front yards must feel for ants. You hug yourself as you walk. Trying to warm yourself up. You make it less than half a second before unwrapping your arms. You're too fat to hold yourself like that. Someone might notice from one of the hotel room windows and laugh. Point down and say, *Look at this obese fuck, thinking he can fold his arms across his chest like someone who's skinny. Like someone who isn't completely pathetic.* So you dig your hands in your hoodie pocket instead and keep on moving. It's too cold to stand still for any significant amount of time. It's windy outside. It's always windy. The hotel's right off the shore of Lake Michigan. The wind here is fierce and often freezing.

To gamble in the state of Indiana, a person must first enter a gargantuan gaming boat. It used to be, apparently, the boat would have to sail out somewhere in the middle of the lake before any gambling could commence, but rules have changed, and now it's allowed to remain perpetually docked. You've never seen inside the boat. Either of them. There are two boats here. One is called the *Majestic Star Casino* and the other is the *Majestic Star II*. But that second boat has just undergone a name change. Up until recently, it had been called the *Trump Casino*.

You imagine, from an aerial point of view, the layout resembles some kind of stupid castle. To get onto the premises, gamblers have to first drive down a long, narrow, curvy road surrounded by wilderness and advertisements.

Then they have three choices. They can turn right into the five-story tall parking garage. They can continue straight and try their hand at the limited parking in front of the main building. This is also a good choice if they are simply dropping someone off or picking them up. Just park next to the front entrance and quickly do their business. The third option is they can turn left and park in front of the hotel. That's where your dad tends to park these days. There used to be a time when you still owned a house, and he'd have to find a spot somewhere in the parking garage. Now there is no need.

If a person continues into the main building through the front entrance, they'll find themselves walking past numerous gift shops offering discounted jewelry and other items that hold little interest to you. Unlike the boat itself, you are allowed inside this building, assuming a guardian accompanies you. Toward the back of the expansive casino lobby is the buffet room, which is probably the only good thing about this whole miserable place. Stir fry, crab legs, shrimp, fried chicken, pizza, endless cakes and puddings and numerous other desserts you've never heard of anyplace else like *crepes* and *ganache*. The food here is undeniably fantastic. You miss it more than you care to admit.

Recently, the casino decided to adjust its policy on who, exactly, can benefit from their complimentary buffet vouchers. Now, if a person is younger than twenty-one, they have to pay the outrageous buffet fee to gain entrance, which your parents refuse to do. Which means you will never step foot in the buffet again. Sometimes your parents still attend it, and your mom sneaks as much food as possible into her purse when nobody's looking, but it isn't the same. She can't smuggle pasta or pudding in a purse. Not without creating a disaster. Mostly you end up with stuff like cold fried chicken and crushed coffee cake. Anything she can easily wrap in a napkin without causing too much of a scene.

INDIANA DEATH SONG

Back before the casino screwed you on the new age limit policy, you can't recall seeing many other children enjoying the buffet. It makes you wonder if this new rule was created solely because of you. Had your presence here annoyed the employees so much that they felt the need to rewrite their entire terms and conditions? What had you done that was so wrong? Sometimes you imagine their conversations from the kitchen about the boy who ate more food than anybody else in the casino. The boy who ate more than they could keep up with. The reason the casino was starting to lose money. Every time you'd ever gone up to collect a new plate, you noticed how they looked at you, and you knew exactly what they were thinking.

Beyond the buffet room is an escalator that leads to the second story. Up here patrons can turn left or right. To the left is an overpriced coffee shop and an overpriced chicken wing kiosk. And to the right is the top of the forbidden ramp. Several guards can usually be found patrolling the area. To walk down the ramp, gamblers have to first present valid identification proving they are old enough to gamble. You do not know what the end of the ramp looks like. You imagine a short plank leading from the building into either of the two boats.

The inside of the boats is another mystery. You've never asked your parents and they've never told you. But you've seen enough movies about casinos to form somewhat of an idea. Movies like *Ocean's Eleven, Rain Man, Casino, Dodgeball*. They all have big casino scenes. Bright lights. Loud music. Drunken idiots. Coins spraying from machines like they have allergies. You never want to step foot in one. As far as you are concerned, there is no place on this earth worse than a casino. If you had things your way, they'd all burn to the ground.

The hotel and casino are connected by a long walkway enclosed by glass walls. The walkway ascends at the halfway point, forming a covered bridge. Strolling along it, gamblers have the option of two views. One wall faces the parking lot. The other wall provides a generous view of Lake Michigan and all its glorious waves. You like to stand in the walkway with your face pressed against the glass and stare at the water. It's nice in here when it's cold. The glass serves as decent protection from the wind, although the walls don't extend to the ground, leaving a foot-tall gap of empty space between the glass and the sidewalk. Stand there too long and your legs will get numb, which is sometimes a pleasant feeling too. If something is numb, then it can't hurt.

At the end of the covered walkway, gamblers can either enter the ground floor of the casino or branch off into an unprotected concrete path that circles the hotel. It also extends across the front of the casino and wraps around the parking garage. The trail doesn't lead behind the casino building. They don't want anybody getting too close to the boat. If the trail led back there, then a team of thieves could easily maneuver around the building and sneak aboard with grappling hooks or something.

You continue along the trail leading across the front of the casino, toward the back of the parking garage. Without the glass walls protecting you, Lake Michigan breathes its violent breath against your cheeks. A tall chain-link fence with barbed wire curling around the top of it prevents anybody from wandering too far off the walking trail. You loathe this fence. Sometimes all you want to do is discover what Lake Michigan actually feels like. Run your hands through the water and splash it against your face. But for some reason, the casino doesn't want you to feel the lake. Everything beyond the chain-link fence is forbidden. The boat. The water. The strip of jagged stones protruding from the mainland toward the desolate lighthouse way out there in the lake.

A *jetty* is what your dad had once called the stones leading to the lighthouse. You often spend hours staring out your hotel window studying that lighthouse. Assuming the day is clear enough. You don't think it's still operational. At least, you've never seen anybody enter or leave it since you moved into the hotel. Not once have you ever witnessed an actual light shining from the top, either. Which, what? Makes it abandoned, right?

Probably not much purpose for a lighthouse after bringing in a giant building with two gaming boats. It's never truly dark out here, not with all those casino lights flashing as bright as they do, as if they're trying to announce to all the martians in space that they are indeed open for business and that they will, in fact, never close.

These boats, they operate twenty-four-seven. There isn't a holiday in the world they'd shut down to observe. It doesn't matter what day it is. Nothing's sacred. All that matters, all that *truly* matters, is that the machines continue running, that the games never stop. People will always have money to piss away. They'll always have children to disappoint. Marriages to ruin. Lives to destroy.

In a way, you're relieved to live at the hotel residing next to the casino. Back when you had a house, your parents would still come here, only you'd be left home, which was a good half hour away, if not more. Maybe most kids would have treated the alone time like a vacation. Do whatever the hell they wanted. No parents to supervise, to tell them no. You wished you could have inhabited that sort of mindset. Instead, whenever your parents left you alone, you only found yourself pacing around the living room consumed by worry. The later the night would get, the sicker you would feel. Of course they never answered their cell phone when you called from the house phone. On the boat, cell phones don't get any signal.

Who else doesn't answer their phones? Dead people. People who crashed on the way home and no longer possessed the ability to move their limbs. People who you would never see again. You'd curl up on the couch, wrapped around a blanket, sobbing so hard your entire body would start sweating, just staring at the blank white wall across from the picture window, hoping, *praying* a set of headlights would suddenly smear itself across the surface.

At least now the constant worry that something would happen to them on the way home is gone. Other concerns are quick to take its place, of course. Concerns over someone finding out about your situation. Concerns over the situation never coming to an end. Concerns over this being the new normal, and anything you might have known before the hotel would forever be considered The Past—a place no person could ever return to again. Concerns over the government taking you away. Concerns over courtrooms and social workers and orphanages and tabloid headlines. There are always concerns. Eating holes in your stomach. Scrambling your brain. Making your skin itch and itch and itch. Sometimes it feels like too much for a kid your age to handle. Sometimes it feels like too much for anybody of any age to handle. Sometimes it feels like this is all there is. All there will ever be.

You push onward down the walking trail until you find what you're looking for. Behind the parking garage, between the building and the trail, the casino has allowed a small strip of grass to grow, along with various bushes and flowers. Halfway behind the garage, a small patch of grass has changed color since the last time you walked over here. It isn't exactly *red*, but red is the closest color you can think of to describe it. More like the grass has somehow turned to *rust*. The new color spreads onto a section of the walking trail, too, and here it's a brighter red, but still not quite the same red your brain is used to comprehending. You've seen blood before, sure, but never this much up close. Not outside of movies, at least.

It's the kind of mess only total annihilation of the human body can create.

∗∗∗

This is the spot. You've been obsessing over it since your mom told you and your dad. Wondering what it would look like. You'd feared all evidence of the suicide would be erased by the time you worked up the courage to explore the area. But here it is. As if it's been waiting for you all this time.

Slowly, you sit down on the walking trail, in the center of the stain. The old blood surrounds you on either side. Like a seal of protection from anything that might mean you harm. You can't believe this area isn't blocked off from the public. You thought for sure the casino would have installed some kind of barricade until they could get someone in to thoroughly clean everything. Maybe they don't care. Maybe sweeping up the corpse was considered good enough. The casino's priorities aren't what's happening outside the boat. It's the gamblers *inside* who matter. The ones actively offering up their paychecks as sacrifice.

You fold your legs inward and rest your elbows on your thighs. Your fingers and hands merge as one. You close your eyes and tilt your head upward, toward the sky, toward the roof of the parking garage. Is this meditation? You think so, but you aren't sure. It feels right. It feels exactly like the thing you're meant to be doing in this specific moment. Any other action would feel wrong— dishonest.

You keep your eyes closed as the wind from Lake Michigan explores your exposed flesh.

You keep your eyes closed and you listen.

This is what you hear:

Cars honking in the garage, in the parking lot, you can't tell where. Somewhere. Everywhere.

Seagulls. So many seagulls. Seagulls circling the garage, perched on the edge of the roof. Seagulls behind you, all over the shore. Seagulls in every direction.

Water. You hear water. Waves slamming against each other. Violent. Thirsty. You wonder what those waves would do to your body. How long you'd survive in the lake. Would it be over instantly, or would you fight back for a little while, spitting out water every time some of it tried to infiltrate your lungs?

You hear something else, too.

Whispering.

You hear whispering.

So loud that the source has to be right in front of your face, leaning down, mouth tongue-length from your ear.

Yet you can't decipher what they're saying.

It's a jumbled mess, like a sabotaged car engine, an out-of-range radio station.

You open your eyes and the whispering ceases and so do the car horns and the seagulls and the waves. Even the wind has paused.

There's nobody here but you.

Complete silence.

Time frozen.

You try to study the ledge of the parking garage roof, but the sun's positioned directly over it, as if it's trying to interrupt your investigation. What doesn't it want you to know? You stare anyway, not caring if the sun melts your eyeballs from their sockets. *Just try me,* you think, wishing it happens. Praying it happens.

The man who killed himself, that's where he jumped. Climbed up on that ledge and stepped off. You wonder what part of his body connected with the ground first. If it was you, you'd go headfirst. Smile the whole way down. Pucker your lips just before hitting the pavement. Your first and last kiss. The more you think about it, the more romantic it sounds.

Why did he jump? And who was he? These are the questions you haven't stopped asking yourself since Jessica gossiped about the suicide in the hotel elevator. You need to know his name. His identity being a mystery is unacceptable. It feels like an itch you can't scratch. The longer you obsess over it, the stronger it becomes. It's the kind of itch you simply can't *forget* about. It is here to stay. The only solution is to scratch, and keep on digging until your nails hit bone.

Breathe in.

Breathe out.

Time resumes.

The breeze welcomes you back.

The horns return. The seagulls return. The waves return.

But the whispering does not. It's gone, if it ever existed in the first place.

You don't know how long you sit on the bloodstain. You don't have a way to tell time. At some point, the sun shifts position and it's no longer blinding the parking garage. By then, though, you've lost interest in the roof. Your investigation has now led you toward the bushes and flowers planted behind the garage. Evidence of the man's suicide has spread from the walking trail through the grass and into these flowers. You think maybe the police missed something over here. You think it's possible whoever was assigned the case got lazy and didn't look under these flowers. They aren't as smart as you. That's how you know to always look for coins beneath vending machines. People don't bother searching somewhere if it's going to be an inconvenience.

You kneel and spread the flowers apart. You lift bush branches and poke your head beneath. Sniffing, listening, searching. Using all your senses. There is something here. You know there is. The blood guided you to this spot. The suicide man left it for you. Whatever it is, he hid it so nobody else would find it. He knew you would come here. He knew you would keep his secret safe.

You crawl into the bushes, deep enough that you disappear. Someone could walk by right now and have no idea you're here. How thrilling that would be. To watch someone so close without them knowing. To see what they do in private. To see how they behave. To see the real them.

But nobody comes. It's just you.

When you try to crawl out of the bushes, your hand connects with something more than just dirt. At first, you think they're rocks. But something about the surface of them, the way they're chipped, it makes you second-guess your assumption. You blindly scoop up a handful of them and exit the bushes. You're out of breath and embarrassed about it, but you're still alone, there's no one here to witness the fat kid wearing himself out in a flowerbed.

You sit in the dirt and open your hand and stare at the rocks you've collected.

Only they aren't rocks.

You already knew that, though, didn't you?

What else is smooth and hard like this?

What else is white?

White and stained pink.

You're holding a handful of someone's teeth.

And not just someone's.

The suicide man.

You've found his secret.

Another hour passes as you thoroughly comb through the flower bed, collecting any teeth you come across and storing them in your pocket. By the time you give up, you've found ten of them.

Ten teeth.

Bloody, chipped, jagged.

These were once in someone's mouth. Someone's jaw.

A jaw that must've exploded upon impact. Sent pieces of the man scattering in every direction. Everything else the police or the seagulls must've scavenged by now.

But not these teeth.

These teeth belong to you now.

You return to the hotel room thinking, *This is the greatest day of my life.*

✱✱✱

Before the hotel, there was a house. You grew up in that house. The first thirteen years of your life, anyhow. You'll never forget the street address as long as you live. 3030 Old Hobart Road. You'll forget the zip code. You'll forget the housephone number. You'll forget where laundry was stored. You'll forget what day of the week the trash truck did its pickups. You'll forget the face of your mailman. You'll forget the names of your neighbors. You'll forget so, so much. But you'll never forget the address.

The winter before you lost the house, the ceiling collapsed. Not all of it, of course. But a decent chunk of the ceiling in the living room, which was where the three of you always slept. The house was big enough to have bedrooms, yes, but from your earliest recollections, none of them had ever been inhabitable. Maybe when you were little, before you could grasp onto memories.

You wouldn't learn the word "hoarder" until after moving into the hotel and seeing that stupid TV show on A&E. Back then, when you were still living on Old Hobart Road, you didn't know *how* to describe the living situation. You knew it was atypical. Other kids in your class had their own bedrooms—or so they claimed. Your friend Ian had a bedroom. You knew that for a fact. You'd slept there on numerous occasions. It was real. So why didn't you have one, too?

According to your mom, you *did* have a bedroom, and so did your parents. Yeah, true, the rooms technically existed, but that didn't mean any of them were in any shape to sleep in, much less *enter*. You struggle now to remember what exactly had occupied each room. Clothes, absolutely. Piles and piles of clothes nobody had worn in years. Where did they all come from? Magazines, too. So many magazines. Magazines that were published before you were even alive. Boxes of junk. Literal garbage. Things your mom had won through internet contests that the pawnshop held little interest in purchasing. Exercise equipment you'd never witnessed anybody use. So many paperbacks. Books everywhere. Books that taught you how to read. Dozens of Stephen King novels. You tried to read them all. You might have succeeded. You can't remember anymore. It's all a blur.

One of the rooms was eventually designated the shit room. The family room is what your parents used to call it.

Different from the living room, somehow, but you don't know why. There was a big credenza in the family room. Every shelf contained outdated electronics. The furniture consisted of a ripped sofa and the backseat of a van your dad used to drive. It was called the shit room because that's where your dog always shit. After so long, everybody stopped trying to pick it up. Maneuvering through most of the rooms in your house was like entering a minefield. It was easier just to leave it. Nobody ever went in there, anyway. Eventually, the smell got so bad nobody *could* go in there without gagging, so they simply didn't. Surrendered the family room to your dog. Someone nailed a bed sheet over the doorway, leaving enough of it loose at the bottom for your dog to walk through without any trouble. It became her new toilet.

You don't want to think about your dog right now.

Before the hotel, this was where you lived. All three of you, cooped up in the living room every night. Almost like a practice run for what awaited you afterward. But at least back then you could leave the house and visit friends. You weren't *stuck* on your property. You could wander Lake Station. You could explore the woods with Ian and set things on fire. You could sleep over at his house and watch funny videos on YouTube. Now you don't have that expanded freedom. Every day you wake up in the hotel and every night you go to sleep in the hotel. If you do leave the room, you aren't going very far. Beyond the parking lot and walking trail is a highway and that's it.

There is nothing for you here, and there never will be. You don't belong here.

Nobody belongs here. It is a bad place. An evil place. And yet . . . somehow, this is your home.

And there is nothing you can do about it.

★★★

You wish you'd never watched *The Truman Show*. For someone in your particular situation, it's probably the worst movie that could have ever broadcasted on the hotel television. It's difficult not to wonder if it was intentional. If somehow someone had known you were alone that night and that you'd be channel surfing at that exact moment. Had the movie served as some sort of message? You can't rule it out.

But ever since that movie, things haven't quite been the same. The situation hasn't changed. You're still living in the hotel. You're still spending most evenings alone while your parents do whatever it is they do next door at the boat. But now you don't feel . . . *alone*, which should be a good thing, but it isn't, it's far from a good thing. Because if you aren't alone . . . then who else is here? As far as you can tell, there's *nobody*, yet that feeling remains . . . and it's only growing stronger every day—the feeling that someone's watching you. But how? A hidden camera, maybe. Multiple cameras, most likely. Just like in *The Truman Show*. They had that guy's entire life on video—cameras planted everywhere he went, tracking him down, streaming his every action to millions of viewers.

Maybe that's why the casino hotel only has twelve channels. Nobody wants to risk you accidentally stumbling on *your* channel. It'd be a nice twist in the show, sure, but once you have your protagonist staring at himself on television, there's no returning to regular programming. The series changes forever, and now it has a ticking clock on its runtime, because sooner or later the hero's going to figure out what's going on and finally put a stop to it.

You don't think any of this began as early as it did for the guy on *The Truman Show*. His show premiered with his birth, right? That doesn't feel right for your situation. Instead, you think, this most likely started with the hotel. It's probably the *reason* you're living in a hotel. Some coked-up television producer thought it'd be a hilarious idea if they removed a child from society and stuck them in one room for . . . how long have you been here now? Has it already been two years? When was the last time you checked the day's date? You can't remember anything. You wish one of the producers of your show would step on set for a moment so you could ask how long you've been on the air, but you suppose that would defeat the show's purpose.

You wonder how they picked you. Out of every kid in America, why you were targeted. How much are they paying your parents to keep this a secret? And how much of it are they recycling back into the casino every night? Assuming the casino's real. Maybe they're seated backstage, watching the show with the rest of the country.

And what is it they're all witnessing?

What kind of content have you been giving your audience?

Masturbating into ice buckets. Crying into your pillow. Pacing the hotel room from one end to the other. Furiously scratching at your flesh until drawing blood. Refreshing your old classmates' MySpace pages on your PSP hoping at least one of them will post something about you and trying not to wonder why none of them have included you on their top eight friends. Not even Ian has you ranked on there anymore. He's moved on. They've all moved on.

This can't be an exciting television show for people. If anything, it's just a bummer. It's depressing. Depressing, and . . .

Boring.

You can't understand why so many people would possibly tune in every night for something so goddamn tedious.

Nothing new happens on this show. Every episode is exactly the same. Why haven't you been cancelled yet? Unless you *have* been and nobody thought to let you know. This could all just be dead air. There might be cameras zoomed in on you right now, but are they actually *filming* anything?

Are they even watching?

Yes.

The certainty is alarming, but you can't deny it.

Someone is watching you.
Right now.
At this very moment.
They are watching.

***

A few months ago, you had to go get a blood test done. Your parents didn't tell you why. All you knew was your dad had experienced some recent complications with his own blood work and now both you and your mom had to get tested, too. You'd never had your blood taken before. At least not that you could remember. You didn't think it would be that big of a deal. You were wrong.

The moment you saw red liquid shoot up the IV and start filling the vial, all sense of calm went out the window. It wasn't so much that you were afraid of needles. It was something else. Something more biological, something . . . *primal.* Something that belonged inside your body was now being removed by an outside force. Nothing about this felt natural. You were being violated. They were *stealing* from you. Pumped dry of the one thing that you needed to stay alive.

You don't remember fainting. It just happened. One second you were staring at the IV in your arm, sucking up blood, then you were looking up at the ceiling, neck cranked back, drenched in sweat. The nurse stood above you, snapping her fingers and repeating your name. You sat forward and asked what happened. They told you. Then they stood there and waited for you to do something. You weren't sure what someone was supposed to say after they fainted, so you just said you were sorry, and they nodded, like that's exactly what they'd been waiting to hear all this time.

The whole incident was embarrassing. Nobody brought up the fainting again at the doctor's office, but you could tell it was what everybody was thinking about for the remainder of the visit. They were thinking about it because *you* were thinking about it, and they knew you were thinking about it. They could read it across your face. It was all you could focus on. Nothing else they said registered. You were too concerned about fainting again. It didn't matter that they were done drawing blood. Maybe now that you'd fainted once, you'd start doing it more frequently, with or without bodily liquids being removed from your insides.

A couple days later, you stopped thinking about the doctor's visit. Other things entered your field of concentration. A new video game for your PSP. New movies added to the hotel TV's rotation. On the Wikipedia page for Pornography, you found a black-and-white video of a woman removing her bra and shaking her breasts. For a while, that was all you could think about. You'd completely forgotten someone had taken your blood.

Until the afternoon your parents returned to the hotel and asked you to sit at the desk. Your dad wouldn't look at you. Just stood in the corner of the room, staring out the window above the air conditioning system and lighting his pipe over and over. Your mom was the one who broke the news. She sat on the edge of the bed opposite the desk. Her eyes were wet and her hair was a mess. She'd been crying before they walked through the door and she was crying now. This was something major. You didn't know how to prepare. You weren't scared. You knew you *should've* felt scared but you just didn't. The whole moment felt distant, like it wasn't happening to you but someone else, and you were watching it all unfold as a mere spectator.

Hepatitis C.

That's what your mom said you had.

Not just you, but her and your dad, too.

All three of you.

She asked if you knew what that meant and you nodded even though you didn't have the slightest clue. Except that it was bad. Something to do with your blood. It was tainted. Poisoned somehow. A disease? But what did it do? Your mom didn't explain it. She couldn't control herself.

You asked how you guys had it, and she shook her head and said she didn't know, that nobody could make any sense of it.

Later, after your parents fell asleep, you'd google hepatitis C on your PSP's web browser and read everything there was to know about it.

It was pretty obvious how the three of you could've gotten infected. Your mom and dad must've known, too, but were too afraid or embarrassed or maybe a little of both to admit the truth.

Before you were born, they once confided in you, your parents had been addicted to heroin. That's why every two weeks they drive down to Chicago at 4:30 in the morning. That's the time the methadone clinic opens. Methadone replaced the heroin. Another drug, but nowhere near as bad as the other stuff they used to do. An opioid substitute. You've known about this for a couple years now. You don't judge them. If anything, you're proud that they got help and stuck with it.

But if they think their years of heroin abuse isn't the cause of their hepatitis diagnosis, then they are in deep denial.

It's a denial you can understand.

Because that would mean you were born with it and had been living with the disease eating away at your liver for the entirety of your existence. All because of their previous addiction. Their life choices. According to what you read online, mother-to-child transmission of hepatitis C occurs in fewer than ten percent of pregnancies. Which makes your situation rare. A crooked middle finger to the statistics.

It'd be easier not to think about it—for everybody involved. To ignore the problem. Which is what they chose to do, after the diagnosis returned positive for all three of you.

It's no longer discussed.

Cataloged away with all the other things nobody in your family is allowed to bring up.

Like what happened to the house.

Or what happens to your dad's paycheck every two weeks.

Or how come you're still living in a hotel.

Or what happened to your dog.

If nobody talks about it, then it's not a problem.

✳✳✳

Your dad is yelling your mom's name. It's late. You don't know what time it is. You keep the blanket over your face and pretend to still be asleep. He's yelling her name, but not full-on shouting. It's more like a loud whisper.

"*Jess! Jess! Jess!*"

Your mom's wet snores crash to a halt, replaced by a single disgusting *snort* as she awakens and says, "What? Jesus Christ, what do you want?"

"You wanna go buy a new car?"

"*What?*"

"A new car. Let's go buy a new car."

"Would you stop it?"

"Stop what? Didn't you win big? You don't got enough to buy a new car now? Because that's not what you said earlier."

"It's the middle of the goddamn night. Would you fucking stop it already? Jesus."

Your dad chuckles. "Sure thing, honey. Whatever you want."

They both go back to sleep.

You wait under the blanket for their snores to resume. You squeeze your fingers into a fist around one of the suicide man's teeth. You don't remember falling asleep holding it, but you must've, otherwise, how did it get here? The jagged points of it dig into your palm. It feels relaxing. This tooth once belonged to someone else and now it belongs to you. You're used to it working the other way. Strangers owning what you once possessed. Things your parents pawned to refill the gas tank or keep the lights on, back when you had lights to keep on.

The rest of the teeth are somewhere safe. A secret stash hidden where housekeeping won't find it should they force their cleaning cart through the door. It's better to focus on one of them at a time, you've learned. Any more and you feel overwhelmed. With one tooth, you can really study what makes it unique from the others. The dents, the texture. Every tooth is different. They might look the same from afar, but you've had time to go over each one recovered from the death scene, and now you understand the truth.

Every tooth tells a story.

Still under the blanket, you carefully wedge the tooth between your lips and wrap your tongue around it. It's a dangerous game, doing this while flat on your back. If you fall asleep again, you might end up choking on the tooth. Dangerous and exciting. There's no point in playing it safe. The threat of it accidentally getting lodged into your throat only improves its taste.

You didn't wash the teeth after smuggling them into the hotel room. Scrubbing the blood stains away felt too dishonest. Like how they brush the dust off dinosaur bones in museums. The dust is natural, and so is the blood.

You don't remember why you started sucking on the teeth. The memory of the first incident is lost, hazy. You also don't know why you continue to do it. They do not taste pleasant. But, then again, the point of this process isn't to feel good. Nor is it to feel bad. The teeth are more meaningful than either of those definitions. Their significance is incomparable to anything you've ever experienced.

When you suck on these teeth, you taste more than simple flavors. You *learn* things. You understand truths.

Truths about the man who killed himself.

You know what he looked like.

Inside and out.

You know about the limp in his left leg. You know about every cold he'd ever recovered from. Every heartbreak. You know he was a tall man. You know he was overweight. You know most of his family was already dead, and what little remained had cut off all contact long before he killed himself. He was an unlikable man and he knew it, just as you know it.

But how do you know it? How do you know *any* of this? You've never seen a picture of him before. You don't know his name. Yet, the longer you explore these teeth with your saliva, the more access you gain to his subconscious. It's as if his body expired and everything else latched onto his discarded teeth as they ejected from the mouth, like ship-wreck survivors grasping the last unoccupied raft in the middle of the ocean. You're suckling the leftovers. The hand-me-downs.

When you drift back to sleep tonight, you will dream someone else's memories. You will time travel through another person's past. A hitchhiking voyeur practicing a bartering system centralized on the loose teeth of suicide victims. You will wake up rich.

✷✷✷

The next night that you're alone, you lock the hotel room door three times and research hepatitis C on your PSP's web browser. No. That's a lie. First, you masturbate into the ice bucket. Then you rinse it out. Then you begin your research. The Mayo Clinic website lists the following symptoms for those infected with the disease: bleeding easily, bruising easily, fatigue, poor appetite, yellow discoloration of the skin and eyes (jaundice), dark-colored urine, itchy skin, fluid buildup in your abdomen (ascites), swelling in your legs, weight loss, confusion, drowsiness, slurred speech (hepatic encephalopathy), and spiderlike blood vessels on your skin (spider angiomas).

Some of these symptoms describe yourself. Some don't appear to have anything to do with your condition. Weight loss is not a symptom anyone in your family has ever experienced—not in your lifetime, anyway. Spiderlike blood vessels sound terrifying, but thankfully aren't apparent on your skin. At least not yet. Things could change, you know. Things could change so quickly. Look at how much time passed between your house losing electricity and your parents withdrawing you from school. Barely any time at all.

Sometimes you bleed easily. When the hotel room feels smaller than it actually is, you like to scratch your stomach and inner thighs with your overgrown fingernails until you see red. The blood doesn't last long, but it *does* make an appearance. Sooner or later, the blood always comes.

You don't know about the yellow skin. Jaundice is the name for it. Icterus is another. Supposedly the white of your eyes get yellow, too. There are photos online that make you want to cry. They don't look like *Simpsons* characters but they don't look *not* like them, either. Every day afterward you spend at least five minutes studying yourself in the mirror, wondering when your skin's going to start looking more diseased. Wondering when the jaundice is going to finally get you.

This is how you're going to die, you decide. It might not be soon, but it will eventually be the cause of your demise. The hepatitis will destroy your liver. Cirrhosis will possess the organ and gnaw away until there's nothing left to scar. It's not the most exciting way to go out, especially for someone who might be the star of a twenty-four-seven television program, but that's the reality of the situation. Few people on this planet are gifted glimpses into their own futures. Thanks to your parents, you've received exactly what so many others waste their lives trying to predict. Knowing doesn't seem to change anything. You're still stuck in the hotel. You're still fourteen, or maybe you're fifteen now. It's so hard to keep track of what year it is anymore. It doesn't matter, anyway. The date means nothing when you're surrounded by four walls day and night, night and day. It's all just one long minute, isn't it? The clock broke before you were born and nobody thought to ring a repairman. It's going to remain nonoperational until . . . until . . . well, that's for someone else to figure out. You'll be long dead by then, thank god.

✳✳✳

The casino gifts your mom a comp for the chicken wing kiosk that resides at the top of the ramp leading down into the boat. Your parents load up on chicken and cups of ranch dip and return to the room. The three of you feast. Your mom and dad eat on top of their bed and you eat on top of yours. Crumbs get lost in the sheets, but it doesn't matter. In a couple days housekeeping will force themselves in and change out all the linen. Until then, you don't mind sleeping on bits of old food. You've slept on worst.

On television, the USA Network airs several reruns of *Monk* and *Psych* back-to-back. They're the only two shows this channel ever seems to broadcast. The volume on the TV is so loud yet somehow it doesn't drown out the noise of your parents greedily sucking meat from bones. Wet slapping noises infiltrate your eardrums and you try not to gag but it's impossible.

Before dinner, your dad had taken off his shirt so your mom could squeeze tiny bits of metal out of his back, which is a common side-effect of working in a steel mill. After she finished, she didn't wash her hands. These are the same fingers you witness her lick clean now while watching television.

You rush to the bathroom and lean over the toilet and open your mouth and you think, *here it comes*, and a tiny chunk of *something* shoots out of your throat and splashes into the water, along with several helpings of thick phlegm.

You stay hovered over the toilet, staring at the object floating below you, then reach into the water and scoop it up.

It's a tooth.

One from the man who had jumped off the parking garage roof.

You don't remember swallowing it.

You don't remember a lot of things.

You set it back on your tongue and run the sink faucet and curl your lips around its cold steel and drink until the tooth has fled somewhere deep inside you again.

It's back where it belongs.

✱✱✱

Sometimes you sit on the ledge of the room's window, legs dangling along the side of the hotel, and try to build up the courage to jump.

There are a few things stopping you.

For one thing, you are a coward.

It takes courage to kill yourself. Courage you do not possess.

Is your room high enough from the ground to do the job, or would it leave you only half-dead? Paralyzed and catalogued away in some hospital for the rest of your very long, very mundane life. Guaranteeing that life sentence of isolation you fear every day you wake up in the hotel and nothing new has happened. Except now you wouldn't even have your parents to keep you company, as awful and intolerable as they are. You know your parents love you, despite everything that's transpired recently, but you also know even the best parents in the world would not be able to dedicate every second of their lives visiting you in a hospital. Their visits would occur more infrequently as the years passed, until they stopped coming altogether. A nurse would be your one and only companion. Someone who would have to give you sponge baths and feed you through a tube. Someone you would develop a crush on at first, which would blossom into full-on *love*. Except she would never share these feelings. To her, you would be another part of her shitty job. Another helpless imbecile unable to take care of himself.

If you really wanted to kill yourself, you'd follow the lead of the man whose teeth you claimed. You'd take a hike up to the parking garage, climb on the tall concrete ledge, and try to fly. Of course, you would fail at flying, but in doing so you would succeed at everything else. Because from that height, there's no trip to the hospital. It's the grand finale.

Which is why you're a coward. Because you know this. You have *evidence of this* hidden away in your room. Yet you refuse to consider any starting point other than the window of your hotel. Because you know it's not a for-sure thing.

It doesn't matter. Parking garage, hotel window—either way, you aren't going to go through with it. It's fun to fantasize. Plus, if someone really *is* watching you, if the cameras *are* rolling, you like to believe it adds some excitement to the program. The viewers must be on the edges of their seats right now. Watching your legs sway in the wind as you stare at the ground below. You wonder if the producers are losing their minds, if they're afraid the show's about to lose their main star, if they've already started the process of brainstorming ideas for recasting the part. You wonder if your parents are watching behind-the-scenes. You wonder what they're thinking. Are they afraid? If so, afraid of what? Afraid they're about to lose their one and only son, or that they're about to lose a steady paycheck?

You glance behind you at the empty hotel room, hopeful you'll spot a camera lens zooming out of its hiding spot, but there's nothing there. Nothing you can see, at least. Just because it's not visible *to you* doesn't mean it doesn't exist.

You shout *Okay!* to maybe nobody, to maybe everybody. You shout that you're going to do it. That you're going to really, for sure do it this time. And, just in case the producers aren't one-hundred percent positive about what you're referring to when you say you're going to *do it*, you elaborate a little further and say you're going to jump out of the window. You tell all the listeners at home you're going to kill yourself, once and for all.

And then you face Lake Michigan and grip the sides of

the windows and lean forward and take several deep breaths, waiting for someone to come barging through the door, for someone to call *Cut!* and pause production, for someone to come tell you it's okay, that you're right, that this has all been some elaborate *Truman Show* scenario and you figured the whole thing out, congratulations, you aren't alone, you've never been alone, and now you can go back to your normal life again.

None of that happens.

You sit on the ledge, watching the seagulls circle Lake Michigan, until the cold grows too unbearable and you crawl back into your room and shut the window.

Next time, you're thinking, next time you won't chicken out.

Next time you'll go through with it.

Next time you'll jump.

Then these sons of bitches can find themselves another television star.

✲✲✲

Before the hotel, there was a house.

You lived in that house until you didn't. But for many years, that was your home. This house. 3030 Old Hobart Road. The address might as well be tattooed in your brain.

The three of you, plus your dog. All together under the same roof, in the living room, which was only slightly bigger than the hotel room you live in now. But at least then you had a dog. At least then you had friends who lived nearby. At least then you had a life.

Before the hotel, *you had a life*.

You had a reason to breathe.

A reason not to leap from parking garage roofs.

A reason that was taken from you. Stolen. So subtle. You didn't know it was happening until long after it was finished.

It started with a hole.

The end of the beginning, the beginning of the end.

A storm hit a year before you moved into the hotel.

None of you knew that the roof was in such bad shape—or, if your parents did, they never bothered filling you in on the details. But you certainly found out. The storm showed you the truth.

All three of you were asleep. Your dad on his recliner. Your mom on the couch. You were curled around the kerosene heater near the TV, desperate for warmth. Your dog snuggled next to you, which was how she always slept. The house had never had a standard functioning heating system. When it got too cold, your parents turned on the stove or ignited the kerosene heater, which they kept in the center of the living room.

When they first brought the kerosene heater home, the odor had given you headaches, but over time you adapted to the smell, and eventually found it pleasant—soothing. The closer you rested your head next to it, the easier it became to drift off to sleep. The fumes scrambled your brain. It cast a safety net for all bad thoughts to suffocate.

Something must've been playing on TV. You can't remember what now. But you also can't remember a time when the television had ever been turned off. It was always playing something. Typically, when it was time to sleep, you guys would pop in a random DVD. Your mom liked to control the remote, even when she wasn't conscious. She often drifted to sleep with the remote in one hand and a Virginia Slim in the other. Which meant she was always snapping back awake moments from setting the living room on fire. If she woke up and the DVD menu screen was playing in a loop, she'd quickly click PLAY before nodding back off. If you tried to take the remote or insert a new DVD, she'd snap and claim that she was watching what was already on, even if the movie had long finished.

There was a bang. Not from the TV, but from the roof. A noise you'd never heard before. A noise you haven't forgotten since.

Which one of you woke up first is unclear. Probably all three of you in unison. It was so loud, you have no idea how anybody could've slept through it. Except for the television glow, the room was dark. A tremendous noise had woken you up, yes, but from where? And why did the outside storm sound so close to your head?

It was raining inside the house. As improbable as it sounded, that's what was happening. You'd fallen asleep with the rain strictly outside, and had awoken with it coming down through the roof. The hole was near the front door. The three of you stared at it from your individual sleeping spots in the living room, struggling to comprehend reality.

There was a hole.

There was a hole in your house.

The house you'd lived in all your life.

It had been penetrated.

Invaded.

The entire purpose of having a shelter—shattered.

Confusion followed. Your parents screamed at each other louder than the storm. Your dog was already over by the front door, trying to lick up all the water soaking into the carpet. You followed her and flipped on the living room light. Puffs of pink, soggy fiberglass insulation spread around the floor like shed flamingo feathers. Your dog tried to eat one of them and spit it out, decided to stick with the rainwater. Somewhere your mom screamed to get a goddamn bucket. You had never seen a bucket in the house for as long as you could maintain memories. What use could your family ever have had with a bucket before? This ceiling collapse was unpredictable. There had been no time to plan.

In the kitchen, you retrieved a large pot from a cabinet. You could still hear the rain falling and your parents screaming in the living room. A part of you wanted to hide here in the kitchen and never return. Besides the bathroom, there were no other rooms in this house a person could easily enter without tripping over something or stubbing their toe. When you were younger, your safe place used to be the crevice between the refrigerator and stove. You'd sit on the floor with your back facing the gap and slowly scoot into it, vanishing from view. Only those who already knew about the hiding spot would ever think to look there. But by the time the ceiling collapsed, you were already far too fat to still fit between the refrigerator and stove. Now it was just a useless section of space, available only to the mice that came to scavenge from the woods behind your house.

You ran back into the living room with the pot raised above your head in case another piece of the ceiling was considering falling on top of you. You laid the pot on the wet carpet where most of the rain was coming down. Within a minute it had filled the pot.

You looked at your mom as if to ask what you were supposed to do now.

But she was looking at you as if she were asking the very same question.

***

There are teeth under your pillow. You have no idea who they belong to or how they got here. The teeth from the suicide man are long gone now. Swallowed away and stored somewhere in your intestines. You'd made them last as long as possible, but the hunger and desperation grew out of control. Once the last one was gone, hidden somewhere deep inside you, a profound emptiness overwhelmed your senses until paralysis induced a two-day-long sleep.

These new teeth are fresh. You can tell from the blood stains.

Louis is already at work. Jessica snores in the bed next to you, not quite lying down, instead half-reclined against the headboard. A Virginia Slim in one hand and the TV remote in the other.

On the television, a judge show plays at a low volume. Someone is suing their former landlord for the way they were treated while living in their building. The judge cracks a new joke every ten seconds, usually at the expense of the ex-tenant's physical appearance. The crowd eats it up and laughs like they're at a standup comedy show.

You roll over and face the window. Seagulls circle Lake Michigan, reappearing and disappearing in the mist, making the sky resemble an optical illusion.

In one hand you grip the new teeth discovered under your pillow. In the other hand you squeeze your balls so tight you want to cry. Or maybe you wanted to cry before this. Or maybe wanting to cry isn't related to anything you're presently doing. It's hard to understand everything all the time.

You pop one of the teeth in your mouth.

You suck the blood off of it before swallowing.

Only then are you able to fall back asleep.

You dream of a woman. She's pushing a housekeeping cart, out in the very hallways you now consider your only home. You recognize this woman. She's often the one assigned to clean your room. You can't remember her name. The tag attached to her chest is too distorted to decipher. You love this woman. You've fantasized about running away with her. You've masturbated to her memory for months. And, yet, you don't know what her name is.

In the dream, you follow her from the hotel to the parking lot. You watch from an unknown POV as she gets into her car. The car is bright yellow. You don't know what kind. It's late in the evening. She's parked away from the other cars. Somewhere isolated. Somewhere alone. Her face is wet and you realize she's been crying since the beginning of the dream. She's never stopped crying. She pops open her glovebox. A bottle of pills rolls out. Like the name tag, the bottle's label is too blurry to read. She unscrews the cap and taps out a dozen tablets. They look like tiny teeth. She plops one on her tongue, washes it down with an old bottle of water, then takes another, and another, until both the pill bottle and water bottle are finally empty. She leans her head back against the headrest. She's no longer crying. Now she's smiling. Laughing. She turns the radio up louder but you can't figure out what song is playing. The housekeeper stops laughing. The noises coming out of her mouth sound more like she's choking. Like her throat's restricting. Her skin color changes. Her lips go pale. Her eyes bulge. Saliva drools down her chin. Her body rocks violently against the steering wheel, setting off the car horn over and over, but nobody's listening. Nobody but you. She stops moving. Everything is still. Her mouth hangs open. You see her teeth. You want them more than anything in this world. Then, one by one, you are given what you crave. The dead housekeeper's teeth begin detaching from her mouth. Dropping from her gums and landing on her chest. Some of them fall into her shirt. They slide down between her cold breasts, waiting for you to push your face between them and dig them out.

When you wake up later that day, your crotch is sticky with cum. You change your underwear and pants in the bathroom and dispose of your soiled clothes in the hallway trashcan. When you return to the room, a new judge show is playing on TV. This time, when you watch it, you laugh along with the audience.

The remaining teeth stay gripped in the palm of your hand, just in case.

***

"You missed it," your mom says, lighting a new Virginia Slim, "when you were asleep, I went down to the lobby to snag us some bagels."

You ask what she's talking about. The bagels are right in front of you. You're eating them now. They're stale and terrible.

"There was an ambulance out in the parking lot, and like three cop cars. All with the lights on."

You ask her what they were doing, although a part of you already suspects the truth.

"I'm not sure. They were all interested in this one car . . . "

You ask if the car was yellow.

And she says, "How did you know?"

★★★

Your dad buys a loaf of white bread and asks if you want to feed the seagulls. The two of you used to do this all the time before moving into the hotel, whenever you were stuck with him at the casino while your mom gambled on the boat—which was by your mom's design. If you were with your dad, then he couldn't leave you unaccompanied to go stop your mom from losing his paycheck. Once in a while, if she was taking too long, he'd ask you to go hide in the public restroom. Just for a couple minutes, so he could run down and give your mom hell. But he never did it, because you would freak out and start shaking and beg him not to leave you alone.

Sometimes he described this scheme as a hostage situation.

At least now he can drop you off at the hotel any time he wants and it's okay. But before then, you had to learn other ways to pass the time together. The two of you read a lot. Sometimes you listened to audiobooks in the car. You walked around the premises. You fed the seagulls.

You didn't realize how much you missed feeding them until your dad brought out the loaf of bread. Your mom's at the boat, but it's a Saturday, a day off from the mill, and your dad feels like doing something fun. So you get your shoes on and the two of you head over to the parking garage roof. It's the first time you've been up here since hearing about the suicide man. It feels exotic and dangerous.

The wind's so strong you have to shout to be heard. It slaps against your face and your clothes and you wonder if you weighed less if it would carry you off the roof and into the lake. Despite the wind, your dad still attempts to light his pipe. He is not successful. The seagulls take one look at the loaf of bread swinging at your side and they immediately know what's about to happen. They start singing their ugly bird songs and flapping their wings with excitement. *Hell yeah*, they're screaming at each other, *hell yeah hell yeah hell yeah.*

✳✳✳

You're convinced you will never grow up. If you grow up, then you can leave the hotel. You won't be forced to stay in this room all day every day. Doing the same things. Eating the same foods. Listening to the same arguments. Your mom demanding your dad's paycheck. Your dad pretending to put up a fight. Money, money, money. Always wondering what happened to all the stuff in your house—the stuff that wouldn't have made sense to pawn, like the cheap plastic Little League trophies with your name on them, or the hundreds of illegal movies your dad downloaded from Limewire and burned onto blank DVDs. Jerking off into the same ice bucket to the same *Girls Gone Wild* infomercial. You will never see their actual breasts. The black censor bar will always be there. Watching the same shows. *Family Guy, American Dad, Roseanne, Seinfeld.* Over and over and over.

Everything is a rerun—including your life.

It's no mystery why the kids in cartoons never grow up, either. That's not what the audience wants. They don't want change. They want comfort. When they tune in, they want to know what to expect.

So yes. You are stuck here. Forever. Eighteen is an impossible number. You will never reach it. Time will continue stretching like silly putty.

There are only two periods of time now.

Before the hotel, and after the house.

There will never be an "after the hotel" era.

Maybe after you are dead, once the reek of decay finally convinces the staff to break down the door to your room and they're forced to call an ambulance to come wheel your corpse away to the nearest morgue in Gary. Except you don't really believe that. You secretly suspect you aren't capable of dying—that, or you've long been dead, and this hotel is simply some fucked-up boring purgatory.

But wouldn't that be a little too obvious?

Wouldn't that be too . . . *on the nose?*

So maybe you can't die, then. Your death would be bad for ratings, right? Isn't that the whole thing you've convinced yourself is true? That this is all a bizarre and cruel reality television program? You suddenly dropping dead might be fun for one episode, but what about the rest of the season? The rest of the *series*?

If production wants to kill you off, it's going to take months of pre-planning. At least nine months. It's not like you have any siblings who can be passed the torch. Plus, your parents haven't exactly been having sex. You've slept one bed away from them for how long now? A year—two? And, before the hotel, you were all cramped together in the living room, anyway. Back then, nobody even used *beds*.

When was the last time your mom and dad fucked each other? You ponder this question constantly. Sometimes it's all you can think about. At least back when you had a house, you were going to school and hanging out with Ian. Plenty of time for your parents to get frisky. But now? Half the time you don't sleep at night, and in the daytime, your dad's at the steel mill. Unless they aren't always at the boat when they say they are, and have instead rented a *second* room down the hallway. But if they can rent two hotel rooms, then surely they can afford to just get a new house—or, at the very least, an apartment.

Unless the reason you're living in a hotel has nothing to do with money. It's less to do with tragic *circumstance* and more to do with pure *entertainment*. It is simple. You reside in the hotel room because this is what the writers' room outlined long before you were conceived. This is the pitch they sent out to studios and distributors. To the financiers. Free will is an illusion when the scripts have already been typed and printed. You were always meant to live in this hotel. Events preceding the hotel were scenes from a prologue. The hotel is the main set. It is the stage. It is the story. It is the lack of story. It is everything.

You so often forget your exact age these days because age no longer matters. Like the children on cartoon sitcoms, you will remain in this state of being until the ratings drop and you are finally cancelled. There is no growing up. There is no anything.

There is only the hotel.

✳✳✳

Every two weeks your parents wake up at 3:30 in the morning and drive to Chicago. Sometimes, if you're awake, you tag along. But if you're asleep, they leave without disturbing you. Usually, you wake up while they're gone and experience a period of absolute terror. You forget that it's a Monday morning, you forget your parents' routine, and instead you curl up in your bed, illuminated only by reruns of *Roseanne*, and you convince yourself that they've finally abandoned you once and for all. They've left you here for the hotel staff to find, for them to claim as their own. They've decided they no longer want to be stuck with some kid, that it's time to move on without you in their lives. You sob into your pillow and pray to god they return until you fall back asleep and wake up to the sound of them opening the hotel room door again.

This is why you prefer to go with them. Plus, there's something comforting about laying sprawled out in the back seat of your dad's Oldsmobile. The scent of his vanilla pipe tobacco drifts over you like pollution. Your parents argue about directions. They argue about traffic. Your mom yells at your dad about making sudden swerves. Your dad asks her if she would have preferred they hit a pothole and blown their tires out. Your mom says to stop being a smartass. Your dad laughs and tells her to count the correct change for the incoming tollbooth. Your mom complains about the old pipe cleaners discarded in the coin tray. Not just pipe cleaners but clumps of dirt he's dragged in from the mill. Dirt and spent tobacco. It makes digging for change a disgusting task guaranteed to leave anyone's fingernails black.

She hands him two nickels and your dad laughs and says, "Jesus Christ, for someone who spends every spare second of their life in front of a slot machine, it's truly amazing you don't know what a quarter looks like."

"What the fuck is that supposed to mean?" Jessica asks, but Louis laughs and ignores the question. He digs into the coin tray and retrieves the correct change himself.

Inside the tollbooth, the operator hasn't looked up from the paperback she's been reading since you pulled up. What a job, you think. Just sitting around reading books while families bicker about money. You wouldn't mind a job like that. It's not like you don't already have the experience. You slip a spare tooth out of your pocket and curl your tongue around it, wondering what would've happened if you flung it through the window into the tollbooth basket instead. How many teeth to proceed? You don't have many left. Your mysterious tooth fairy hasn't returned since leaving the dead housekeeper's teeth under your pillow.

You try not to think about the *how* too much. After all, this is television, isn't it? This is just some fucked-up show. Leave the exposition for the writers. All that matters is they keep restocking you with other people's memories.

You zone out after the tollbooth. Head pressed against the cold window, sucking on the tooth, eyes closed. If your parents are still arguing, you can't hear them. You can't hear anything. Not even the traffic.

You're somewhere else.

The housekeeper.

She had a child. A daughter. A little girl.

She never felt happier than when she was holding her. The warmth is unlike anything you've ever felt before. It's like you're there, holding her too. You don't know the child's name. You just know her face. Her scent. When she smiles up at her mother, she's also smiling at you.

Except this already happened, and it'll never repeat itself. Not really. Because the baby's mother is dead.

The housekeeper.

The housekeeper and her yellow car.

The housekeeper and her bottle of pills.

It isn't a dream. None of this is a dream. They're memories. They're histories. The housekeeper's life, processed and transferred via teeth. What happens once it loses its flavor? You swallow it whole before you find out. There it will stay, in your stomach, in its new home. Teeth can't be digested. They remain inside you always. It feels true. You don't know if it actually is. But there's nobody to tell you differently. So you decide it must be. Teeth are forever.

You snap awake back in the Oldsmobile. Drenched in something cold and sticky. You hope it's just sweat but you can't tell for sure. Either way, there's not much you can do about it now.

You and your dad are parked next to the methadone clinic. Your mom has already gone inside. The clinic is nondescript. There aren't any signs outside advertising its business. Just a plain brick wall with two windowless doors. The kind of establishment regular passersby wouldn't give a second glance. Which is the point, your parents once told you. Most of the people who have to come here, they're deeply ashamed. They don't want anybody else to know what's going on inside.

When you originally had this conversation, you asked them if they were ashamed, too.

"Yes," your mom said, "but it's better than what we were doing before this."

Your dad didn't respond. He didn't need to. You can't remember a single time he's ever discussed your parents' past experience with heroin addiction. You know he's ashamed. You wish he wouldn't be. Not once have you ever thought less of him or your mom because of it. You're just grateful they trusted you enough to share this kind of secret. You know it couldn't have been easy. It's not exactly the kind of thing adults typically talk about with children.

Most parents pretend people don't make mistakes—that, or they judge them with the utmost cruelty. You've never judged your parents for their drug addiction. You judge them for other things, constantly, but not for the heroin. A weird, sick part of you even thinks it's cool. You'll never admit it out loud, but it's true: you like the fact that they used to do drugs. It makes them more interesting. Everybody else's parents are too boring and perfect. Not yours. They're weird and insane fuck-ups and you wouldn't trade them for the world. Even if it means living in a hotel. Even if it means being exploited on reality television.

Or maybe you're still high from the dead housekeeper's teeth.

On the radio, the "Mad World" song from *Donnie Darko* starts playing. You used to watch that movie with Ian in his basement all the time and the two of you would take turns quoting it. *How exactly does one suck a fuck?* was a favorite line to shout between laughter.

Attempting to light his pipe, your dad says, "You know, son, if you ever wanted to kill yourself—I'm not saying you should—but if you ever decide to do it . . . to, uh, kill yourself, that is . . . this wouldn't be such a bad song to have playing."

You nod and tell him you know exactly what he means.

More time passes outside the methadone clinic. People trickle in and out. Most of them with hoods over their heads. They keep their hands in their pockets and shrink into themselves, as if to appear as small as possible.

A man with a burned face briefly glances at the Oldsmobile before turning away. You remember your mom telling you about how a lot of the clinic's patients first got hooked on pain medication prescribed to treat injuries. Horrific burnings, gunshot wounds, car accidents, back problems, whatever. They're given stuff like OxyContin and then when it's time to stop taking them, they can't. The addiction's too strong. They start abusing the medicine. Sometimes this leads to heroin since it's cheaper than the pills, especially without health insurance. It's a downward spiral, every time. Sometimes they get help before it's too late, sometimes they end up overdosing in an alley.

You asked your mom if she and your dad had been prescribed pain medication for an injury, too, if that's how they started doing heroin. But their story was a little different. The heroin started with your mom, before she was dating your dad. She and a previous boyfriend were into it. After they broke up and she got with your dad, he joined in on the fun.

At the time, when you were first talking about all of this with her, you couldn't understand why she'd *chosen* to do it in the first place—why she hadn't simply *not* injected herself with poison. Why she couldn't just . . . *resist*.

But now?

In the back seat of your dad's Oldsmobile, parked next to a methadone clinic at 5:00 in the morning freezing your ass off, frantically searching your pockets for another spare tooth despite having *just* swallowed one?

There's no longer a question.

It all makes perfect sense.

✷✷✷

There's a McDonald's near the methadone clinic that's two-stories tall. The Rock N Roll McDonald's, is what it's called. World-famous for reasons that don't make any sense to you. If they have the money, sometimes they take you there after your mom finishes in the clinic.

Fortunately, Louis had only gotten paid a couple days ago, and there's still some of it left. Not much, but some. He gives Jessica a fifty-dollar bill and says, "Make sure you bring me back the change," despite everybody in the car knowing that's never going to happen.

Your dad finds a spot in the parking lot and leaves the car idling as you and your mom go inside. Louis never comes into fast food restaurants unless he's eating inside, which he also despises. He prefers to listen to the radio and smoke his pipe as Jessica places the order.

Despite it being so early in the morning, the Rock N Roll McDonald's is packed. You and your mom have to wait almost ten minutes in line. It's the only fast food restaurant you've ever been in that has an escalator. You don't know why it's so big. Neither does your mom. But it feels nice to be inside it, and sometimes that's enough of a reason.

Something's been on your mind lately, probably since learning that all three of you tested positive for hepatitis C. You know your mom won't want you bringing this up in public, but you can't stop yourself from blurting out the question. With the methadone clinic, only your mom has an account with them. Your dad is nowhere in their system. Yet they both take the medication. Your mom shares it with him. So your question is, what will happen if she dies before he does? She's previously told you it's a huge hassle to even get enrolled in the methadone program, and one slip-up (such as being late for an appointment) can set patients back significantly. So if she dies, isn't your dad going to experience a painful withdrawal as he goes through the process of trying to enroll? Isn't it illegal for the two of them to be sharing? What's going to happen? What needs to be *done?* The interrogation bursts out of you like machine-gun fire, and by the end of it, you're out of breath.

Jessica looks pissed and embarrassed. She keeps glancing at the other patrons in line, but nobody's paying any attention. They all have their own lives to dwell upon.

"Would you knock it off with that?" she tells you, in a half-whisper half-shout. "I'm not going to die. Jesus Christ."

You wonder if she honestly believes that, and consider sharing with her that you suspect the same thing about yourself, but before you can say anything else your mom's been called to the register by a cashier with terrible acne.

The counter consists of three registers, and all of them are occupied by tired, hungry customers. You and your mom are on the far left register. Another woman at the middle register wears an extravagant fur coat that hangs down at her ankles. When she orders, her deep smoker's voice commands the room. She exchanges eye contact with your mom and you know immediately your mom is convinced this woman overheard the methadone clinic conversation. Her cheeks turn red and she focuses on the menu above the counter as she recites the breakfast order to the cashier. Biscuit sandwiches, breakfast burritos, lots of hash browns, a couple coffees, and an orange juice. Your mom pays with a twenty-dollar bill, different from the fifty your dad handed her out in the parking lot.

Next to you, the fur coat woman slides a thick white envelope from her purse and pulls out several bills to pay the cashier at the middle register. Meaning the rest of the envelope is also full of cash. You can't help but stare. You've never seen so much money before in one place. Your mom nudges you in the ribs and whispers, "Stop that." You turn around and face the other direction. You don't trust your eyes not to return to the envelope.

Then your mom jabs her elbow at you again and says, "Let's go, let's go." She shoves the drink tray into your grasp and clutches the two fast food bags against her chest as the two of you head toward the exit. You're surprised that she's in such a hurry to leave. Usually, your mom pulls out everything on the counter and unwraps the sandwiches to make sure the order is correct, and you have to stand there next to her as everybody in the restaurant stares with shock and amusement and disgust. You're grateful she decided to skip this part of the routine, for whatever reason that might be.

Behind you, the fur coat woman's shouting something at the cashier, and the last words you hear before you step outside are:

"—*right fucking here*—"

✱✱✱

Back at the hotel, your mom can't sit still. In the mornings, she's normally passed out—*especially* on the mornings they've driven to Chicago. Except for your dad, who still has to go to work. After dropping you guys off, he uses the bathroom real fast then kisses your mom goodbye. He looks like a zombie. You worry he'll fall asleep on the way to the steel mill. Your mom's too distracted to notice. She keeps glancing at her purse on the edge of the bed.

Halfway through eating breakfast, your mom hands you the rest of her food and says you can finish it, she's not hungry. You ask her if she's okay. She says she's fine, just a little hot, says maybe she'll go for a walk and get some fresh air. You ask if you can come with her. She says it's best if you stay in the room. She goes to the bathroom to fix her hair and brush her teeth. You get up and tiptoe to your parents' bed.

Her purse is wide open, revealing the white envelope of cash stuffed inside it for the whole world to see.

✷✷✷

Once she's gone, you sit on the bed and finish your mom's breakfast while watching judge shows on TV. Then you throw away the trash and try to sleep a little. Nothing happens. You remain awake. You pull open the blackout curtain and let the sun cook your face. Not a cloud in sight. The abandoned lighthouse looks like it's melting off in the lake. Next to it, you can see the back of one of the gambling boats. You wonder if that's the one your mom has fled to. You wonder how long it'll take her to feed the entire envelope of cash into a slot machine. You wonder if the cameras at McDonald's caught her stealing it. You wonder if the police will be able to track her down, if they'll come busting into this hotel room with their guns drawn. You wonder if you will pretend to have a weapon. You wonder how many bullets it will take to bring you down.

You decide to masturbate.

You turn on the correct channel and wait for the *Girls Gone Wild* infomercial to broadcast. It doesn't air often in the daytime, but you're feeling lucky today. The ice bucket is on the bed next to you. It feels cold against your thigh.

You wish you had another tooth to suck on right now. You wish it more than anything in the world.

You close your eyes. You try to lick your own teeth but it's not the same. You wedge your tongue in the missing spot in your gums where you recently lost a tooth of your own. It feels wrong. Like you're violating yourself. Your cock hardens. You try to penetrate your gum with your tongue. It *hurts*, which doesn't make sense, because hasn't it been weeks if not months since you lost it? Shouldn't the wound have healed by now? You're glad it's not healed. The pain is good. You stroke faster. You can't believe how much it hurts. You hope it never stops.

Is this the kind of entertainment people want? Is this what the sponsors of your show are paying good money to advertise on? A twenty-four-seven stream of a teenager masturbating in a hotel room? If anybody is actually tuning in to this, they're sick, they're perverted and fucked up in the head. You realize right now, right this very second, the entire country—or, possibly, the entire *planet*—might be watching you pleasure yourself. Everybody you knew back in Lake Station. Your friend Ian. Your teachers. The crushes you were too shy to approach. Your parents. Everybody. They are watching. They are leaning forward. They are glued to the screen. And you couldn't be more turned on by the thought of it. You *want* them to see. You want them *all* to see.

You sit up and reach for the ice bucket with your free hand, and—in that moment—your vision happens to catch something on the wall directly across from the bed. *Movement*? On the wall itself, next to the television display. Below a painting of a fruit bowl.

What is that?

You stop stroking, but don't take your hand off your shaft. You grip it tight, more out of fear than pleasure. There is something there. In the shadow of the painting. A *hole?* Yes. A small hole.

But it's not the hole you're staring at.

It's what's *through* the hole.

An eyeball.

Yellow and diseased, but an eyeball all the same.

You see an eyeball and the eyeball sees you.

Watching you from inside the wall.

Not just any eyeball but *my* eyeball.

For the first time since your family moved here, you are finally seeing me.

Just as I am seeing you.

Neither of us move or make a sound for an extraordinary length of time. We share the silence together, just as we have shared many other silences.

Without looking away, you continue stroking yourself.

This time, when you are about to finish, I do not blink.

And neither do you.

✶✶✶

It's only after you've rinsed out the ice bucket that the reality of the situation fully registers.

Someone is watching you.

It's no longer just a suspicion. You're not just paranoid. You saw me. You fucking *saw me*. And I saw you. There was a moment, a long moment when our vision crossed paths, when one eye bled into the other and they became one. My eye. You saw my eye. It's yellow, you're realizing now. My eye is yellow. The skin around the eyeball, yes, but also the eyeball itself. A sickly yellow.

Not a television show, after all. Something else. Someone in the walls. *Someone is watching you through the walls.* You wonder if I can see you right now. The answer is no, not *physically*. I'm not in the hotel anymore, I've fled out of fear, too terrified of being confronted, but that doesn't mean I don't *know* what you're doing, anyway, that we aren't connected on a spiritual level, that I can't hear your thoughts, that I can't feel everything you feel. Of course, there's no way for me to tell you that. Not yet. But soon.

You pace around the bathroom, still naked from the

waist down, heart racing. The same question pounding in your skull over and over: *what is happening what is happening what is happening—*

Stop. Breathe. Think.

There is a hole across from your bed. A hole big enough for a single eye to press against. Has it always been there, since you first checked into this room? The same room the hotel always gives you. Room 333. How has nobody noticed this hole before? How long have I been watching you? What have I seen?

The truth you're afraid of is the correct answer.

Everything.

I have seen everything.

It takes a while to build up the courage, but you eventually leave the bathroom. You run to your bed and quickly wrestle your pants back on—facing away from the peephole, just in case I'm still there. But when you turn around, the hole is unoccupied.

Your body trembles as you approach the hole. There's no ignoring it at this point. You can't continue as if it doesn't exist, as if you didn't see what you saw—as if you didn't see *me*. You study the hole for minutes that seem more like hours. Nothing happens. You reach up and softly probe your index finger in it. The edges feel wet and warm. You slide your finger as far as it can go, convinced someone or something is about to bite it off, yet you're unable to resist the urge. A part of you wants me to do it. The idea of losing your finger is somehow the most exciting thought to ever cross your mind. When you remove it from the hole, a heavy disappointment washes over you when you discover it's still intact.

But even if I were still there, I wouldn't have done it. I would never do anything to harm you. I am here to protect you. I *love* you. You don't know that yet but it's true. You are the best thing to ever happen in my life.

You go back over to the bed and sit along the edge, next to the nightstand. You go to pick up the hotel phone but you pause before releasing it from the cradle. Who are you going to call? There's no cell phone signal on the boat, which means you can't call your mom. Although, if she *did* manage to latch onto a signal, the odds of her answering while gambling the money from McDonald's don't seem too significantly in your favor. So she's out.

Which leaves your dad. You've never called him while at work before. You don't know the steel mill's number, although you assume it's listed somewhere in the phonebook stored in the nightstand beside the Holy Bible. You try to imagine getting through to him, and you can't figure out what you would say. There's a hole in the hotel room and someone was watching you masturbate? No, of course not. You can't tell him what you were doing. You can't tell anybody. Imagine how they would look at you. Imagine the shame.

So what then? You were just . . . watching television, yes, and that's when you noticed the hole. The hole that, for some reason, none of you have noticed until today.

Suppose he believes you.

What is it, exactly, you are hoping he does about it? First, he's going to ask to speak to your mom. What are you going to tell him then? That she's at the boat, gambling money she stole from an old lady while ordering breakfast this morning? He'll want to know why you didn't tell him about this sooner. He'll want to know why you kept it a secret. He'll get so worked up about your mom gambling that he'll forget the reason you called him in the first place.

And, once again, what is he supposed to do about the situation? He's at work. He can't leave. He shouldn't even be talking on the phone so long. The mill will write him up. They'll fire him. Then where will you stay? Where will you go? Because, despite everything, you don't want to actually leave, do you? Not now, not when things are finally getting exciting. You want to stay right where you are. You want me to come back. I know this is true. I know what you want. I know what you need. I am never wrong about these things.

Which is why, when you put your shoes on and run out of the hotel room, I'm genuinely surprised.

＊

Before the hotel, there was a house.

A house with a hole in its ceiling.

A house that cried every time it rained. Its tears soaked into the ceiling. Into the carpet. Over time, it contaminated too much.

The ceiling turned black.

Like an infected wound that needed to be amputated.

Its sickness spreading throughout the rest of the body.

The rest of the house.

You didn't realize it was mold until one of your parents mentioned the word during an argument. You didn't quite understand what mold *was*, but you knew it was something bad. Something unhealthy. When you slept, you tried to scoot closer to the kerosene heater and breathe in its fumes to counteract the toxic mold from above.

One day, your dad came home from work with several rolls of duct tape and plastic wrap. He covered the gaping hole in the ceiling with plastic. The next time it rained, the plastic sagged down, creating a huge egg-shaped nest that stretched toward the floor like silly putty, until it finally burst.

Then your father brought home a blue tarp, and taped that over the hole instead. When it rained again, the tarp maintained a sturdy hold. But where did the water go if not through the hole? Somewhere in the attic. Somewhere above you. You asked your parents about this but neither of them had a good explanation. They just said it would be fine. They said to stop worrying.

The mold continued to spread.

The house took on a new scent, something you'd never smelled before. Like the whole place had gone . . . stale. Expired. Like old, rotten trees you sometimes found out in the woods while exploring with Ian. The kind of trees that caved in with the slightest pressure. You wondered if the walls of your house would do the same if you touched them.

Several months after the ceiling initially caved in, you woke up and discovered the house had lost electricity. This wasn't atypical. The electricity and water were frequently shut off due to failure to pay bills on time. Sometimes when the water went out, your dad would take a big wrench and go around to the backyard and tweak the meter himself. Somehow he never got in trouble. But there was nothing he could do about the electricity, except pay them to come out and turn it on again. Usually, your parents got it straightened out within a day—at the most, two. Usually, this meant making a trip to the pawnshop. Usually with something they'd gifted you in the past. Which was why, as you rode the bus to school that morning, you regretted not reminding your mom that the Xbox 360 still had the *Kiss Kiss Bang Bang* rental in its disc tray.

After school, the Xbox was gone and the electricity was still off.

"Tomorrow it'll be fixed," your mom promised.

When you got home from school the next day, your mom was sitting on the porch waiting for you to get off the bus. Smoking a cigarette and drinking a warm can of pop. As you approached the house, you asked what was going on, and she told you to pack a bag. "We're staying at the boat tonight," she said. And you looked at her, confused, not sure what she meant by that, forgetting that there was a hotel there. You'd hung out in the parking garage so many times with your dad that you'd blacked out any existence of an additional building on the property. "I have a comp," she added. "It'll just be for the weekend, so bring something to do. And extra clothes."

Inside the house, you found an empty grocery bag and gathered some books and clothes and crammed it in your backpack. Your dog followed you around the house, panting, obviously hot, looking at you for answers you didn't have. Nobody took her out anymore. If she needed to poop, she could just use the family room at the back of the house. It was fine.

There were blood stains all over the carpet and furniture. The dog seemed to be in a perpetual state of menstruation since finding her off the street the year before and taking her home. You asked your parents if she was sick and they told you it was perfectly normal, that there wasn't anything to worry about.

You poked your head out through the front door and asked if you could bring the dog to the casino hotel.

"Oh my god," she said, rage on the edge of her voice, "she'll be *fine* here. *Relax.*"

You patted her on the head and made sure her food and water bowls were refilled and told her you'd be back soon.

A couple hours later, your dad pulled up from the mill. He never got out of the car. You and your mom met him in the driveway and he backed out and headed in the direction of Gary. You watched the house disappear out the back window and hoped your dog would be okay over the weekend.

Several weeks later, your dad returned to the hotel after stopping at the house to get the mail and check on things. He told you one of the windows in the living room had been cracked open. Broken from the inside. Meaning your dog had smashed her way out of the house. He said he looked everywhere, but there was no sign of her. She was gone.

Then he handed you a PlayStation Portable.

It was your fourteenth birthday.

⋆⋆⋆

You know you're not supposed to be outside alone. At least when your mom's in the hotel, there's a safety net. If someone catches you, you can lead them back to the room and show them that you haven't been abandoned. But when your mom's somewhere worshipping a slot machine, things get a bit trickier. Casinos enforce strict rules when it comes to unsupervised minors. It doesn't matter if you aren't technically on the boat. The fact that you're *near* it is enough to raise alarm.

The consequences of getting caught terrify you enough to keep you in the room—most of the time.

Right now, it's the last thing on your mind as you run across the covered bridge and down the walking path leading into the casino lobby.

You aren't thinking about Child Protective Services. You aren't thinking about your mom yelling at you for disobeying her orders. You aren't thinking about your parents going to jail. You aren't thinking about anything except for the hole back in the hotel room.

It's not the first time a hole has changed the course of your life, is it?

Holes follow you like insects attracted to your scent.

They are inescapable.

One of these days, you're going to stop running away from them.

One of these days, you're going to create a hole of your own.

That's what you're thinking as you huff and puff, out of breath, onto the lobby escalator. You know you're drenched in sweat. You know your cheeks are red. You know you look crazy. But you don't care. Right now, you need to speak to your mom. You need to tell her what's going on. You can't handle this alone. You need her *help*.

Usually, there are two or three guards positioned outside the ramp leading down to the gambling boat. They check IDs of anybody attempting to enter. Any time they've ever seen you get remotely close to the ramp, they tense. Sometimes, in the past, when you and your dad were waiting down at the chicken wing kiosk, you would inch closer and closer just to study their different responses.

But, when you ascend to the top of the escalator, the ramp appears empty of life. You don't question it. You run down the slope without a second thought. At the bottom of the ramp, you push open the doors and emerge onto the *Majestic Star Casino* boat and you are assaulted with noise and lights unlike anything you have ever encountered. Bright, flashing lights that remind you of Christmas Eve. Sounds that you've heard in arcades dozens of times. People everywhere. People drinking. People offering more drinks. People laughing and cursing and sweating. So many people, more than you ever imagined would be here in the middle of the afternoon. What are they all doing here? Don't they have jobs? Don't they have families? Where are their *children*? None of them care. Not really. The casino is more important. This is where they'd rather be. Sitting in front of a large slot machine, hitting buttons and pulling levers while ignoring all other responsibilities, while pretending their lives outside this boat are mere fictions.

Everything becomes dizzy. You lean against a trash can and dry-heave over plastic cups that reek of alcohol. Nobody notices you. Everybody's too zoned in on their individual games. You might as well be a ghost. You've certainly had enough practice.

First you were the ghost of Lake Station, now you are the ghost of the *Majestic Star Casino*.

It is a role you've found comfort in embracing. Especially now, when you don't want anyone to catch you. This is the boat, after all. This is the *forbidden area*. The place you've only visited in nightmares. A long time ago, you made a promise to yourself that you'd never step foot in a casino. You would never gamble. You would never *touch* a slot machine. This was your mom's curse that you had no intention of inheriting.

Yet here you are.

You're on the boat.

The place that has ruined your life. That has taken away your childhood. Stolen you from your friends. Deprived you of forming normal high school memories. The place that corrupted your mom. Turned her into someone you didn't recognize. Turned her into *a stranger*.

And now it has her again. You just have to find her. You have to find her and tell her enough is enough, there's something urgent going on at the hotel, and it's time to leave. It's time to go home. Not home as in the hotel but home as in your real home, as in the house on 3030 Old Hobart Road. It is time to return to Lake Station. *Please,* you want to shout at her, *please can we please go home now? Can we please?* You'll do anything, you want to tell her. You'll do whatever she wants. Just as long as you can finally leave this miserable place and never come back.

Except your mom isn't here. Or, if she is, she's nowhere in sight. You've searched all the slot machines. You've gone into the women's restrooms. You don't know anywhere else she could be. This is the only place she could have possibly gone. But that isn't exactly true, is it? Because this establishment consists of *two* gambling boats. She could be on the other one. The *Majestic Star II,* formerly the *Trump Casino.* Somehow that feels unlikely, though. Your mom is a creature of habit. She's always gambled on the original *Majestic Star Casino.* Why would she change her routine now? No. If she's gambling, then she's *here.* Somewhere . . . you just haven't looked in the right spot yet, is all. You need to keep looking.

And that's when you feel someone tapping on your shoulder, and your body freezes, statue-still, waiting, waiting, waiting . . .

Slowly, you turn around, knowing your mom wouldn't simply tap you. She would shout your name. She would throw something at you. She would scream and curse. She wouldn't tap.

Of course, you are correct. It's not her.

It's a man. A tall, bulky man. A man dressed in a maintenance person's uniform. A man looking down at you. Looking down at you with sickly yellow eyes.

But that isn't all that's yellow, you see now.

His flesh is the same.

His cheeks. His neck. The top of his bald scalp. His hands and his long, pointy fingernails.

Yellow.

The word that comes to mind now is something you read while researching hepatitis C.

Jaundice.

This man is jaundiced.

This man is me.

***

I unlatch my walkie talkie from its belt hoop and inform my supervisor that everything's under control, that I've located the unaccompanied minor and will deal with him swiftly. That there's no need to be concerned. Everything is perfectly okay down here.

Meanwhile, you're backing up, mumbling an incoherent language, oblivious that there's nowhere for you to escape. Behind you is a wall. The exit is the other direction. Predictably, you run out of space. You start shaking and cower to the carpet. I tower above you and try my best not to appear menacing but I understand this isn't the easiest task, considering my appearance. I know what I look like. I know why you're afraid of me. Soon that fear will be gone. I promise you. Things will make sense. You will grow to love me, just as I've grown to love you.

I tell you to come with me and you ask me where your mom is. I repeat myself and this time you listen. You get up. I grab your shoulder and lead you away from the gamblers. The moment you turned around and saw who had tapped you on the shoulder, you recognized me for what I am. You knew I was the one you caught watching earlier. There's no use denying it. Neither of us need to vocally address the circumstances. Instead, we move in silence. Away from the noise. Away from the lights. Away from the cameras. Away from the other people.

Until it's just the two of us, alone in the maintenance office. Surrounded by tools. Sitting across from each other. One brown, flimsy wooden desk serving as our only divider.

This is the moment I've been dreaming about. No

longer hiding behind a wall. Not just me seeing you but you also seeing me. *Really* seeing me. You have no idea how many imaginary conversations I've played out between us in my head. Anybody else and I'd consider it embarrassing. But somehow this is different. This is meant to be. This is destiny.

Right?

You ask me again about your mom, but I don't want to talk about her yet, so I pull out the necklace tucked into my work shirt. It's a thin, black string—a torn shoelace—that I've tied a single object around. An object I hope you recognize. An object that once belonged to you. An object that was once *part* of you.

You instinctively wedge your tongue against your gum, where you recently lost a tooth.

Although—how recently was it? Can you even remember?

It's yours, this tooth. After you flicked it out of the window, I scavenged it. I don't know if you realized back then that you were giving it to me, if you had *intentionally* discarded the tooth for me to find. I like to believe that is the case, but I also understand sometimes happy accidents happen.

But this wasn't an accident. You were meant to lose that tooth, and I was meant to find it. As if it were already written. Not by the television producers you imagined were watching you, but by the secret shadows that chaperone all living life. The shadows that decide when it's time for something to cease living. I know all about these shadows, and I suspect you aren't as uneducated as you feign.

I give the tooth a soft lick before pushing it back under my work shirt. I've been savoring it, you see. Trying to stretch out its flavors. You of all people should understand the kind of great temptation I've had to face. It is almost impossible to resist succumbing to these memories once you've had that first taste. If anything, you should be proud of me. You should be impressed.

You ask me what I am.

Not *who*.

What.

It's a fair question, but I promise you, I am not a monster. Believe it or not, I'm just like you. At least, I used to be. I was a man. Maybe I still am. Sometimes even I can't figure it out. The specifics of my history are not important. Later, we will have plenty of time to browse my own memories. I will break you off a fang and let you binge and you will see everything I have ever seen, just as I have seen everything you've ever seen. Then, truly, we will be complete.

But yes. I am human. I have a job. I work as head of maintenance for the casino. Before this, I worked at Lehigh Cement along the harbor until it closed its doors. I used to have a family but none of them have been alive for many years now. I've lived in this city all my life. I've witnessed it prosper and I've witnessed it die. Things happened to me during that time. Bad things. Things that no soul on this planet should dream of experiencing. Things that forever innovated my biology.

Just like you, I also lost my house.

The state foreclosed on it. They wrapped chains around the door and secured it with the biggest, sturdiest padlock available in the Midwest.

But that's okay. Because I have a new home now.

I know you've seen it before. Let's be honest, you've done more than just see it. You've sat in your hotel room window and yearned to visit it.

The lighthouse.

You thought it was abandoned, and that was only partially correct. Abandoned, yes, but also *reclaimed*.

Well, I am here to tell you that you can do more than just visit it, that you don't need to stay in the hotel room one moment longer.

You can live with me.

You can be with someone who actually loves you,

someone who will do whatever it takes to protect you from harm. You can change the direction of your life forever.

You can do something *different*.

I know it's a lot to spring on you at once. You hardly know me. Who *am* I, right? Just some creep you caught watching you through the wall. There's no quick way to convince you that I am someone you can trust, that I am someone you can love, but I have patience, and I am confident you will see that I am being one-hundred percent honest right now. Everything I am saying is the truth. I would never lie to you. I may do a lot of terrible things—some of which, you have probably already guessed by now—but one thing I will never do is hurt you. I can promise you that right now with absolute certainty, that it is a promise I will never break, under any circumstances.

But before you say anything—before you make a decision—I have a present I want to give you. Your parents might have forgotten, but I didn't.

I know what today is.

It is your sixteenth birthday.

Did you also forget?

I didn't. I would *never*.

Today is your birthday and I have a birthday gift for you. I even wrapped it.

You take the small box from me without uttering a single word. You untie the ribbon and tear open the gift wrap and lift the box lid and stare down at several dozen, nicotine-stained teeth.

You ask me who they belong to.

And I tell you to go ahead and try one. I can see from the way your hands are trembling that you're dying to put one of them in your mouth. So why don't you go ahead and do it? It's your birthday, after all. Why not treat yourself a little?

That's all the convincing you need.

As I whisper-sing the happy birthday song, you lift the box and pour every tooth into your mouth at once.

***

You see a little girl. Younger than you by a few years. She's sitting on a hospital bed. Her face is bruised and swollen and her arm is in a cast. The girl's mom is in the room with her. She's telling her something, you can't tell what exactly, but it has to do with who caused these injuries. Her mom keeps shaking her head *no, no, no,* and the little girl keeps nodding her head *yes, yes, yes.*

***

The girl's face is wet with tears and her clothes are filthy and she's running through a forest. She still has a cast on her arm and her bruises have yet to fade. You don't know what she's running away from and you don't know where she's heading but she seems determined to get there in a hurry. Then she's at a cabin. It's dark out and the cabin doesn't have any working electricity. The girl curls up into a ball on the floor and shivers. She stays like this for three days—no food, no water, nothing—before her stepfather tracks her down and drags her back home.

***

The girl is older now, but only slightly. She's alone, with another man close to her age. Both of them are naked. The room is a disaster. They're listening to music but you can't hear how it sounds. The man is showing her a syringe and a spoon. He's whispering something beneath the music. The girl looks nervous, but she doesn't look afraid. She's smiling.

***

A different room. The girl has aged a couple years. The man who introduced her to the syringe lies on the floor. His body is stiff and cold. The girl stands above him, screaming, screaming, screaming—

***

Another room. The girl is now a woman. She's with a different man. They're naked and cuddling in bed. The woman's belly is swollen as if pregnant. She opens a nightstand and pulls out a black pouch. She unzips it and retrieves a spoon, followed by several other items. The man kisses her and holds out his arm as she ties a rubber tourniquet around it.

✳✳✳

Hospital room again. Nighttime. Through the window, fireworks illuminate the sky. The woman is on the bed, wearing a gown. She's sweaty, clammy, but otherwise looks happy. She's holding a baby. Staring down at him. Smiling, kissing his cheeks, loving on him. The man sits next to them, watching his wife and son with the same excitement as the explosions outside. They're exhausted and perfectly content with each other. This is the best night of their lives.

✳✳✳

The woman joins a long line of people waiting outside a nondescript city building. She sticks her hands in her pockets and shivers. The wind is brutal against her face but she doesn't leave. Everything in her body hurts. She can't stop shaking. But she sticks it out. She is determined. The line shortens. Eventually, someone invites her inside and they ask how they can help her.

✳✳✳

The woman and another woman—a neighbor—take a drive. It's the middle of the afternoon. The woman's son is at school. Her husband is at work. Everything is fine. There is plenty of time. The two women pull into a massive concrete parking garage. They get out and head toward a building. The sign consists of bright, white bulbs that spell out ***MAJESTIC STAR CASINO***. Both of them glance around the inside as if they've never been here before. This is all new to them. The woman sits at a random slot machine. She struggles for a moment as she tries to operate it. Her neighbor shows her where to insert the coins and what buttons to hit. It's simple, once she gets the hang of it. A baby could do this, she thinks, which reminds her of her own son, but only momentarily because the slot machine *explodes* with noise and lights. She jumps back, afraid she's broken something, but it's the opposite. She's won. She's won *big*. Everybody in the casino applauds and celebrates. They're thrilled for her. She's done something amazing. She's conquered the machine. She's won. She's actually fucking won. The sparkle in her eyes now is the same sparkle she had when she gave birth to her son. If anything, it's brighter. When she gets home later that night and shows her husband the amount of money in her purse, he kisses her with the same passion and intensity as he used to when they were shooting heroin together. She melts in his arms and has never felt more loved. Every decision, every mistake, every action she's made, it has led her to this moment. The moment she won.

★★★

You vomit your mom's teeth all over my desk. They scatter to the floor like dice. A part of me is tempted to lean down and slurp them up. Maybe later, once we've come to a better understanding. After all, I don't want to scare you. Not when you're so close to accepting—

Then you start screaming.

You demand to know where your mom is. You threaten me with violence. You tell me I'm a monster. You say you want to see your mom right now or else.

But I don't understand what you mean. Because I just showed you your mom. What did you think this was? What did you think *any* of this was?

Now you're knocking things off my desk. You scream that it isn't true, that your mom is okay, that nothing happened.

But it *is* true, and you know it.

Your mom is very much not okay.

How else do you think I collected her teeth?

You shout the word *TEETH* at me over and over, like it's a curse, like it's supposed to scare me, and it works, especially when you pick up the hammer from my toolbox and start swinging it around wildly.

TEETH TEETH TEETH you scream.

Something in your brain has short-circuited and, for

once, I don't know what to do. I try to tell you to calm down. I suggest you take a seat. Maybe a deep breath. I reach out to touch your shoulder and you bash me with the hammer and I cry out and flee across the room.

You're not supposed to hurt me. You're supposed to be *grateful*.

I've given you the best birthday gift any kid your age could hope for, haven't I? The one thing you've wished for every day since moving into the hotel. No, before then. This is what you've always wanted. Why are you pretending like it's not?

Next time you raise the hammer, I yelp and flinch, convinced you're going to strike me again—but instead of hitting me, you open your mouth, jaw unhinged like a snake, and swing the weapon inward. It bashes into your teeth, and you scream and swing it again and again and I'm on my knees, arms out, begging you to stop, please stop, but you won't, you swing the hammer until every tooth in your mouth has cracked and broken and your mouth is gushing blood and you're smiling with complete and total mania.

At the sight of loose teeth scattered at your feet, I finally lose control. Because these aren't just *any* teeth. These are *your* teeth. I dive to the floor and I press my mouth against the globs of bloody teeth and I suck and lick the carpet dry. I can taste the hepatitis in your blood and it only enriches the feast. It is delicious. It is perfect. Pure ecstasy overload. Everything tingles with pleasure.

I don't even mind it that much when you stand over me and swing the hammer down upon my skull.

As everything in my head leaks out of my eyeballs and ears and mouth, I can't stop grinning.

You will never have any idea how happy you've made me today.

Thank you.

Thank you so much.

***

Nobody notices you as you stumble out of the casino. Your mouth is full of blood and it doesn't matter how many times you spit some out. More regenerates instantly. There is no pain. There is no anything. There is just you.

You make it back to the hotel room without anyone bothering you. You are a ghost. A literal ghost, not just metaphorically. If nobody stopped you in your current state then that can only mean you no longer exist. The alternative is too cruel to entertain—that they *did* see you and they just didn't care enough to offer any help.

So then you are a ghost.

Maybe you've always been a ghost. Either way, you are fine with it. There is nothing wrong with being a ghost, you decide. Ghosts don't feel pain. Ghosts don't need teeth.

You think about showering and cleaning yourself up, but decide you prefer the way you look. You look scary. You look crazy. If you aren't a ghost then, you're something else unexplainable, and that's just the way you want it to be.

You collapse on the bed and turn on the television.

As luck would have it, USA has just started airing *The Truman Show* again.

You crank the volume to its maximum level and throw the remote out the window.

The time on the alarm clock reads 3:00 P.M, which means your dad won't be home from the steel mill for another couple hours.

So you stay in bed, and you watch TV, and you wait.

And you wait.

And you wait.

YOU ARE MY NEIGHBOR

I USED TO break windows. One window in particular, really. Our neighbor had a basement and we didn't, and I always thought that was unfair. Growing up, all I wanted was to live in a basement and invite all the kids from school to hang out and drink beer with me while listening to Black Sabbath. But we didn't have a basement and nobody ever came over because Mom was too embarrassed by how messy the house was and Dad was paranoid someone would swipe their oxys while he was asleep.

He always accused me of taking them, but I never once dared. One night, around two in the morning, I woke up to his hand squeezing my throat. He was above me, tears pouring down his face and splattering against my own, and demanding I tell him what I did with them. The way he looked at me, I could tell he didn't want to be doing what he was doing, but something beyond human consciousness had him under its control, and I had to beg and beg for him to let me go, whimpering that I didn't have his pills, and eventually Mom stumbled in and reminded him they'd already finished off their stash the night before.

So sometimes I broke the neighbor's basement window, the one at foot-level along the side of their house, half-hidden in dirt. It was a thing to do while Mom and Dad were down for the count and I was bored because I couldn't invite anybody over. I wasn't allowed to walk along the interstate to visit anybody so what the hell was a kid to do besides break windows?

The first time it happened, it was just about twilight and everybody next door had left. I'd watched all four of them pile into their tan station wagon and drive off. Who knew where? Maybe to go get ice cream or watch a movie. Stuff families did together on TV. The household consisted of a mother and father and son and daughter. I didn't know any of their names, but they always seemed busy doing bizarre activities. Having barbecues in the back yard and going on vacations and playing catch in the street for the whole wide world to see. The shame of my own situation just about killed me.

I was sitting on our porch as the family next door drove off, all smiles and bubblegum as the station wagon disappeared beyond our little subdivision. The anger in me bubbled like a welt. I stomped across our front yard and maneuvered around the fence separating our property. One glance at the basement window along the side of their house made me tremble with rage. Musings of what could be beyond the glass did not occur. The fact that it existed here and not at our house spoke plenty of the situation.

From the grass, I unearthed a fist-sized stone and hurled it at the window. It bounced off without inflicting any damage, like it was mocking me, laughing at the pathetic boy too weak to even break a window.

On the second throw, the rock shattered it to bits.

The noise echoed far and loud. Scared me so bad I fled back inside our house and hid in my bed. Through my bedroom window, I could hear the neighbors return home several hours later, although none of them seemed to notice the damage I'd inflicted. Perhaps it was simply too late and they'd immediately succumbed to exhaustion. I waited all night to hear a scream that never arrived.

Two days later the window was fixed. Almost like it'd never been broken, like my actions were meaningless. No one had even come to talk to me about it. I stood near our fence, unable to stop staring at the flawless fixture. Behind me, the school bus pulled away and the other kids in my neighborhood laughed and shouted, relieved to have finished another day of education. I could not share their excitement. All I felt was the absolution that my existence didn't mean anything and nothing I did would ever alter this truth. I could break every window in the world and within a week they'd be replaced with new ones.

I fled inside our house and found my parents on the couch, entwined together like the infinity symbol. Although they were both stripped naked, inappropriate activity was not present. The oxys had already knocked them out. I sat on the floor in front of the couch and leaned my head against an empty space on one of the cushions and closed my eyes and visualized glass shattering and reforming over and over until sleep came knocking.

I woke up to a stinging sensation across my face and Dad standing over me, still naked, pointing at me like I'd been up to no good.

"What'd you do with it, you little shit?" he said.

"I didn't touch them. I swear."

He shook his head, the sound of his teeth grinding loud enough to penetrate my own skull. "The Xbox, goddammit. It ain't in your room."

"Wh-what?" A coherent response failed me. Paranoia raised the question of whether or not this was a test. Either way, he didn't like my answer. Slapped me so hard my head just about performed a three-sixty. I felt like a cartoon character without an audience, no laugh track or anything.

Dad grabbed my shoulders and leaned his face in real close to mine and demanded my Xbox. Behind me, still on the couch, Mom rolled in her sleep and groaned for us to keep the noise down. Instead of giving him an answer, I started weeping, which only pissed him off more. The reason he wanted my Xbox was he hadn't gotten paid yet and they were already out of oxys, so he'd drop the Xbox off at the pawnshop and go restock their pill supply. The only problem in this plan, which I couldn't find the courage to tell him, was he'd already pawned my Xbox last month.

He wouldn't have believed me even if I did remind him, and if he *did* remember after the fact, he sure as hell would never have admitted it. So, instead, he squeezed my face and screamed for something I couldn't give him, and then eventually he got bored and got dressed and stormed out of the house. The sound of his car screeching from the driveway relieved an enormous weight from my chest and I settled back against the couch. Mom shifted again and asked me to fetch her a cup of water. Her mouth was dry.

✶✶✶

The second time I broke the window came a couple weeks later. I had decided to do it the night before. Nothing specific prompted the decision. I had simply been lying in bed, listening to Mom and Dad arguing in the living room, when the thought crossed my mind. *Tomorrow I will break the window again.* It generated not as a question but a fact. Tomorrow I would break the window, and when tomorrow arrived that's exactly what I did.

Sunday mornings always mystified me. We'd never been a church-going family, never discussed religion or the possibility of deities. Kids at school referenced Christianity as if it were a common limb attached to everybody's bodies. Weekly visits to wooden pews. God and Jesus and all that trash. Waking up early dressed like rich folks. What a scam. But our neighbors fell for it every Sunday without fail. That specific morning, I sat next to my bedroom window early enough to beat the sun, waiting for them to pull out of our subdivision. Eventually, they emerged from the house wearing clothes our family could never hope to afford. All four of them smiling and enjoying each other's presence. It made me want to break all the windows in the world.

But I'd settle for the one in their basement.

At least for now.

This time around I came prepared with a baseball bat resting along my shoulder. The aluminum rattled against my palms with each contact it made against glass. It took five good swings for the window to spiderweb, another two for it to completely surrender. My former cowardly self would have fled at the sound it made, but something inside of me had changed. Now, I feared nothing.

I knelt in the dirt and stuck my head through the window, careful to avoid slicing my throat open with the remaining shards sticking out along its sides. Sunlight reflected off the broken glass on the floor below. Winking at me. Inviting me inside. Instead of accepting its offer, I scanned the rest of the basement from my vantage point outside. The interior disappointed curiosity. Boxes covered with sheets were lined up against the wall. A wooden staircase led from the floor to a door several feet up, into . . . what? The kitchen? This was the first basement I'd ever seen in real life and out of all the emotions I expected to feel, I had foolishly omitted "boredom" from the list. Now that the window was broken, nothing further seemed to offer much excitement.

Then I saw it.

On the opposite side of the basement, nearly swallowed by darkness: a door.

But not only a door . . .

. . . a door with a padlock attached to it.

✳✳✳

The rest of the week moved at a glacial pace. Whenever I closed my eyes, I saw the door in our neighbor's basement. The mystery followed me like disease. What awaited beyond it remained an intangible black hole that irritated my flesh and swallowed my concentration. At night, I rolled around in bed fantasizing the myriad secrets hidden inside their locked room, imagination running the gamut of potential treasures. Money, of course, but money seemed too obvious. What kind of secret could a family keep that would require a padlock? Locks kept things from escaping. It seemed logical to assume whatever was in that room could be alive. Could be dangerous. A prisoner, but why?

Several days after the second window breaking, I asked

Dad about the neighbors. He was in the kitchen sprawled out on his back, halfway under the sink with a wrench as he attempted to fix a leaky pipe.

"No," he said in the midst of struggling, "they don't talk to me, and I don't talk to them. If you was wise, you'd do the same. Nothing good ever happened from letting goddamn strangers in on your business."

"Did they live here when we moved here, or did they come after?"

Dad sighed and slammed the pipe on the floor and sat up. The look in his eyes was the same look he always gave me. It was the only look.

"Do you think I have the kinda time to sit around paying a single goddamn second to who lives in this neighborhood? I worry about me and my family and that's it. The hell's got you so interested in this shit, anyhow?"

I shrugged. To admit the truth would be the same as issuing a death sentence upon myself. "Nothing. Never mind."

"You ain't been fucking around, telling people things that's no concern to them, have you?"

"No."

"Denny . . . "

"I promise."

He stared at me for several seconds before returning to the sink. The moment he broke eye contact, I fled to my bedroom and shut the door.

The next day, I found the courage to sneak back across our property line. Someone had boarded up the window. What had our neighbors thought, coming home to find the very same fixture shattered again? Would they bother replacing it a third time, or instead stick with wood and nails forever? I did not want to break wood. I wanted to destroy glass. I wanted to hear the sound of something shatter.

Before I could process the actions of my limbs, I was already standing on their front porch and ringing the bell.

WHAT AM I DOING WHAT AM I DOING WHAT AM I DOING, my brain screamed.

The door opened and before me stood the residence's father figure, sometimes referred to as "the man of the house" on TV. He smiled down at me. Although he was not dressed for church, his clothes still seemed infinitely nicer than anything my family could ever dream of owning. "Hello there, son. How can I help you?"

My throat threatened to close. *Son?* He had called me his son. Why had I come here? This was never part of the plan. *What plan?* No such thing existed. I was here because I was meant to be here. I opened my mouth to speak but words refused to form beyond a soft croak. The man of the house stepped back, his initial welcoming posture rapidly deteriorating.

"Son, is something wrong?"

He knelt so we were eye level and clamped a hand upon my shoulder. The contact weakened my knees and I nearly collapsed right there on his front porch. Memories of the last time an older man touched me exploded like lightning. Dad squeezing my throat, both of us crying, screaming loud enough to rupture the universe.

I swallowed.

Took my time.

Then said, "Sugar?"

"Excuse me?"

I pointed behind him, into the house. "My mom needs to borrow sugar. Can we borrow sugar?"

"Sugar?" He hesitated, chewing over what I said, still kneeling, then smiled. "Your momma fixing a cake, son?"

I nodded, enthusiastic. "It's my birthday."

"Today?"

"Yes."

The man's face morphed into pure excitement. "Well, how about that!" He ran his hand through my hair and stood. "Come on in, son."

I followed him into the house and shut the door behind

me. It felt good to lie. Almost as good as breaking windows. My heart started beating like I'd been sprinting through a field. I wanted it to beat so fast it'd burst through my chest and paint the neighbor's kitchen with my blood. The ultimate shattering.

The inside of their house looked just as fancy as their church clothes. I wanted to burn it to the ground. I wanted to live there forever. The man fetched a bag of sugar from a cupboard and asked how much we needed. I stared at him for several seconds, trying to decide how much sugar a cake could possibly need.

"A lot," I finally said. "A whole bag."

He cocked his brow. "A whole bag?"

"Yes."

"How much cake is your momma making, son?"

"A lot."

"Well." He hesitated, glancing at the bag of sugar in his hands and then back at me. "Okay, I suppose since it's your birthday and all, why the heck not?"

"Where are your kids?" I asked.

"What?"

"Your kids."

"Oh." He bit his lip, the warmness to him briefly evaporating before returning. "They're in the basement, with my wife."

"The basement?"

"Yeah." He nodded, completely unaware of the concert of noise thundering inside me. "They're playing."

"What are they playing?"

"Say, son . . . " He touched my shoulder again. This time a little tighter, a little rougher. I thought of Dad again. " . . . don't you think maybe it's about time you went back to your momma? Otherwise, how else is she gonna make a birthday cake for the birthday boy, right?"

He led me back through his kitchen and living room and out the front door. He stood on the porch and watched me walk back to my house. Something told me, even after

I entered and closed the door, he remained out there, watching . . .

 . . . Waiting . . .

★★★

That night, curled up in bed, I dipped my finger in the bag of sugar and sucked it dry. I kept repeating the action until a headache emerged, then I did it a few more times just for the hell of it.

Next door, the family had been playing in their basement. *Playing what?* I didn't just want to know. I *needed* to know. Playing in the locked room, surely. Playing with whatever they kept hidden from the rest of the world. Playing with some*one* or some*thing*?

I did not have a clock in my room to obsess over, so instead I watched the headlights shine against my wall through the window. Cars passing in the dead of night to places I could not imagine. None of them knew the truth. None of them knew they were driving past a house with a locked door in its basement. None of them even cared.

I cared.

I cared so much.

It was easier to sneak outside than I anticipated. All I had to do was tell myself I had fallen asleep and everything that followed was simply a dream. In dreams, consequences did not exist. A person could do anything in a dream and it always ended the same. You woke up and after a couple minutes you forgot it ever happened.

Turned out wood was much easier to remove than glass. I sat on my butt, took out dad's wrench and pried the boards loose. It created a soft thud in the dirt, but nothing too distressing. Nothing that would alarm the floors above—or at least I hoped. I slid through the window and let gravity drag me down several feet to concrete. I hadn't expected the drop to be so high and it was a miracle I didn't break my ankles. It only occurred to me after infiltrating the basement that I'd neglected to form an escape plan. But that was okay. I would worry about that later.

After I discovered what was behind the door.

All the nights I'd spent fantasizing about being in this basement, and the moment had finally arrived. The musty scent made my eyes water and nostrils twinge. I moved slowly across the dusty concrete, taking it slow, enjoying every second of my limited time here.

I'd brought the baseball bat with me, intending on using it to bash open the padlock. Of course I was aware of the noise it would make, and what that would mean. The family would wake and come downstairs to investigate. I didn't care about being caught. As long as I made it inside the room first. As long as I *saw*.

Something shiny gleamed in the corner of my eye as I neared the room, a small key winking at me from the edge of a table. I didn't want to feel disappointed, but if I could control my emotions then I wouldn't have been down in this basement in the first place. Finding the key felt wrong. Like it'd been waiting for me. I set down the bat and held up the key, feeling its various ridges before giving up and inserting it into the padlock. The mechanism popped open.

Maybe this really was a dream, after all.

I opened the door.

Inside the room, I was met with total darkness. The odor shifted from a strong musk to something . . . rancid. Like meat that'd sat out too long. I gagged, shot both hands up to my mouth, terrified of breathing in whatever awaited inside. The time for retreating had expired. I stepped forward and felt around the wall closest to the door. Eventually, a light switch materialized in the darkness. One flip and a dim bulb dangling from a chain in the center of the room buzzed to life.

A dim bulb, dangling directly above a small figure.

At first, I mistook the shape for a mannequin. Like something displayed in a shopping mall. Except . . . it was hard to tell at first, but the thing's chest had a steady rise and drop to it. I assumed the figure was a child based on its height, which nearly matched my own. As to its sex, I could not venture a guess, as its entire body had been wrapped in an old, mildewed cloth material. Even its face had been confined in the stuff. The nearer I approached, the worse its stench became, but I would not allow something as trivial as a horrid odor to prevent me from fulfilling what I'd set out to accomplish tonight.

We stood inches apart from each other in an otherwise empty room. No toys, no books. There wasn't even a goddamn mattress. How long had the family kept this child here, and for what purpose? Something sinister. Something evil.

"Hello," I whispered. "My name is Denny."

The child did not react to my voice.

Could it see me?

I raised a hand, palm out. *I'm friendly,* the gesture represented. *I come in peace.*

"You are my neighbor," I said, and softly touched the child's shoulder.

Somewhere from behind its face wrap: a gasp.

Then the figure jerked forward, wrapping its arms around me.

Hugging me.

I tried to jerk away but its grip solidified like concrete. I stopped resisting and embraced the situation. It wasn't hurting me. I felt nothing but desperation from its touch. A plea for help.

"Okay," I finally whispered by where I assumed its ear was located, although who could tell for sure with the cloth wrapped around its head? How could it even breathe like that? "Okay, okay, okay. Let's get you out of here."

✱✱✱

I led the imprisoned child up the basement steps and through the house. We moved slowly, careful not to bump into anything in the darkness. I expected the father of the family to be waiting for us somewhere upstairs, somewhere in the shadows. But he never showed. We slipped through the front door without incident. I led the child across the property line and into my own house, not thinking about my parents until I saw them in the living room, passed out on the couch. Crushed up pills all over the coffee table. Empty beer cans discarded on the rug. I was relieved the child couldn't see any of this. The embarrassment would have killed me. Gripping its hand, I whispered for it to follow me, we were almost there, and up the stairs we went to my bedroom.

I kept the light off and the door locked. After some guidance, the child sat on my bed. Somehow its stench had started to become tolerable. I could live with this smell. Live with it? Already I had fantasized a life with this stolen child in my bedroom. I would share my meals with it, read it bedtime stories, raise it as my own. We'd be best friends, forever and always. Someone I could talk to and share my deepest secrets. This could work. This could actually work.

I snuck a glance out my bedroom window. The neighbor's house still appeared dark. Nobody was awake. Nobody had noticed a goddamn thing. My heart wouldn't stop racing and I never wanted it to stop. I sat on the bed next to the child and tapped it on the thigh. It didn't react.

"Can you hear me?" I asked.

Nothing.

"How long have they kept you prisoner?"

Nothing.

"What . . . what were they doing to you?"

Same response, rinse and repeat.

I wasn't going to get anywhere using words. I reached up and touched the thing's face, intending on peeling off its wrapping, but couldn't locate the end of it. I trailed my hands along its body and came up with nothing to grab. The child wasn't wrapped in anything.

This was its flesh.

"Oh my god."

I tried to leap off the bed but the child lunged at me, wrapping its arms around my shoulders again. It lay along the bed, dragging me down with it. I did not resist.

Together we spooned in the darkness. My body still tense, expecting the door to burst open any second, either Dad or the next-door neighbor; I couldn't decide which possibility I feared most. Despite the anxiety, the child's embrace felt comforting. I never wanted it to let go.

I fell asleep in its arms and woke up the same day.

When I rolled over, I had to bite my lip to prevent screaming.

Its no-face had morphed into something somewhat resembling a human being's. Like its skull had been made of clay and someone had pressed their fingers against it, molding the template for eyes and a nose and mouth.

"What the hell," I said, reaching up to touch them.

Its face felt hot.

Overheated.

"What are you? Oh my god, what are you?"

My neighbor continued to hug me and I was left with no choice but to stay in bed. Its grip tightened, like it was restricting my lungs from breathing properly. I had slept most of the night, yet I was still dog-tired.

I woke up before I realized I was even going to sleep.

The child's face had continued evolving. Now it had pupils, teeth, and pores.

And hair.

No longer an *it*, but a *him*.

I'd seen this face before.

Chills trickled down my body.

My body, which felt drained of all energy. I couldn't have gotten up now if I wanted to. There was nothing left.

This thing was doing something to me.

Emptying me.

Of what?

Goddammit, *of what?*

Before I could give it any more thought, I was already asleep again.

The next time I woke up, I thought I'd melted into the

mattress. I tried to move something as simple as my toe and failed. I couldn't talk, either. I couldn't do anything.

The boy was smiling now.

"Hello," he whispered into my ear. His voice sounded like metal. "My name is Denny." He hugged me tighter. "You are my neighbor."

✶✶✶

I woke with just enough energy to stand from the bed. If I turned my head to the side, everything became blurry, so I kept my focus straight ahead as I stumbled downstairs. In the living room, I stopped in front of a mirror and confirmed what I'd already expected.

I found my parents still on the couch. The crushed-up pills had disappeared from the table. Sometime during the night they had woken up, snorted them, then passed back out. The boy sat on the floor next to them, legs Indian-style, staring up at me.

Smiling.

"Go home," he told me. "It's time to go home."

If I still had a mouth, I would have told him okay.

I would have told him good luck.

Instead, I walked outside and headed next door. I crawled through the basement window, easing myself down carefully this time. Despite no longer having eyes, somehow I could still see. Everything seemed blurry. Like a camera lens contaminated with a fingerprint. If I walked any faster I would have fallen, but there was no need to rush. I was where I was supposed to be. Where I was always supposed to be.

I entered the empty room and closed the door behind me and stood under the dangling lightbulb and waited.

Eventually, my family would come down to check on me, and together we would play.

There were no windows here.

BLOOD DUST

I.

A WILD PACK of dogs got in the trash last night. I could hear them from my bed, knocking over the cans and digging in. Mother had thrown out a half-eaten dish of casserole that had spoiled. They'd hit a goldmine.

Everybody in the hills knew these dogs. They moved fast, like a shadow in your peripherals. Some thought they slept all day and only roamed the land during nightfall like bona fide vampires. But I'd seen them a few times when the sun was out. It was rare, but I'd seen them. They liked to frequent the junkyard. So did I. The junkyard was neutral ground for both boy and dog alike.

Back in my bedroom, I remained quiet and still, listening to the dogs feast upon our leftovers. I imagined myself sneaking outside, on my hands and knees, facedown in the trash. I thought about the moon hanging over my naked body and gifting me with just enough light to see. No parents, no rules. Complete and total freedom.

If I snuck outside, would the dogs welcome my presence?

Or would they rip me to pieces?

The front screen door swung open and Father ran outside, screaming and shooting his shotgun. The dogs barked and took off into the night. Father's screams sounded farther away as he chased after them, following each yell with another buckshot. My own dog, Toad, was losing his mind in the backyard, where he was tied to a pole. He was probably watching the whole scene, desperately wanting to contribute.

It was like this every night. Soon, Toad would break away from his pole and tear after them. I always wondered why the pack didn't mess with him. They typically ignored his existence. What did my dog have that they didn't?

And the answer was that Toad had a master, and the pack of dogs did not. They answered to nobody. Humanity did not control their lives. The dogs controlled humanity.

A half hour later, Father returned to the house, panting heavily as he got a glass of water from the kitchen. Mother was awake too, and she was lecturing him about giving himself another heart attack. Father told her it was too early to listen to that kind of shit. He was tired and sore, and the last thing he wanted to hear was a bunch of nonsense about heart attacks.

"Besides," he said, "those goddamn dogs will be the death of me long before my ticker kamikazes."

II.

That morning, during breakfast, Father drank his coffee one gulp after the other. My little sister, Mel, was sitting next to me at the table, smashing potatoes with the bottom of her fork. Father finished off his second cup of coffee and cleared his throat. He waited until Mel and I gave him our full attention. "Now, kids, I'm sure you both woke up last night from all the racket. As you know, those damn dogs have been getting in our trash every night, making a mess of things. I just wanted to tell y'all not to go messin' about with these dogs. I know some of your friends like to play with 'em, but hear me right now, these dogs are dangerous. Some dogs you pet. These are not those types of dogs. They're vicious and hungry. They got that ache in their stomachs."

Mel nodded. "I heard you shootin' at 'em."

"You heard correctly."

"Did you kill any of the doggies?"

Father shook his head. "No. I wasn't trying to kill them. I was shooting up, toward the sky, just to scare them."

"Oh," Mel said. "I hope you didn't hit the moon."

"The moon's invincible, baby."

"Are you like the moon, Daddy?"

"Yeah, baby, I'm like the moon."

III.

After breakfast, Mel and I went down to the junkyard. We took Toad with us and we met up with Billy and Gunther next to the perimeter gate. At the sight of my sister, Gunther sighed and asked why I had to bring along a snot-nosed girl.

"I ain't snot-nosed," Mel said.

"Sure you are," Gunther told her, and looked back at me, awaiting a response.

I shrugged. "Mel's all right. Don't be so harsh."

"Just don't let her get any snot on me."

"I'll punch your face in, you call me snot-nosed one more time," Mel said, making fists. And even though she was a few years younger than us all, Gunther still flinched and stepped back.

"Besides," I said, "Mel's smaller than us. She can fit into places we can't."

Gunther seemed to contemplate it, then nodded. "Good point."

One by one, we crawled through an opening in the gate where someone had split apart the wiring. I held Toad's leash tight, paranoid that he'd go running off and get lost in the depths of the junkyard. This place was a labyrinth of hidden paths and dead ends. Decomposing cars waited in the shadows to swallow us as soon as we let down our guard.

We breathed through our mouths. The rot of the town's

leftovers invaded our senses and filled our lungs with vomit. To take our minds off the stench, me and Mel told the others about last night.

"Yeah," Billy said, "they got our house, too."

Gunther shook his head, amused. "One day, all the dogs of the universe will eat us humans and rule the stars."

"My daddy says the moon is invincible," Mel said.

"Nothing's invincible," Gunther said.

As we walked deeper into the junkyard, Toad grew agitated. Something up ahead gnawed at him, and when we rounded a corner, we understood.

The dogs stood in a circle, feasting on an animal carcass. At the sound of our arrival, they stopped eating and lifted their heads to stare at us. Billy muttered an obscenity and stepped back.

"Don't run," I told him. "They'll chase us if we show 'em our backs."

Toad growled at the pack, and the pack growled back.

"This is gonna get bad," I said.

"What do we do?" Gunther asked, shaking.

"It's okay." Mel stepped forward and waved her hands out at the dogs. "It's okay, doggies. Don't be mad. We're not gonna hurt you."

"Your sister's gonna get us killed!" Gunther said.

I didn't say nothing. Mel continued soothing the dogs, and after a minute, they stopped growling and returned to their carcass.

"Let's go," I whispered. We slowly backed away, and once we were out of the dogs' sight, we ran like hell. Once we'd made it to the other side of the fence, we collapsed in the grass, out of breath.

"I told y'all," Gunther said, "them dogs are gonna rule the stars."

IV.

We went home for lunch. Mother already had some sandwiches prepared. Mel told Mother about the incident at the junkyard.

"What did your father say about them dogs?"

"We know," I said. "We didn't touch 'em or nothing. Once we saw 'em, we left right away. They didn't really care about us, anyway."

"They was busy," Mel said.

"Doing what?"

"They was eatin' dead things, Momma."

Mother shook her head slowly. "You don't go messin' with them dogs."

"But we eat dead things, too, Momma," Mel said. "We eat dead things just like the doggies."

"We aren't dogs, honey."

V.

The dogs came back that night. They weren't as loud this time, and managed to eat our trash without being disturbed. Maybe they learned noise meant buckshot. When Father woke up in the morning, he raised all sorts of hell. He dragged me out of bed and instructed me to clean up the mess.

"It's your own damn fault," he told me. "The trash cans are right by your window. You should've heard 'em and woke me up."

Outside, Toad was missing. His rope hung from the pole, but the end of the rope was chewed and torn.

VI.

Mel was heartbroken. During breakfast, she refused to touch her plate. Father and Mother told us Toad would come back when he got hungry. He was just out for a run, stretching his legs.

Mel sat by Toad's pole all day, crying. I asked her if she wanted to go play at the junkyard, and she shook her head, told me she wasn't leaving the pole until Toad returned. So I left her there and met up with Billy and Gunther outside the junkyard. I told them about Toad. They all seemed to have their own theories.

"Maybe aliens from outer space sucked him up into the sky," Billy said.

"That's stupid," Gunther said. "He probably just ran away. Hell, he might even be here."

We looked at the fence, then back at each other. Suddenly it felt like Toad could be no other place but the junkyard. We slid underneath the fence, running blindly through the alleys of trash.

But all we found were animal carcasses, covered in flies and maggots and smelling so foul we had to go vomit our breakfasts. It was a ghost town and we were the ghosts. We walked around for a little while, throwing rusted cans at each other, but it just wasn't as fun without Toad keeping us company.

I returned home, mind racing with curiosities. Mel was still sitting by the pole, only now she wasn't alone. The dogs stood around her, snarling. Toad stood in front of them all, and at that moment I realized he now belonged to the rest of the pack.

Mel smiled at Toad, holding her hand out.

But Toad wasn't smiling.

"Mel, no!" I screamed, and ran toward them.

When I reached the backyard, the dogs were gone and so was my sister's soul.

VII.

Nobody slept that night. Mother sat on the porch and cried. Cried 'til her eyes were raw and leaking blood dust. Father drank in the living room. I stayed in bed, looking through my window at the pole in the backyard. It was stained red.

In the morning, I sat alone at the kitchen table. I fixed some toast and dragged the breakfast on for hours.

Billy and Gunther stopped by my house later that afternoon. They wanted to know why I hadn't met them at the junkyard. I told them what happened. Afterward, they both stared at me, then left without saying another word. Our young minds couldn't contemplate these sorts of horrors. If given the choice to flee, one would flee. But I didn't have that choice. I was stuck here in the house, the same house my sister used to run around in, laughing and playing with our dog.

There had been a time when this kitchen was full and bright with love. Mel, Father, and Mother had all once sat here with me, as a family, Toad under the table, searching for dropped food.

Now it was just me.

I was alone but still trapped in this miserable house.

I wanted to run but my legs would not behave.

When Father came home that night, he told me he quit his job.

"If your mother comes home, tell her not to wake me up in the morning," he said, and kissed the neck of a whiskey bottle. I watched him drink himself stupid on the couch, staring blankly ahead and losing his mind in the cracks of the wall. I wanted to know what he was thinking. I wanted to know what he was going to do about everything. Where was Mother? Where was Toad?

What were we going to do with Mel?

Who was gonna bury her body?

But I couldn't ask him that. He wasn't himself, and I doubted he would be himself ever again. I'd lost more than just a sister.

Father told me he hadn't quit his job. He'd been fired. He'd broken down at work and punched his boss. He couldn't think straight anymore, he told me. Couldn't see what was right in front of him.

"Is Mother coming home?" I asked him.

"Home is gone, boy. Home is gone."

VIII.

I sat in bed all night, leaning against the wall, my bedroom window wide open as an invitation to the ghosts. The dogs were somewhere outside, howling at the moon in search of dead things to eat.

Toad was with them. I could hear his bark. It was the same bark I'd grown up listening to ever since I was a baby.

These dogs were his new family. I tried to accept that, but couldn't. I'd grown up with Toad. Toad was my everything. My dog. My best friend. I needed him.

I prayed to God and promised that if Toad returned then he would never have to be tied to a pole again. I'd convince Father to let me keep him in my room so we could sleep together every night. And then after Toad was back, maybe somehow we could bring Mel back, too. Maybe we could reverse all these horrors, recycle these nightmares into pleasant dreams where happy endings weren't fairy tales.

If only I could just pray hard enough, I could make everything right. Mother would come back home. Father would quit drinking. Toad would still be our dog. Mel would still be alive.

I sat in my bedroom a long time before eventually falling asleep. My mind raced and so did my heart. I did not know what tomorrow would bring but it was bound to be another round of depression. Another hour of blood, of tears.

Tomorrow would be today, but it would never be yesterday.

IX.

Morning came and Mother still wasn't home. Father was passed out in the living room, his whiskey bottle now empty. I kicked it across the room and winced as it shattered against the wall. But still, Father did not wake.

I left the house and sat out by the pole. I leaned my back against the metal, against my sister's dried blood. I stayed out there all day, just as Mel had before she died. I thought about running through the hills, wild and hungry. I thought about hunting and eating anything and everything. I thought about shedding my clothes and howling at the moon. I wondered if maybe I wasn't supposed to be born human after all. Maybe someone, somewhere, had made a mistake.

The dogs eventually returned. Toad led them past me and to the trash cans, only the cans were empty because nobody had thought to fill them.

I tilted my head back and watched the clouds slowly fade from the sky like they were dissolving into coffee. They were going away, and so was I.

The dogs may not have ruled the stars, but they did rule the hills.

They were free.

FISH

PAUL DESPERATELY WANTED to fuck.

He was seventeen years old for Christ's sake. Everyone he knew was fucking except for him. It didn't make any sense. Statistically speaking, there were more girls at his high school than boys. He should have been chosen by now. He didn't even care by who—anybody would do. If all the girls at his school were getting laid, then why was he still a hopeless, pathetic virgin? Were the girls sharing dicks? What was wrong with his? It worked perfectly fine and he wanted to prove it.

He *needed* to prove it.

He couldn't explain it. Maybe it was a feeling of inadequacy. Everywhere he looked, people were fucking. On the TV, on the Internet, in school; people fucked there, too. He had caught Shawn Callahan and Nancy Hiaasen in the football parking lot the other week; her legs stuck out the windows, her white tennis shoes still tied to her feet. Her panties were hanging from her ankles, and all you could see in the car was Shawn's bare, hairy ass thrusting into the car seat like an animal. Paul remembered her panties had been red. Silky, he thought.

He wanted to be the wild animal in the car, succumbing to all his urges once and for all. He had them just like everyone else. He wanted to fuck. Everyone wanted to fuck. He was the only one who couldn't seem to, though. No one wanted him. They would take Howard Larsen over him, and that was really saying something. Howard Larsen worked at Burger King after school. His face was covered with zits the size of those mini bouncy balls you'd get out of a quarter machine. You would take one look at those things and just want to thwack it as hard as you could until it exploded hamburger grease all over the place. Plus he had glasses—huge, black-framed sons of bitches that he constantly had to push up the bridge of his nose on account of sweating so much. That was Howard Larsen for you. It was also the same kid that had gotten a blowjob from Cindy Grace in the Burger King public bathroom. At least that was the rumor. It might have just been a handy.

Still, though. Paul would have killed for a handy. He would have killed for anything.

He needed a release, and jerking off just wasn't doing it anymore. It was too lonely and depressing, hiding away in his bedroom, playing the Rolling Stones to drown out the noise, and just whacking away over muted sex videos online. Even the sex videos were depressing. Watching these women whom he would never meet in real life, knowing that deep down, they didn't give a single shit about Paul. They were just there for the money. Most of the time he wasn't even able to come because he'd sit there imagining what they were thinking. Sure, they were moaning and doing a convincing enough job of enjoying getting pounded in the ass, but he was convinced that in their heads, all they could think about was how a thousand creeps would be watching this, touching their pathetic small cocks, and drooling. It must have creeped them out. It creeped Paul out.

No, he couldn't do the sex videos anymore. He wanted his own movie star just for himself.

He needed to *fuck*.

✱✱✱

It was Bobby Wilburn that first told him about the woman living on Rosewood Boulevard. They were in the woods behind the high school, sharing tokes off a badly wrapped blunt. P.E. class would not miss their absence.

Bobby was probably Paul's best friend, and they weren't even that close. Bobby only hung out with Paul because they'd been thick as thieves back in elementary school. So maybe it was a kind of pity thing, Paul guessed. Bobby had sex all the time. They were nothing alike, anymore.

Paul inhaled on the blunt a little too strong and became lightheaded. He worried about falling down and embarrassing himself in front of his pseudo-friend, but then decided he didn't care. He kind of hoped he did fall.

"Have you done it, too?" Paul asked, trying to take his mind off the fact that the trees were swirling around his face in kaleidoscope-vision.

"Done what?" Bobby took the half-smoked blunt and inhaled deep like he'd been doing it for years.

"You know," he said. "Visited her. That woman."

"Oh. No, I haven't. Lucy would cut my nuts off if I ever did something like that. But like I was saying, Steve did. He told me about it last month."

"What happened?"

Bobby laughed. "What do you think happened, man? They boned. He said she was the best lay he'd ever had in his life, but between you and me—I doubt that's really saying much, considering who we're talking about."

He stopped and gave Paul a look similar to a look Paul had given a schoolmate when he'd made a suicide joke to her in math class, only remembering afterward that her mother had hung herself the previous summer.

"Oh, shit. You're a virgin, aren't you?"

"*What?*" Paul squeaked. He'd been caught. The charade was over. "Of course I'm not a fucking virgin. Jesus Christ."

Bobby looked at him suspiciously, not fooled. "Who have you been with?"

Paul didn't have to think hard. He simply recalled the image that came to mind whenever he didn't have Internet access.

FISH

"Morgen Summers."

"You're full of shit," Bobby said, laughing louder than necessary.

Paul shook his head. "No, really. Last fall, at that Halloween party. We both got wasted off spiked punch and did it in the backyard."

In reality, however, he had gotten drunk at the party alone, wandered outside, and found Morgen fucking the captain of the football team on the grass. He liked to imagine it had been him, though.

Maybe one day it would be.

Bobby stopped laughing and gave a serious look; impressed. "Damn, bro, I actually heard about that. But I thought that'd been with Ronnie."

"That was all me," Paul confided, smiling at the idea.

"Wow. Never thought I'd hear that one. Hot damn."

Paul finished off the blunt and flicked it into some leaves. It was most likely a huge fire hazard but he was simply too high to care. "So anyway, about this woman."

"Yeah."

"What do you know?"

"Well, Steve told me that he'd found out about her on account of some dumbass cousin of his or something. She's just this prostitute, man. Some whore. But I guess she's amazing. Like, from out of this world. Cheap, too, apparently. Real cheap. He told me she suffers from nymphomania or some shit so it's not really like she's doing you a favor, but the other way around."

"On Rosewood Boulevard," Paul said.

"Yeah."

"Where at, though? What house?"

Bobby tried to think but his face made this scrunched up look like he'd swallowed a lemon. "I don't know. I think it's the one with that crazy tree out front."

***

The tree was indeed crazy.

Paul stood out on the sidewalk staring at it. There were

no leaves on it, emphasizing the stripped branches springing from the base like dying hands sticking out of the grave. Arms twisted and curved at impossible angles. It made him sick to his stomach just to look at it.

Yet he couldn't look away.

Beyond the tree was the house. It looked like every other house on Rosewood Boulevard; the only differentiating feature about the place was the tree. Beyond that, it was basically identical to the rest of the neighborhood.

But inside this house, there was something new. Something Live Oak was not used to. This was a town of high standards. It prided itself on its football team, on its politics. It did not tolerate filth.

It did not know about what was living inside the house on Rosewood Boulevard. It did not know about the prostitute.

Paul brought twenty-five bucks with him. He wondered if it would be enough. Maybe he should have just gone back home; do it another day. One of his favorite television shows would be starting soon. Plus his mom was making tacos. They'd be cold if he didn't leave soon.

No.

He mentally punched himself in the face. If he didn't do this—*right here, right now*—then he would forever hate himself. Every night he lay in bed, depressed because he never got chances like this. And now he had one of those chances. A chance to change everything. This was his moment. He wanted to fuck; well, this was where you fucked.

Paul rang the buzzer and waited on the porch. He waited a good five minutes. The day was quiet, the day was still. Just when he was about to give up and go home— tacos once again on the brain—the door swung open, revealing a tall, gorgeous woman standing behind it. Not a *girl*, but a *woman*.

Paul gave her one look and forgot all about tacos and

FISH

TV and everything else. She was a little taller than Paul, with red hair that dropped all the way to her ass. The outer edges of her eyes were shaded purple, as were her lips. She wore a black dress; kind of see-through and silky, but it didn't reveal much skin—like a dress you'd wear on Halloween, Paul thought. But that was all he thought, for his breath had been stolen.

The woman stood there at the door and looked Paul over slowly, then smiled a smile that made his heart skip a beat.

"Hi there," she purred.

All he could do was stare.

"You gonna say anything, stranger?" she asked.

Paul coughed. His skin felt radioactive. "Uh. Hi."

"Can I help you with something?"

"Uh, um, well. I . . . uh."

The woman smiled. "Yes," she said, "yes I can help you with something. Come on in, boy."

Paul did what he was told. It was almost dream-like, how he followed her through the darkly lit house. There was a long hallway, then they were in the kitchen. She told him to have a seat, and asked if he wanted a glass of iced tea.

"Yes," he mumbled. "That would be nice, thank you."

"Sure thing, honey," the woman said, bringing two tall glasses of iced tea to the table and sitting down next to him. She handed him one of the glasses and watched him take a drink. It was good. Very good.

"My name is Lilly. What's yours?"

"Paul."

"Well, Paul, would you like to tell me who told you about me?"

Paul gulped, suddenly feeling like he was in trouble. Jesus, what had he been thinking? Stupid, stupid!

"Paul . . . ?"

"A kid at school," Paul said, finally.

"What's his name?" Lilly asked.

Not wanting to squeal on one of his only friends, he said, "Steve, Steve Luntz."

The woman nodded. "Ah." She took a drink of her iced tea and said, "I know Steve. Steve was a bad apple. He didn't listen to what I said. Are you a bad apple too, Paul?"

"No, ma'am."

"That's good," Lilly said, "because I like my apples to be good." She gave Paul a playful squeeze on the knee and he flinched. He had to adjust his legs to hide the sudden erection rubbing against his jeans.

Lilly smiled. "You ever have sex before, Paul?"

"No, ma'am."

The kitchen was becoming very, very small. He wanted to leave. This was wrong. But it was right, too. He didn't know what to think, so he took another drink of his iced tea.

"Mmm," she said. "That's good, that's real good."

"Ma'am?"

"I like 'em when they're innocent like you. They give me their all."

"Oh."

"That's why you're here, yes?" the woman said. "You want to go to bed with me."

Paul hesitated. "Yes, ma'am."

"Tell me."

He decided to stop thinking. It all felt so much like a dream, he figured he might as well treat it as a dream. A dream, which is like life, only without consequence.

"Tell me, Paul," the woman said again, leaning closer. Her hand traveled from his knee and rubbed up his leg, stopping at his crotch. She gave it a soft squeeze. "Tell me."

"I want to go to bed with you," he whispered.

"How bad?" she asked, leaning closer than any female had ever been to him. She nibbled on his ear and he felt his whole body tighten.

"Bad!"

"What will you do for me?"

FISH

"Anything! Anything you want!"

"Good," she whispered. "Because I'll also give you anything *you* want."

It felt like the buttons on his jeans were going to pop off and go shooting across the room. "*You!* I want *you!*"

"Well, then. Let's go."

The bedroom was dark. The woman wasted no time in pushing Paul onto the bed. She carefully stripped him of clothing while he lay there helplessly. This was really happening. Jesus Christ.

Then she took her own clothes off, the thin rays of sun from the closed blinds revealing pale, white skin. She got on the bed with him and slowly crawled up his body. He felt her nipples rubbing against his skin and he didn't know what to do. Then they were face to face, and she was prying apart his mouth with her own mouth, and penetrating his face with her tongue. It welcomed itself among his teeth and gums and tongue. The woman was hungry and she was feeding. He was her meal. Paul could only lay there, arm on either side of him, and let it happen. He wanted it badly; he wanted it more than anything in the world. He didn't know what to do about it, though, but this woman knew exactly what to do. And that's what she was doing—taking charge.

Then he noticed the smell.

Before he'd been too distracted to notice. But now, in the dark with her tongue going nuts in his mouth, all he could focus on was the smell.

Like fish, he thought. Like a bucket of dead, half-gutted fish left out in the sand all day under the sun.

It smelled *warm*.

It made him want to vomit.

Then she sat up, straddling his lap, and slid down his painfully hard cock. It was wetter than he expected. Almost sickly wet. It reminded him of that time when he was a kid, and his parents had taken him to that haunted house for Halloween. There was this special attraction there where they blindfolded you and made you feel all these different horrorish sensations. They were all supposed to be body parts, according to the haunted house. Like the meatballs were eyes. The egg foo young was a heart.

And the bowl of spaghetti, that was supposed to be guts.

He remembered how old and stale it felt, and how much sauce they'd dumped in the bowl. His hands slid into that bowl and he was greeted with this warm, disgusting sauce. He wanted to pull out, but there was so much goddamn sauce that his hands slid even deeper, until they were rubbing against the bottom of the bowl, nearly elbow-deep in the stuff.

It was the spaghetti he thought about now.

The woman, Lilly, rocked her hips on top of Paul, moaning louder than he expected. It was all very exciting and frightening. The smell grew stronger as the sex continued. He almost started gagging, but stopped himself by reaching around and squeezing her ass, pulling himself closer against her. He felt trapped underneath her, and he loved it.

"Yes, oh yes," the woman moaned. "You are a good one. Yes, you are going to be very, very special. Oh yes."

"Yes," Paul moaned back. Then he came. Hard. His body convulsed and he wrapped his arms around her, squeezing her tight like she was the only thing stopping him from freefalling a thousand feet. Everything went dizzy, and he heard her moaning softly next to him, breathing just as heavy as he was.

"We are going to do wonderful things together," she whispered.

"Yes," he said.

***

Afterward, she turned on the nightstand lamp and went into the bathroom next to the bedroom, leaving Paul flat on his back in bed. He didn't move. He felt completely content. No wonder everyone did this. He couldn't imagine anything better. This . . . this was the meaning of life, right here. For as long as he lived, he would simply need no other answers.

He sniffed and grimaced. The smell still hadn't left. Jesus, what the hell was that? It was awful.

He followed the smell and glanced down his body.

His eyes widened at the sight of himself.

Blood. It was blood.

All over him. On his stomach. On his thighs.

On his cock.

The head looked like it'd been dipped in a jar of pasta sauce. Only this wasn't pasta sauce. It was fucking blood.

"Oh, my god," he cried quietly, and jumped off the bed. He ran into the bathroom with Lilly, almost to tears.

"*What did you do to me?*"

Still sitting on the toilet, the woman took one look at him and frowned. "Yuck. That was a lot messier than I thought it'd be."

"What are you *talking about?* What *happened*?"

She shook her head dismissively. "Nothin' happened to you, honey. That's all me. Sorry, should have told you. I bleed."

"You bleed."

"Many women do, honey."

Paul paused. Looked at Lilly, then back down at his cock. Blood was running down his leg. He sniffed. The smell made him want to kill himself.

He turned and stepped into the glass shower and turned the HOT faucet all the way to the left.

★★★

Over the next two weeks, Paul visited Lilly every other day. He couldn't help himself; it was like an addiction. She was the heroin and he was the pathetic junkie, totally lacking a will of his own. Even when they were in the middle of fucking, he was craving the next time they'd be able to do it again.

And the best thing was, she didn't even charge him

money. Whenever he asked how much she wanted, she would just smile and kiss him and tell him that he was enough, that she just wanted him. Nothing else would compare.

Every man wished to hear those words. He couldn't have been luckier.

The only thing he didn't wish for was the blood. And, of course, the accompanying smell. He had always thought that it was only supposed to last like a week, and then go away for the rest of the month. Yet, it still persisted—if anything, she bled more as they continued the sex.

The thought revolted him. It'd make him gag just thinking about it, and afterward, he would swear never to do it again, not until the menstrual cycle finally passed. But then a day would go by and he would find himself running back to her house on Rosewood Boulevard, knocking feverishly and taking off his clothes before he was even through the front door. He would forget about the blood until they were in the bedroom, and she was sliding down his dick, that smell of rotten fish defiling his nostrils.

One afternoon, a month or so after their relationship began, Paul was in the bathroom wiping himself off with a towel. Lilly was standing in front of the mirror fooling with makeup. Paul couldn't take it anymore. He felt that he'd had enough sex by now to begin questioning things. Sure, he was by no means a pro—but he felt like he at least knew a little bit, now.

"Lilly," he said, trying to breathe out of his mouth.

"Yes, baby."

"I want to ask you something."

"The blood," she said. It wasn't a question.

"Yes."

She nodded in the mirror. "I know, you're probably confused. You think I should have stopped by now."

"It's been over a month."

"I know. But here's what you don't understand, baby."

"What?" Paul asked, not sure if he wanted to know what she was about to say next.

FISH

"It never stops," she said. "I always bleed."

He paused, not knowing what to say. "How? Why?"

"It's my curse," Lilly said. "Some women, they're only cursed once a month. Me, I'm cursed for life."

"I don't understand."

"Neither do I," she said, "but that's just the way it is. Always has been. I hate it just as much as you do. I wish it would go away. Do you wish the same?"

"Of course," he said, then added, as an afterthought, "But I still want to be with you regardless."

Lilly smiled. "That's sweet, baby, but it doesn't have to be so bloody, you know that? We can make the blood go away."

Paul was confused. If she could make it go away, why hadn't she before? "How?"

"I would need your help."

"I don't understand," he said, "what would you need from me?"

She closed her eyes and sighed. It was obvious she didn't want to talk about this any more than Paul wanted to hear it. But these things couldn't be avoided.

"I would need your total devotion," Lilly said at last. "I would need you to be mine, and myself to be yours."

He could feel his dick shriveling up into his body as he stood there in the bathroom, the coldness of the tiled floor sending shivers up his legs. "I thought I *was* yours," he said, confused. "I thought you *were* mine."

She reached over and touched his cheek. "Not yet, baby. You have to really mean it. You have to tell me that you would do anything for me, and promise to devote the rest of your breaths to serving my needs."

Her hand trailed down his naked body and cupped his balls. She squeezed gently.

"Anything you want," Paul whispered. "I am yours forever."

"Good," she said, and kissed him.

Paul felt a chill zap through his whole body. He

suddenly became much lighter than he was used to—he almost felt *weightless.*

She led him back into the bedroom and pushed him onto the mattress. Despite having just ejaculated, Paul had no trouble growing erect again. She straddled on top of him and went wild. Paul watched in awe, stuck in a dream-like state, studying her face as she moaned. He didn't move; even when he finally came again, his facial expression did not alter from the same drugged, monotonous look.

Then she lay down beside him, breathing heavily, and the trance broke. "Jesus Christ," he sighed, ready to pass out from exhaustion.

"No," she whispered in his ear. "He has nothing to do with this."

When he went into the bathroom to shower again, he noticed that his cock was bloodless. It had worked. What he'd said, he'd fixed her. She was better now. Normal.

He looked at his cock for a long time before returning to bed and falling asleep. This was the start of something new.

∗∗∗

Paul heard the words but he didn't quite understand what she meant. Of course, deep down, he knew damn well what she meant, but another part of him found the words she spoke completely alien. This just didn't make any sense.

It shouldn't have been a surprise. Not once had he used protection when they fucked. They warned you about these kinds of things in school all the time, but . . . he didn't know. Once she pulled him into her house, the thought never crossed his mind.

But now . . .

Now she was pregnant.

"How is this possible?" he said. They were sitting at the kitchen table, drinking iced tea. He couldn't remember the last time he'd been home.

"I think you know how it's possible," she said. "Last night, you gave yourself to me, and I accepted. These are

FISH

the consequences. Now, are you man enough to accept this new responsibility?"

He didn't think he was. Then she kissed him, and suddenly he felt like he could take on the whole world. "Yes," he said. "I'm ready."

"Good," she said. "Because we're going to have babies, and I need a man who will be there."

"I'll be there for our baby."

"I'm going to need someone to protect our family," she said.

"I'll protect our family with my last dying breath."

He realized he couldn't remember his mother's face, and wondered if she was worried about him. Then he decided he didn't care. He had a new family to look after now.

★★★

"There's someone you need to deal with."

"What?" Paul said. They were cuddling in bed a few weeks later. He was rubbing her swollen stomach. He could already feel their baby kicking at them. Everything he had learned about pregnancies no longer voiced itself in his head. This was what was real. The woman on Rosewood Boulevard was his only reality now.

"Do you remember that boy, Steve?" Lilly asked. "The one who told you about me?"

He didn't like where this was going. "Yeah. Of course I remember him."

"Well, he used to visit me, like you. But he wasn't good enough. He left me, he called me names. He called me a whore."

"No."

"Yes," she said. "The other day when you went out to the store, he came back. He was mean to me, Paul. He said he was going to tell the whole town about me, about what I'm doing."

"What do you mean?" Paul asked.

"He knows about me and you, honey. If people found out

-121-

about this, there would be hell to pay. People wouldn't approve; they'd hate me and make sure I burned. They'd make me and our baby go far, far away. Do you want that to happen?"

He felt the baby kick again.

"No," he said seriously. "Nothing bad will happen to you. I promise."

"Will you take care of this boy?"

"Yes."

"You'll make sure that he'll never be able to hurt us?"

"Yes."

"Promise me, Paul. For our baby. For our family."

"I promise."

✶✶✶

He had never been good friends with Steve, but they'd spoken on occasion. He'd been to his house a few times to play videogames. It wasn't that far of a walk from Rosewood Boulevard. The house overshadowed his presence like the sun over the earth.

He didn't know what he was even doing here. But he had a feeling he would know when the time came. He was just going with it.

He tried not to think about the knife sheathed in the back of his pants.

The doorbell rang, and after a few moments, Steve's mother answered the door. She took one look at Paul and grimaced, taking a step back.

"Oh my god," she said, "are you okay?"

"Yes, of course, thank you," he said. "Is Steve home?"

She gave him another doubtful look and said, "Uh, yeah, he and Bobby are in his room. Go ahead."

She left the doorway and allowed him entrance. He walked down the hallway to where he remembered the bedroom being, and pushed open the door.

Steve was sitting on the ground playing his PlayStation. Bobby Wilburn was next to him, also gripping a controller. They both turned their heads at once and gave Paul a look of absolute horror.

"Jesus Christ," Bobby said, "what the hell happened to you, Paul? Where have you been?"

Steve jumped to his feet. "You were with her, weren't you? I fucking knew it! Everyone was saying you'd skipped town, but no, not me. As soon as Bobby said he'd told you about that whore, I knew right away what happened. Holy shit. She really got you bad, didn't she? Are you okay?"

"Don't call her that," Paul said, sternly. He took a step forward.

"What?" Steve said. "Listen, you need to sit down, I'll call the police. This time they'll believe me. That fucking bitch . . . I don't even know what she is. I'm just glad I got out before it was too late. I was there the other day, trying to find you . . . and I swear to god, I thought she was going to kill me."

"Shut your mouth," Paul said.

"Hey, uh, Paul, relax," Bobby said, standing up and putting a hand on his shoulder.

Paul reacted almost instinctively, reaching behind his back, pulling out the kitchen knife and thrusting it into the side of Bobby's stomach. Bobby let out an unnatural gasp and bent over. Before anyone could react, Paul took the knife out and slammed the blade down through the back of Bobby's neck.

Bobby fell to the ground, still.

Steve stood on the other side of the room, dazed. The crotch of his blue jeans had turned dark.

"No," he whispered. "Please don't do this."

Paul moved forward. He did not blink.

"You threatened my family," he said.

"What?" Steve groaned, pressing up against the wall with no chance of escape.

"You want to kill my baby?" Paul asked him, holding the knife up against the boy's throat.

"Your *what?* I don't know what you're talking about, man. Please, don't do this."

Paul cocked his head and growled, like a dog on the

prowl. "My family is all I have, and I must protect them. I have no choice."

Steve tried to push him away, but Paul was too powerful, as if overwhelmed by supernatural strength. Paul countered with a headbutt, breaking Steve's nose instantly and sending him flying back against the wall. He leaped on top of his prey like a hungry animal.

"Oh, shit, get off of me, no, please."

Paul drove the knife into Steve's stomach, pulled it out and stabbed him again. Then again. With each thrust, Steve let out an exhausted breath. It excited Paul and made him wish he was back home with his woman. His family.

Paul paused, looking Steve in his dying eyes. He held the tip of the blade up to his neck, panting.

The last thing Steve said was, "Jesus, that smell, it's all over you," and then the knife slit his Adam's apple to shreds and he said no more.

"Oh, god," said a voice from behind him.

He spun around, spotting Steve's mother in the doorway. She was shaking something terrible, looking at Paul like he was a monster.

"What have you done?" she cried.

"What was necessary," he whispered.

She turned around and ran down the hallway. Like a lion, Paul took off after her, the knife gripped in his fist. His eyes stung from the blood caught in them.

The front door swung open, and Paul's heart sank.

He couldn't let her escape. She would tell everyone, and his family would be ruined.

He had to protect his family.

Paul sprinted outside and leaped off the porch steps. Steve's mother was already in the middle of the street, screaming bloody murder. He had to silence her before it was too late.

Paul ran up from behind and punched the knife into her spine, causing her to bend at an odd angle and collapse

FISH

to the ground. The street was empty save for the two of them. No cars in sight. The neighborhood was theirs.

Paul got on top of her, screaming that he had no choice, there was no other way. Then he began to slam the knife in her cheek and he didn't stop until her face was the equivalent of a gutted jack-o-lantern.

"I'm sorry," he whispered again, dropping the weapon on the street. "My family . . ."

And with that, he ran.

✷✷✷

Back home, in the house on Rosewood Boulevard, Paul lay cuddled up to his one and true love. They couldn't have been more content.

The bedsheets were soaked in blood, but it didn't bother him so much this time. It wasn't the same kind of blood.

Paul smiled at the sight of his new babies. Just a few hours old, and they were already scuttling around. He watched them climb up the walls, then onto the ceiling, looking back down at him as they explored this new world he and his darling had brought them into.

They were beautiful.

The woman kissed him softly on the lips and he kissed her back.

His family was safe for the moment. And the next time a new danger threatened them, he would not hesitate to do what was necessary.

He would protect them with his last, dying breath.

IN THE ATTIC OF THE UNIVERSE

STUART HELD THE pistol up to his two-year-old son's skull and closed his eyes. All he had to do was squeeze his finger and everything would be fixed. There would no longer be any reason to worry about Evan, and no longer a reason to not turn the gun on himself and end this horrible fucking excuse of a life once and for all.

Just pull the trigger, and the complications of life would forever cease.

But goddammit, why did the baby have to look so peaceful sleeping like that? Maybe if he looked a little more evil, like one of those goddamn ghouls outside, Stuart would have an easier time doing what needed to be done.

Only that wasn't true at all, because it sure as hell didn't help with Caren. He couldn't end her misery. And now he was bitten and soon he would turn and rip his son's throat out while the poor little baby cried himself to death. It didn't have to be that way, of course. He could prevent the worst of it. Put a bullet through his own skull before it managed to turn against him.

But if he did that, then there would be no one around to care for Evan—which meant Evan had to be taken out first.

Just the thought alone was enough to send Stuart over the edge. The pistol shook in his hand. Tears streamed down his face and his lips quivered and yet the baby didn't so much as fidget in his crib.

He's just a baby for fuck's sake. Why? Why does it have to be this way?

Stuart sighed, blinking the sweat and tears away, and sheathed the pistol back in the leather holster he had scavenged from the police department. Away from the crib, he banged his head against the wall. It wasn't an accident. He kept doing it, and doing it, and doing it.

He invited the pain and the pain accepted.

Most of the walls were covered in egg cartons he'd nailed there; an attempt to soundproof the room from Evan's cries. If enough of those things heard his wailing, then . . . well, it didn't really matter anymore, now did it? He *was* one of those things—or at least he would be relatively soon. He didn't think the egg cartons worked, anyway.

His forearm was wrapped in white gauze, but you couldn't tell the color now, so much blood had soaked through. One stupid mistake, that's all it had taken. One stupid mistake and their lives were ruined.

Stuart flexed his arm and the red in the gauze grew darker.

"Fuck," he said.

He looked back over to the crib, his son sleeping inside, and felt the gun at his hip. He shook his head.

"I can't do this."

Like you have a choice.

"No," he said, voice trembling. His eyes retired to the floor, vision blurred. "I can't."

Stuart headed over to the trapdoor and lowered the dropdown staircase. Evan would be waking up from his nap any time now. He didn't want to be around when he did. At least not right now. He didn't think he could stand looking into his son's eyes, seeing his smile, knowing full well that he would have to put a bullet into it within the next day or so.

The cabinet above the sink was full of various bottles of booze he'd boosted from the liquor store some odd weeks previous. Now he grabbed a bottle of whiskey down, twisting the cap off and splashing it in the general proximity of his mouth. It felt so warm and welcoming. How easy it would be just to drink the whole bottle; lose control of everything, blackout from reality and do whatever he wanted. His inability to shoot Evan would cease, and everything would be taken care of. Just down the bottle and let the rest work out by itself . . .

Stuart threw away the bottle and left the kitchen, disgusted with himself. That was his *child*, for Christ's sake. He couldn't *kill* him. He just couldn't.

One way or another, you're gonna. Best do it the easy way now or else it's bound to get a helluva lot messier.

Stuart walked through the house into his old bedroom; the one he had once shared with his wife of three years. The mattress was upstairs in the attic, leaving behind just a lonely box spring. He stood in front of the steel structure and closed his eyes, reminiscing of a time when the bed was still together in the room and he was under the covers spooning next to his wife; his arm wrapped around her, hand massaging her tummy. He could still feel Evan inside, evolving into the beautiful baby boy that he was now.

The same beautiful baby boy he now had to kill.

Stuart wiped his eyes and approached the bathroom in the bedroom, reaching into his pocket and pulling out a key. He cautiously inserted it into the padlock he'd installed in the door, and stored both the lock and key back into his pocket.

Caren had heard him pacing in the bedroom, so when Stuart entered the bathroom she was already standing and reaching out toward him, fully alert. Fortunately, her hand was cuffed to the railing in the shower, forcing her momentum to come to an abrupt stop before it even began. Stuart didn't flinch; just leaned against the sink with his arms crossed, looking at his wife. He realized that he was trying to hide his gauzed arm from her, and quickly loosened up, thinking how ridiculous it was to worry about what his wife did or didn't see.

Caren was trying with all her strength to come after him, but she couldn't gain another step forward as the steel handcuffs held her a good two feet away. And even if she could, it wasn't like there was much of a risk of being bitten considering he had long ago removed all of her teeth. Her cheeks now were sunk deep into her face, like a blowfish who had forgotten how to blow back out.

Besides, did it really matter anymore if he was bitten?

Stuart opened his mouth to talk, but instead of a voice, only an awkward guttural cough came out. Clearing his throat, he tried again.

"Hi, honey."

Caren recoiled back, eyes widening, like a dog whose food bowl suddenly started talking. This defensive reaction only lasted a few seconds, however, as she was quickly right back to reaching out toward him with her desperate fingers, tongue curling out from her opened mouth, yearning to taste him.

Stuart tried to ignore all this and instead pictured his wife how she had looked back in bed, when he was spooning up against her, rubbing her swollen tummy, feeling the life they had made together. It proved damn near impossible seeing how she barely even had a stomach at this point; her ribs sticking out through the Chicago House of Blues T-shirt he had dressed her in. He opted instead to look at the tiled floor, training his vision on a patch of mold growing on the marble.

Caren started making this low, screeching noise under her breath, sending goosebumps down Stuart's spine. He tried to drown it out with his own voice.

"I fucked up," he said. "I fucked up real bad." He cleared his throat again. "I don't know how to say it, baby, but everything is fucked. I'm bitten, Caren. I'm gonna turn. I don't know what's gonna happen with Evan but it's not gonna be pretty."

He wiped his eyes and sniffled a little, saying, "I woke up early, the boy was still asleep, usually wouldn't have woken up for another hour or two, so I thought maybe I'd slip out and find something good for breakfast, you know? Most of everything is looted, but, you know, sometimes you get lucky and find something. Yeah, well, not this time. I didn't find a fuckin' thing. And as I was leaving . . . "

He stopped talking, remembering how the creature had jumped out at him from behind the door, like he'd been hiding there, waiting in that spot for somebody to come walking past. Caught off guard, Stuart was easily tackled to the ground. He lifted his hands to shield his face and that was when the fucking bastard sunk his fangs into his forearm. His subsequent scream was loud enough to echo throughout the grocery store. It was a scream rooted not in pain but out of the agonizing knowledge of the path this bite would lead to.

The blood spraying like a slit hose, Stuart knocked the monster to the side, fumbling at his hip for the pistol. He pulled it out, aimed it at the sonofabitch who'd just murdered him and his son, got ready to pull the trigger and then thought better of it. Who knew how many walkers he'd attracted from that scream; any further noise would be a guaranteed death sentence.

The creature was crawling to his feet, looking at Stuart like he planned on murdering Evan himself. Stuart dived at him, slamming the butt of the pistol into the monster's face. He picked up his arm and swung down again, then again and again and again, the whole time the zombie's claws digging into Stuart's back as the pistol smashed further into his skull until all that was left was a bloody pulp of a head. Brain matter and other repulsive oozes dripped down Stuart's own face, staining his clothes, contaminating his eyes and blurring his vision.

But it still wasn't enough. He shoved the gun back into its holster and proceeded to punch and stomp the stupid motherfucker between the shoulders until there was barely even a skull left, just a thick puddle of death with white shards poking out.

Back in the bathroom, Stuart couldn't control himself anymore.

"I killed our baby boy," he said. "I killed him."

Caren had stopped trying to attack him and was now sitting there on the shower floor with her legs crossed, watching her husband talk. He didn't know if it was because she was truly sad or if it was just the whole being a zombie bit, but Stuart swore her eyes were beginning to water.

"Are you there?" he asked, suddenly excited, and stood up. But as soon as he moved, Caren snapped out of her little daze and was scrambling to her feet and clawing toward him. He stood mere inches from her touch. Her jaw snapped up and down; eyes no longer watery but wide and dry, pained by her eternal ache.

Stuart shook his head; considered shooting his wife in the head and ending this pathetic charade, but heard his son up in the attic making a fuss, and instead locked the bathroom again and went upstairs to attend to him.

His arm was throbbing.

***

Evan was standing up in his crib, leaning against the railing, shaking the whole thing in his grasp. He was yelling, "Daddy! Daddy!"

It took all of Stuart's strength to respond with the usual banter of yelling back, "Son! Son!"

The baby smiled.

How could he ever be expected to put an end to such a smile?

He laid the baby down on the crib mattress, changing his diaper and tickling his tiny feet. Evan giggled and giggled without a hint of knowledge of the inevitable events ahead of them.

Stuart yearned for such ignorance.

"You hungry, buddy?"

Evan smiled. "Mmm hmmm."

Stuart picked him up out of the crib, hugging him close to his chest.

"Well, what should we have for lunch?"

"No!" Evan yelled at him.

"Oh, you want 'no'?"

"No."

"How about a peanut butter and jelly sandwich instead?"

"No!"

"Hmm," Stuart said, and smiled in spite of his pain. "What about a . . . PB&J sammich?"

"Yeah!"

"That's what I thought."

"No," Evan said again.

"Oh? What did I think then?"

The baby shrugged and started kicking to be let down. Stuart set him on the floor and walked over to their food shelf. There were only two slices of bread left in their stock; both of them heels, too. He spread the peanut butter and warm jam and cut it up into fours, putting it all on a Styrofoam plate and setting it on the cardboard box they were using as a table. Evan quickly scurried toward it, cradling a Power Rangers action figure in his arm like a football.

Stuart sat on the floor with his back leaning against the wall and watched his son dig into the sandwich. When Evan was done, he went back to playing with his Power Rangers and Stuart dug out his old train set from one of the Christmas boxes and set everything up. It'd been quite a while since the last time he took the trains out, and Evan was excited to see the tracks being laid out on the floor. Of course, there wasn't any electricity, so they had to push the trains around themselves, but considering the eagerness of his son they would have probably ended up doing just that even if there had been a steady feed coming from the now defunct outlet.

"It's a train, daddy! A train!" Evan exclaimed.

"I know."

"A train!"

Stuart sat back and closed his eyes as his son played with the train set. He held his forearm in his hand, rubbing the damp gauze. He wanted to nod off for a little bit but feared waking up as one of those god awful monsters. He forced his eyes open, watching his son play and laugh and enjoy life without any worry.

He wanted to be like that. So bad.

They stayed up in the attic for the rest of the evening playing trains and Power Rangers. For dinner, he gave Evan a cup of fruit and a can of cold raviolis. For dessert, he let him have two chocolate-covered rice crispy treats.

Evan tapped him on the shoulder, hugging his blankie close. "Night night," he said.

Stuart shook his head. "No night night, baby. You can stay up."

The boy yawned. "Night night."

He crawled up in Stuart's lap and fell asleep. Stuart thought about shaking him back awake. He didn't want him to go to sleep yet. He wanted to keep him up all night, play with him, give him all the rice crispy treats they had left in stock. He wanted to see him smile more.

"Evan," he whispered, but it was no use. The baby was out.

Stuart sat there for an hour or so longer not moving, just holding his sleeping baby boy in his arms and replaying the countless memories he kept stored in his head. He remembered the first time he had taken him out to the park on a swing, the boy had gone so high up, and he kept shouting to go higher and higher, but would cry when he got too high, so Stuart stopped pushing him but that only made him mad. The boy had wanted to go high. The crying was only part of the fun for him. Stuart remembered how he had laughed, pushing his son higher again while Evan shed tears of enjoyment and how all the other parents gave him strange looks.

He slowly stood, placed his boy in the crib and covered him, planting a wet kiss on his sweet cheek. He was down the attic stairs and headed into the kitchen before another thought was allowed to process through his brain. He grabbed the bottle of whiskey he had left on the counter and took a deep chug. The energy pumping through his body was too great for him to taste the liquor pouring down his esophagus, so he kept on sucking the bottle until the liquid shot back out of his throat, sending a wild flame in his mouth and trickling the booze down his chin.

He didn't bother to wipe his mouth. He stormed into the bedroom. The padlock dropped to the floor and he barged into the bathroom. Caren was already to her feet, clawing for him, her jaw unhinged and yearning.

Stuart sat on the sink, looking at his wife and drinking whiskey.

"Well, not much longer now."

Caren screeched.

"Fuckin' tell me about it," he said. "You should've seen him today, babe, he was so happy with those trains. It was so great. I wish you were there. Soon we'll all be together, right?"

She did not answer.

"God, do I miss you," Stuart said, breaking down. "I miss you so goddamn bad, baby. I need you here. I'm so fuckin' helpless without you. What am I even doing? I don't know, I don't fucking know . . . "

He dropped the bottle and it rolled along the floor, the last of the whiskey spilling out into a puddle.

"I just want you back."

No longer able to think logically, Stuart stepped forward and entered the shower. Caren lunged forward, and he perceived it as a loving embrace, and wrapped his arms around her, pulling her in close. The nails digging into his back were done out of passion. He squeezed his beloved wife tight, even as she opened her mouth and wrapped her lips around his neck, sucking on his skin as she attempted to rip his throat out with teeth she no longer possessed. Her gums felt warm and slimy and perfect.

He ached to hold her this close for the rest of his life, and for the rest of the life that followed, and then forever after that, too.

Stuart moved to look Caren in the eyes and then kissed her deep on the mouth, tears blinding the true state of his decomposing wife. She was his soul mate, his everything, and here she was, in his arms, and they were content with one another. He held her tight in his embrace and kissed her a moment longer before reaching his hands up and gripping his tender wife's skull and bashing it back into the shower wall.

"I'm so sorry," he sobbed, and slammed her head back again. Caren let out a long screech, prying with her one free hand at Stuart's face, but he paid it no mind as he continued to bash the back of her skull into the wall over and over again, blood and brains splattering all over the bathroom, segments of marble chipping off and clattering to the floor.

"I love you so much," he cried, and using the last bit of strength he still possessed, slammed her head one last time. Her body slid quietly to the floor, motionless. He looked down at her, trembling.

"It's okay now," he said. "It's okay."

Limbs feeling like rubber, Stuart stumbled out of the bathroom and climbed back up to the attic of the universe. He got two feet in before his legs gave out and he retired to the floor, flat on his stomach, his wife's blood sticking to his skin.

He heard his son snoring and he smiled.

✳✳✳

When he opened his eyes again, a blinding ray of sun coming from a crack in the ceiling sprayed across his face, sending a sheet of red in his vision. A puddle of drool lingered on the floorboard against his lips; the taste of wood and dirt strong in his mouth.

There was something wrong.

The pain that had previously stayed in his forearm had

now progressed to the entirety of his body, affecting every nerve from head to toe. Stuart shot up into a sitting position, jaw clacking as he suppressed a scream. He arched back in a spasm, smacking his head against a plank of wood.

It felt like there were insects convulsing in his skin, pulsating against his organs, gnawing on his spinal cord and drinking his blood.

Consuming him from the inside out.

"No, no no," he gasped, clawing at the phantom parasites destroying his innards. "Not yet, not *now,* goddammit!"

The transformation was starting. He could feel the monstrous genes multiplying in his veins.

"No, please . . . "

Mouth open, heaving heavily, painfully, Stuart grabbed at his own throat in an attempt to choke the evil out of himself. Turning blue and bug-eyed, his vision fell upon the crib at the other side of the attic. His chokehold relented.

He couldn't be here. Not now. Not with his son. But he couldn't leave him here alone. Fuck. *Fuck.* There was no time to think. The infection was spreading by the millisecond; gripping him and pulling him down deep like an anchor. He felt so tired, so weak. He tried fighting but it only made him weigh heavier.

All the while, his beautiful little boy lay sleeping there in the crib, unaware and innocent. Everything was about to change.

Why did it always have to change?

"*Fuck!* I can't! I fucking *can't!*" he shouted. The thought of holding Evan up in his arms and sinking his teeth into his little neck was too much. Too damn vivid. Sitting there shaking on the floor and looking at the crib, Stuart lost his mind.

"*I JUST CAN'T!*" he screamed, and pulled his gun out of the holster and pointed it at the crib and squeezed the trigger.

The sound was deafening in the small confines of the attic. This attic that represented everything; life, death, heaven and hell and the whole damn universe.

Stuart pulled the trigger a second time, and then a third, and a fourth, and a fifth, and a sixth, and then the gun was empty and the crib was a splintery mess of exploded wood.

"Fuck fuck fuck fuck *FUCK!*" he cried, and threw the empty gun at the wall. He crawled frantically to the open attic door and fell down the stairs, hitting the floor with a thud. Barely a moment passed before he was up to his feet and fleeing through the living room and bursting out the front door. The sun looked so alien up there in the sky, so different from the rest of this miserable place.

Rather than squint, he opened his eyes as wide as they could and allowed the radioactive rays to swallow his eyeballs whole as he took off in a dead sprint down the street, crying loudly and swinging wild fists at every stray monster he came across. Dozens were already heading in the direction of the house, following the sound of the gunshots.

He spotted a large crowd of the bastards a few yards down, stumbling awkwardly forward, their stupid mouths open and drooling for a potential meal.

Stuart pointed at them and yelled with all the energy he still possessed: "*YOU KILLED MY LITTLE BOY!*"

And then he charged.

***

"Did you hear that?"

Jack stopped walking and cocked his head. "Yeah," he said. "Gunshot."

Jennifer looked around. "I wonder where it came fro—"

They both jumped as another shot rang out, and then another, and another, and so on. Jack took out his pickax.

"Jesus Christ!" he said, heading with a quickened pace toward the sound of the shots.

"What are you doing? *What are you doing?*" Jennifer

cried out, following closely behind and fumbling in her pocket for the snubnose they kept. There were only three bullets left.

"Someone needs help," Jack said, driving the pickax into the head of a naked woman lunging toward them. "We gotta help them."

"What if it's too late?" she asked.

"What if it's not?"

They both stopped suddenly when a man burst through the front door of one of the houses, screaming impossibly loud and attacking a couple walkers by a lamppost.

"Holy shit!" Jack said, and started heading for him.

Jennifer grabbed his arm and yelled, "Wait!"

"What?"

"*Look!*" She pointed down the street at a large group of walkers. They were all stumbling toward them. "We can't fight all of them. We'll die."

"What about *him?*" Jack asked, gesturing toward the man covered in blood. He was now standing there in the street, looking at the zombies ahead.

"I think he's crazy," she said.

"So?"

They watched as the man pointed a finger and screamed something, then he charged forward. By then, it was too late to help. The man was a lost cause. He plunged into the immense undead mass, then they saw him no more.

"Jesus," Jack said, wiping sweat from his brow. "What the hell was that about?"

"What did he scream?" Jennifer said. "I don't like this. We need to get out of here."

"Yeah, but first we should check out his house. See what supplies he had."

She nodded. Jennifer wasn't going to argue. They'd been wandering far too long to know not to pass up such an opportunity. "Okay."

In the living room, there was a couch and recliner and a huge plasma television with a cracked screen. All the windows were blocked off with blankets and sheets, shielding them from the cruelty that was the outside. A few zombies were roaming around the house now that the door was left wide open, but Jack was able to take care of them easily enough with his pickax. It was just a matter of searching the house quickly before giving a big enough horde the chance to gather around them.

The kitchen was mostly empty save for a couple boxes of crackers that they stashed in their bag. The house smelled of death.

And so did the whole world.

Jack opened up the cabinet above the sink and smiled.

"Well, will you look at this . . . " He reached up and pulled out a bottle of liquor, holding it up for Jennifer's approval.

"Just what we needed." She sighed and ventured out into one of the bedrooms.

Jack stayed behind, loading three of the bottles into the bag. As far as he was concerned, today was a new holiday. And why couldn't it be? It wasn't like there was anyone else around to prove him wrong.

"Jack," Jennifer yelled. She rushed into the kitchen and grabbed his hand. "I wanna leave. Right now."

"What's wrong?"

"There was a woman in the bathroom," she said, eyes watery. "She was . . . I . . . I just wanna go, okay?"

Jack hesitated, then nodded, throwing his bag back over his shoulders. "Okay, sure, let's go."

They were almost out the front door when he stopped. "Wait a second," he said, but Jennifer tugged his arm.

"You have enough booze," she said. "Let's go."

"Just hold on," he said, looking up at the ceiling.

"There are more coming, Jack, come *on*." She yanked his hand again but he stood his ground.

"Will you shut the hell up for a second? Don't you hear that?"

"Hear *what?*" she said. But then she did hear it.

Jack led her through the house and into the hallway. There was a set of steps sprung from the ceiling, resting at the carpet floor. At the top, there was a rectangular opening leading into an attic.

They stood at the bottom of the steps looking up, and all they saw was darkness.

"Is that what I think it is?" she asked.

He nodded.

"Oh, my god."

Hands gripped together, the couple slowly climbed the steps leading into the attic, and they found exactly what they had been searching for.

DISINTEGRATION IS QUITE PAINLESS

I.

THE SHERIFF DANGLED from a streetlight in the center of town. What had once projected light now cast a sinister shadow. Nathan watched from across the street, mesmerized by the mayhem he'd witnessed—the total destruction of one little suburbia. A place he'd once considered home—now nothing more than an above-ground cemetery. A landfill for the dead.

The wind pushed the sheriff's lifeless body back and forth, animating his shadow on the hot, bloodstained concrete. Nothing could kill a shadow. Shadows were infinite. Until the darkness came, at least. Then all realities fell into a free-for-all.

A wake of vultures circled the lynched lawman. They took turns swooping down upon him, clawing his eye sockets bare, leaving behind empty, dry holes. His sight now belonged to the nevermore.

The urge to approach and touch the lawman's feet hit him hard, but the fear of interrupting the vultures' feast hit him harder.

Nathan broke away from the sheriff's dead, hypnotic trance and continued down Main Street. A flock of corpses mirrored the sheriff's approach to decomposing, each suspended like a pair of shoes dangling from telephone wire. He waded through a sea of shadows, fighting off the suburban rot.

His mother greeted him a few blocks down, mouth slung open, tongue missing. Maggots spilled from her lips onto the pavement. Had they always been inside her, waiting for the right opportunity to make their escape?

Nathan rubbed his own stomach, wondering if there were maggots in him, as well.

2.

Some kids used the summer as an opportunity to take advantage of extra sleep. Other boys—boys like Nathan— spent the whole season outside, and only returned inside well past curfew, completely disregarding the universal streetlight rule. They longed for great adventures, for explorations into the unknown.

Today, however, was not meant to be one of those days. It was simply too damn hot.

After breakfast, Nathan rendezvoused with his friends at the corner of the drug store and they all unanimously agreed to grant the forest a reprieve for the day. They could climb trees and dig holes some other time. So, Nathan, Bobby, Carl, and Henry mounted their bikes and pedaled across town to one of the easier-accessed spots of the lake. They hid their bikes behind bushes, stripped to their underwear, and dived into the startling cold water. They howled and splashed each other under the cruel sun, laughing and shivering and flexing their prepubescent muscles.

If Nathan had had his way, he would have stayed in the lake for the rest of the summer. This was how you were supposed to live. Calm, at peace, completely satisfied with your surroundings. He could never be satisfied at home. Not while his parents still lived there. Not while they did the things they did, said the things they said.

The boys might have stayed like that all day, too, if not for the rogue tire that floated down their way, unnoticed until it bumped into the back of Carl's head, inspiring a scream equivalent to a thousand embarrassing baby stories. The other boys flinched and gasped at the sound of his voice, but upon discovery of the scream's source, all erupted into fits of laughter.

"Every nightmare Carl has ever had just came true at once," Bobby said.

"Ah, that classic tire-monster-in-a-lake nightmare," Henry said.

Carl swiped his hand down and splashed them. "Fuck you guys. That thing nearly decapitated me."

Henry laughed. "'Decapitated'? Where'd you learn such a big word?"

Carl grinned. "Your mother."

Henry narrowed his eyes on Carl and lunged at him. "You're dead!"

They wrestled and pretended to drown each other for a few minutes, until noticing Nathan climbing on top of the tire.

Nathan smiled. "This is great!"

At the sight of his happiness, the other boys decided they wanted a turn on the tire and started fighting and pushing each other off it. It was an aquatic version of king of the hill that eventually ended when Henry swallowed a bug in the water and started choking. The boys guided him to land and took turns slugging him on the back until Henry vomited up lake water and told them all to fuck off.

"You're not supposed to punch someone when they're choking," Henry said, wheezing and attempting to maintain a normal heartbeat.

"Hey, we saved your life," Carl said. "You owe each of us a million bucks."

"I'd rather burn a million bucks than give it to any of you." Henry smiled and flipped them off.

"I'd take a million bucks even if it were burnt," Bobby said. "A million bucks is a million bucks.

"Dumbass, you can't spend money if it's all burnt up," Henry said.

"I don't know," Nathan said. "Once my dad had a twenty-dollar bill with a bunch of blood on it. The grocery store took it just fine. I think burnt money would be okay, too, probably just depends how burnt it is, I guess."

"Why was there blood on the money?" Henry asked.

Nathan shrugged, blushing. "Sometimes people bleed."

They were preparing to return to the lake when the sound of laughter erupted within the trees. They turned and spotted a group of teenage boys approaching, smoking cigarettes and cradling beer bottles. Nathan recognized most of them from the high school. The one boy, Conner Trivet, easily ranked as one of the meanest people he'd ever laid eyes on, except perhaps for Nathan's own father. A rumor around town claimed Connor had once broken a kid's arm for bumping into him in the hallway. There were many rumors about Connor. Judging by the cruel smirk across his face, they were probably all true.

The teenagers stopped when they saw Nathan and his friends. Connor smiled and pointed at them. "I think we just interrupted a circle jerk."

They made sounds of disgust and amusement. Nathan gulped. He wasn't even sure what that meant, but it sounded mean. He turned to his friends, who had all turned white. "C'mon, let's get out of here."

Nathan attempted to walk away, but a hand grabbed his shoulder and turned him back around. Connor stood in front of him, sneering.

How did he get to me so fast? Nathan wondered, shivering. "Leave us alone."

Connor cocked his head. "What the hell did you just say, faggot?"

"I said to leave us—"

Connor punched Nathan in the face and he fell down, hard.

Blood oozed out of his nose and his eyes burned. He waited a moment, hoping his friends would jump Connor and defend him, but when he finally opened his eyes, he realized his friends were gone.

Connor stood over him. The other teenagers hung out in the background, taking drags off their cigarettes and sipping their beers. "Your little faggot friends done ditched you. So it looks like it's just you and us. What say we have some fun, huh?"

Nathan felt his nose again, wet and sticky. The pain was so intense he couldn't prevent tears from streaming down his cheeks.

Connor laughed. "Ah shit, the little pussy's crying."

The teenagers laughed on cue. "Kick his ass!"

Nathan lifted his leg and shot it forward. His foot crushed Connor's balls and the boy screamed, doubling over and falling down beside him. Nathan did not hesitate. He jumped up and took off in a dead sprint before the other teenagers were able to react. He ran and ran, through the trees, through the mud, ran faster than he ever ran in his life. The pain in his nose no longer existed. He didn't know if they were chasing him but he wasn't about to find out.

3.

Nathan continued down Main Street. He thought maybe after a while he would become accustomed to the smell of rotting bodies hanging from streetlights, but he'd been wrong. Every new decaying corpse gut-punched him with nausea.

Desperate, bloody footprints littered the sidewalks. Some made by humans fleeing town, attempting to avoid their inevitable deaths, other prints more paws than feet. The marks of the Discovered. The marks of the hitherto buried.

Nathan followed the bloody prints until he ran out of sidewalk. He climbed over a small wooden fence and landed in his backyard. He paused in the grass and stared at the back of his house. Last month, his father had cooked out in this backyard. He grilled hotdogs and hamburgers and got drunk with his friends while he made Nathan pull weeds. When he'd asked his father for a hotdog, he was told not until the backyard chores were finished. After he finished his chores, his father told him he was too fat for hotdogs, and to go inside for water and carrots, instead.

Now, nobody would ever grill in this backyard again. No one would ever pull these weeds or mow the lawn. Nature would continue, uninterrupted by man, just as it was always meant to be.

Nathan entered through the backdoor. The house was so silent it made his heart race. It'd never been this quiet. There was always a football game or something playing on the TV. His father was always yelling about one thing or another. His mother was almost always crying, and if she wasn't crying, then she was yelling at Nathan about upsetting his father.

Now the house was silent. But it was not empty.

He moved down the hallway and opened the basement door. The creaking of the hinges sliced through the silence like a knife through butter. He flipped the light on and walked down the stairs, never taking his eyes off the grotesque display in the center of the basement.

He had to walk very slowly, careful not to slip on all the blood.

4.

Henry, Carl, and Bobby were halfway down Main Street when Nathan caught up with them, wheezing and gagging, on the verge of heatstroke. Before he doubled over, he managed to get one good whack against Henry's arm.

"Ow!" Henry cried out. "What the hell was that for?"

"You all ditched me. You left me alone with those jerks to get my butt kicked."

Carl shook his head. "We were on our way to get help."

"Yeah," Bobby said. "We were gonna get Sheriff Spooner."

DISINTEGRATION IS QUITE PAINLESS

Nathan spotted the police station a few blocks ahead. He sighed. "It's okay, I got away by myself."

"What did you do?" Bobby asked.

Nathan smiled. "I kicked him in the nuts and ran."

Henry laughed. "No way."

Nathan nodded.

Everybody was quiet for a moment.

Then Carl said, "Well shit, man. He's gonna kill you."

"Yeah," Nathan said. "Probably so."

Henry pointed at his face. "Your nose looks awful. We should take you home. Go to the hospital. Is it broken?"

Nathan shrugged. "I don't know. I don't want to go home."

"Well, what do you want to do?" Bobby asked.

"I don't care. Anywhere but home."

"Let's go to my place, then," Henry said. "We can read comics or something."

They headed toward Henry's house, every few minutes looking over their shoulders, fearing Connor and his gang would be on their trail. Fortunately, they made it without incident. Henry's parents were out for the day, so they didn't have to bother with excuses concerning Nathan's injuries. His nose had stopped bleeding, but there was still plenty of blood dried on his face and shirt. Henry gave him a new T-shirt and guided him toward the bathroom to wash up and change.

Nathan pulled his bloodied shirt off and ran a wet washcloth over his face, letting the warm water soak his skin. He'd taken one hell of a punch, and he did not expect the pain to go away any time soon. When he removed the washcloth, a girl was standing in the doorway, staring at him. Henry's older sister—Elizabeth.

He jumped, almost yelling out a swear word, but managed to catch himself.

She smirked. "Hi."

"Uh . . . hey."

"What happened to you?" She gestured to his face.

"I got punched."

"By who?"

"Some jerk."

She nodded, as if that was enough explanation. "Does it hurt?"

"Yes."

She reached out and touched his cheek, softly caressing it. "You poor thing."

He felt grateful for all the blood on his face. It was covering up his blushing. Besides his mother, no girl had ever touched him like this.

"I'm okay, thank you. Uh, I gotta go."

Not knowing what else to say, he threw on the new T-shirt and fled to Henry's bedroom, finding them all sitting on the floor, going through stacks of comic books.

"Your sister's home," Nathan said, joining them.

"So?"

"She saw me without a shirt on."

"Uh-oh," Bobby said. "Now you gotta fuck her."

Henry punched him on the arm. "Shut up, man."

Nathan stayed quiet. He wasn't quite sure what Bobby meant by that, but he knew it had something to do with adult kissing. Sex. It was called sex. No one had ever explained to him what sex meant, not even his friends, who all seemed to know somehow. It was like the whole world was in on this big secret that no one would share with him.

Sometimes he felt like he did not belong in this world. This world of secrets and bullies, of sex and blood.

Maybe he didn't belong anywhere.

"Ugh, this is boring." Henry tossed his comic book down in the pile. "It's summer. We should be outside or something."

"We could play some ball," Carl said.

Nathan shook his head. "Those guys are still after me, I bet. I don't want to go outside. They'll kill me."

Henry sighed. "Don't be such a wuss."

"Hey, at least I fought back. At least I didn't leave you alone, like a coward."

"Go to hell. We're leaving. You can stay here and read these comics if you want, just don't take any of my stuff. Wuss."

"Ass."

Henry, Carl, and Bobby stood and left the room with a football. Nathan stayed on the floor, staring at an open comic book but not really reading it. If one of them had been attacked by a jerk like Connor Trivet, he would have stayed behind and tried to help. At least, that's what he liked to think. But who really knew what he would have done?

Nathan chucked the comic book across the room and leaned his head against the wall. He dozed, and when he opened his eyes again, Henry's sister was standing in front of him, watching him sleep.

"How long have you been in here?" Nathan asked, yawning.

Elizabeth shrugged. "Why are you here by yourself? Where's my brother?"

"They left to go play football."

"Why didn't you join them?"

Nathan looked away from her and stared at the floor. He didn't want to talk about this with her. He didn't want to admit to a girl that he was a coward. The thought made him teary-eyed with embarrassment.

"How's your nose?"

"It's okay."

"That's good."

They stayed quiet for a spell, awkwardly avoiding eye contact until Elizabeth sighed and held out her hand. "Come on, I'm bored. Let's go do something."

"But . . . "

"Let's go."

Even though Elizabeth was only two or three years older than Nathan, she still managed to possess an

authoritative attitude. Her fully blossomed breasts also
made her hard to ignore. Nathan stood up and put his
shoes on.

"Okay," he said. "What do you want to do?"

Elizabeth paused. "Hmm, I don't know. Wanna go to
the lake?"

Flashes of Connor and his gang waiting for him in the
woods made his heart race. "No. Anywhere but the lake."

Elizabeth eyed him oddly. "Uh, okay. Hmm. Do you
have any ideas?"

He wanted to say, *We could fuck,* but feared her
reaction. What if she screamed and smacked him? Or what
if she wanted to fuck? Nathan had no idea what he was
supposed to do when you fucked. He would embarrass
himself to no end. But at the same time, he still wanted to
try. He'd be King of the World.

Fortunately, Elizabeth saved him the trouble of coming
up with an answer. "I know, let's find the Cannibal."

5.

Nathan's father sat in the center of the basement, chained
to a metal support beam, skull half-crushed in yet
somehow still breathing.

Nathan approached him, vision fueled by pure hate.
He stood above him and spit down, but his father didn't
seem to notice.

"Wake up."

He did not stir.

Nathan knelt and smacked the unconscious man. Then
he did it again and again. Sooner or later his old man would
wake back up.

And when he did, Nathan would be ready.

6.

Nathan walked a few paces behind Elizabeth. His eyes

stayed glued on her butt, watching it bounce up and down as she moved down the street. Once in a while, she would look over her shoulder to make sure he was keeping up, and he would pretend to be staring at his shoes, but then quickly return his gaze as soon as she redirected her head forward.

They were heading a few streets down, toward the sand hills in the middle of the woods. Once they reached the forest entrance, they followed a bike trail until branching off to freely roam nature, the sand hills not far ahead.

It was rumored that an old, homeless man lived somewhere in these dunes. Children who ventured deep enough in them never returned. Sometimes, hikers and joggers found strange bones in the sand—leftovers of the Cannibal's feasts.

Once, Jeremy Krall told Nathan he'd gone down in the dunes and met the Cannibal. The Cannibal tried to eat Jeremy's feet, but he never washed, so his feet smelled too nasty to taste. Out of disgust, the Cannibal fainted, and Jeremy ran away.

Another kid, Allison Maddux, told Nathan the Cannibal was her senile grandfather, who ran away from a nursing home after biting a nurse's ear off.

Nathan knew nobody was living in those hills. Just a bunch of fairytale hogwash. Other boys had tried convincing him to explore the dunes in the past, but he'd always declined. However, when *Elizabeth* brought the topic up, he couldn't bring himself to reject her offer. Sure, he knew there wasn't anything evil in the sand, but more importantly, he was convinced Elizabeth knew there wasn't anything there, too. So why would she want to take him out there? To be alone with each other, maybe. To kiss him, maybe. To fuck him, maybe.

Nathan would go out in the dunes to kiss a pretty girl. He would go to the end of the world to kiss a girl. He would travel multiple universes and slay dragons to feel Elizabeth's lips upon his own.

The dunes would be a piece of cake.

He forgot all about Connor Trivet and the pain in his nose.

All he could think about was Elizabeth's butt, and how mad Henry would be once he found out Nathan fucked his sister.

"Where do you think he is?" Elizabeth asked, standing atop a particularly high hill, scanning the area with an intense determination in her gaze.

"I don't know," Nathan said, trying to play along. "Maybe he's asleep."

"Well, where the hell does he sleep? If you were a crazy cannibal living in sand, where would you keep your bed?"

Nathan shrugged. "Probably in the sand."

"How are we supposed to find a bed hidden in sand?"

"That's the point. We aren't supposed to."

Elizabeth clenched her fists. "I've been trying to find this guy for months. He's nowhere. He's everywhere. Why can't I find him? Where the fuck *is* he?"

Nathan had never heard such foul language from a girl. It excited him, scared him. She really believed the Cannibal existed. Maybe he did exist. No, that was crazy. There was no such thing. But did that mean Elizabeth was crazy? Did Henry know?

He didn't know what to do. He didn't want to leave her here alone. He wanted to be close to her. He wanted to kiss her.

"Let's keep looking," Nathan said. "Maybe if we dig in the sand a little."

Elizabeth sighed. "Yeah, maybe."

They found a few small logs and started digging into the sand. It was hot, tiring work, and after only a few minutes they both collapsed in the sand, exhausted. They sat together, sweating and panting. The sand was hot against his skin, but he tried to ignore it and instead focused on her leg touching his leg.

They hadn't managed to dig deep at all. Every scoop of

sand flung to the side seemed to regenerate before their eyes. The work proved pointless, but it seemed to satisfy Elizabeth, which, in turn, satisfied Nathan.

He wondered what his friends were doing. Had they come home yet? Were they looking for him? For Elizabeth? Was Bobby cracking jokes about sex?

Sex, sex, sex . . .

He reached out and touched her shoulder. She didn't flinch, just looked at him and smiled. "It's pretty hot," she said.

"Yeah."

"Do you think the Cannibal's real?"

He wanted to tell her the truth, but he couldn't. "Yes."

She smiled wider. "Me too."

"Where do you think he is?"

Elizabeth scanned the sandy waves surrounding them. "Somewhere. The son of a bitch is somewhere."

"Let's just rest for a while, okay? I'm tired."

They sat in the sand, not talking, just staring at the hills and sweating oceans of sweat. Elizabeth turned to him and asked if he'd ever kissed a girl.

Nathan looked down at his lap, nearly shaking. "No."

"Well, do you wanna?"

He didn't know what to say. Slowly, he lifted his head back up. His heart pounded against his chest in painful bursts. She stared at him, awaiting his response.

He opened his mouth to tell her he did, he really, truly did want to kiss her, but was cut off by the sound of Elizabeth screaming.

Before he could react, her body fell through the sand, leaving him all alone under the sun.

"What the . . . ?"

Something powerful grabbed his legs, and gravity intensified as his body sunk into the sand. He tried to scream, but no sound came out.

There was only darkness.

7.

Nathan's father opened his eyes. Nathan stood in front of him, holding a hammer he stole from the toolbox.

"Nathan . . . what . . . what's happening? Why are you doing this?"

Nathan pushed his shirt up, showing off the scars across his stomach. The bruises, old and fresh. He dropped his shirt and stared.

"Son, I'm sorry. Please. What were those . . . things? Jesus Christ Almighty, *what were they*?"

Nathan knelt, gripping the hammer tightly. "Those are my friends, Daddy."

He swung the hammer at his father's face, laughing and crying at the same time.

Then he swung it again, and again, until his hand was consumed by blisters and there was nothing left to swing at.

8.

Nathan found himself in some sort of cave. Icicles hung from the dark ceiling and dripped water down upon him. Elizabeth lay at his feet, neck twisted at an impossible angle. Her eyes were open, but they couldn't see anything.

Nathan screamed, backing away from the dead girl. He eventually hit a wall behind him and stopped. The only dead thing he'd ever seen before was a squirrel on the side of the road. Its guts were all over the pavement and maggots were feasting upon its intestines. But Elizabeth was so much worse than a squirrel. She was a person. A kid, just like Nathan. And now she was dead. But how?

Nathan looked up at the icy ceiling. Somehow, they'd fallen from the sand into this cave. Was the cave beneath the sand, though? How could these icicles exist? How could any of this exist?

How could Elizabeth be dead?

No, this was not real. He was surely dreaming.

A nightmare.

He stared at Elizabeth and continued telling himself none of this was real, but he didn't sound very convincing.

This was real. This was just as real as the dead squirrel. Just as real as those things his father did to him with the lighter.

Nathan ran through the darkness, refusing to look back at Elizabeth. If he didn't see her, then she was no longer dead. She was still sitting on the sand, asking if he wanted to kiss her.

She couldn't be dead when only a few minutes ago she had been so *real*.

He ran deeper into the unknown. He didn't care what was ahead of him as long as it wasn't what was behind him.

What would he tell Henry?

Screw Henry. Henry had ditched him. They had all ditched him. They were *always* ditching him. They weren't his friends. He didn't have any friends. Now that Elizabeth was gone, he didn't have anybody.

No one would ever want to kiss him again.

He was alone, so miserably alone.

In the darkness, under the sand, in a world different from his own.

Nathan ran into the mouth of shadows and let them swallow him whole.

9.

After setting his house on fire, Nathan continued down the street. He kept the hammer with him, despite all the gore dripping from it. Soon the entire neighborhood would be up in flames. The suburbs would be no more.

The world would be his to claim.

Nathan, King of the Here and Now, the Always and Forever.

He found Connor Trivet by the lake, half-buried in

mud. Both his arms and legs had long been torn off and consumed by the Discovered. He hadn't stopped screaming all damn day. The sound was heaven to Nathan's ears. He could listen to this boy's agony for the rest of his life.

But Nathan could not afford to stand by the lake for all of eternity. No, there were other towns to destroy, other suburbs to burn to the ground.

Other worlds to obliterate.

"Who's the little pussy now?" Nathan said. He thought about smashing Connor's face in with the hammer, but tossed it to the ground instead. He moved closer to Connor and grabbed him by the jaw, dragging him on top of the discarded tire. Once Connor's body was in the center, Nathan pushed it into the lake and watched it float away.

Connor continued to scream even as the Discovered rose from the water and finished their leftovers.

All the jigsaw pieces were finally falling into the right places.

10.

Nathan could not see the creatures in the darkness, but he could feel them—slimy and scaly, reptilian and revolting. He ran his hand along one of their limbs, his legs paralyzed, his arms possessed and devoid of freewill. He could hear their heavy breathing, their soft moans of pleasure as he caressed them.

No matter how hard he strained his eyes, he still couldn't see. He tried to imagine their appearance but the image he conjured was simply too horrifying.

"What are you? Where am I?"

One of the creatures purred in his ear, then started wrapping around his body. A tail of some sort, or maybe an abnormally long arm. It squeezed itself around his abdomen and pulled him deeper into the cave.

Something wet and warm touched his face, and he found himself suffocating as his head was swallowed by a thick gelatin texture. He tried pushing away from it, but the blob proved strong and pure.

The darkness faded away, an intense light welcoming him. He thought for a moment that he had gone to Heaven, but the smell was too foul. His nostrils fought back in disgust at the smell—the smell similar to rotting garbage, to something dead and abandoned.

He was in these creatures' home. No longer in the cave. No longer in the sand. No longer anywhere.

These creatures, these discovered beings, they lived in the Never Before and the Forever After. And Nathan had entered their lair.

One of the Discovered slowly approached him. It was so close he could touch it. The ball of slime hovered before him, slithering its many tentacles in a circular motion. It possessed no eyes, yet sensed him all the same. It sensed him and breathed him in, investigating his every feature. They were both alien to each other.

Nathan wanted to ask it a thousand questions, but he couldn't seem to talk.

The creature seemed to understand him, anyway.

It moved closer.

Before Nathan passed out, a wet voice snuck into his ear: *"We love you, Nathan. Now you will love us."*

SCRAPS

THE DINER DOOR chimes and by the time I turn around, coffee pot in hand, the boy's already standing next to the PLEASE WAIT TO BE SEATED sign. All thoughts of taking my 2:30 AM lunchbreak and smoking a cigarette in the alley while scrolling through my dead wife's Facebook account vanish. My brain freezes at the sight of him. For a second, I swear to god I'm staring at my son, but that's impossible. Muddy hair hangs past his shoulders, his body skeleton-thin, his skin pale, his eyes dark. He's young—ten, eleven max. A rank odor rises. A garbage smell. A death smell. The boy had dragged the stench in from outside.

I set the coffee pot—freshly brewed—down on an empty table waiting to be bussed and rush over to the checkout counter, slowing as I get closer, afraid of spooking him away.

"Holy shit, are you okay, kid?"

The boy wears a plain T-shirt that had probably once been white but is now mostly black and jeans filled with holes. He's barefoot, and judging from the dirt and blood smeared across his toes, he hasn't owned shoes for quite some time now. A thin jagged cut runs across his face, from the right side of his forehead down to the left of his jaw, skipping over his blackened eye, sloping over his crooked nose, and digging through his lips.

He licks those lips now. "Hungry."

I gently touch his shoulder and lead him across the

diner. "Of course, come sit down, I'll bring you something. Are you okay?"

"Hungry."

Once he's seated in an empty booth, I race into the kitchen in search of something to bring him. On the counter next to the sink, in queue to be tossed in the trash is a plate of fries and a half-eaten burger. I fill up a clean glass with tap water and bring that and the plate back out into the dining area. The boy's head rests against the Formica tabletop and for one terrifying moment I'm convinced it's too late and he's already dead. Died of hunger, died of the smell attached to his presence, died of whatever caused him to be here, right now, at 2:30 in the morning, who the hell knows. I stand above him and clear my throat and wait. The boy stirs and raises his head. When he sees the food in my hand, his dark eyes widen.

But they do not brighten.

I place the plate and glass on the table and the boy dives into it, ravenous. I watch him feast, unsure of what to do with my hands, eventually settling on folding them behind my back. "So, uh, what's going on with you? Should I . . . call the police? Do you need an ambulance? Are you hurt?"

The boy shakes his head as he chews. "No police. No ambulance."

"Are you alone? Where are your parents?"

"No parents."

"Okay, uh . . . " I scratch my head, wishing like hell I knew what to do. "Maybe you have some kind of other family I can call. Someone who could come get you?"

"No family." The boy shakes his head again then swallows what was in his mouth and meets my concerned eyes. "Call no one."

I lean forward, afraid to disturb the boy's eating. "Can I get you anything else, at least?" The question comes out in the form of a timid whisper.

The boy nods enthusiastically, crumbs falling from his dirty mouth, and points at the plate. "More."

"Okay, sure." I return to the kitchen and bump into Beth, the manager-on-duty, waiting for me by the sink. Bitch is eager to pounce, like she's been hiding in the back watching the whole time, just waiting for me to screw up.

"You care to explain what's going on with that . . . kid?" She grimaces at that last word, like it physically disgusts her just having to say it. Beth works the night shift because she is the only manager who doesn't have a family waiting for her at home. The other managers, they all got loved ones who depend on them. But Beth. Beth's more like me. Neither of us has got a single soul other than our own. She goes home every morning to an empty apartment and eats junk food while watching some dumb shit on Netflix then falls asleep on the couch. If she never wakes back up, the only person who will feel anything at all is the poor sap who ends up having to cover her shift. And I'm no better.

"I don't know who he is." I gesture to the dining area, keeping my voice low. "He just came in here. Saying he was hungry."

Beth sighs and rubs her hands through her hair. "Everybody who comes in here is hungry, Owen. That doesn't explain why you're feeding him trash. Or why you even gave him a seat. He smells *awful*."

"What was I supposed to do? Make him leave? He's just a kid." It's then that I realize for the first time who he reminds me of. Of course I'd known it the second he walked inside the diner, but a wiser part of me had refused to acknowledge the similarities until now.

If I'd never gotten behind the wheel that night, back in 2013, Bobby would be about this kid's age now.

Jesus Christ.

"He's not our responsibility. If he can't pay, then he has to go. Call CPS if you have to, I don't care, just make him leave." She pauses, cheeks swelling like she's swishing wine. "And besides, given your history, do you really think it's a good idea to be . . . *socializing* with children? Especially the way you look right now. I mean, *God*."

She's talking about my fading black eye, my broken left pinkie still in a splint, yes, but she's also talking about much, much more.

My right fist tightens at my side. Teeth grind against teeth. Flashes of cuffs, flashes of my P.O. shaking his head and telling me I blew it, I blew everything. Fist loosens. Teeth remain grinding. I turn and stomp back out into the dining area, back to the kid who looks like my son, but isn't my son, can't be my son. I lean over the booth and whisper into his ear, ignoring the rancid stench clouding so close to his face.

"Sorry, kid, but my boss says you got to leave or she's calling the cops. You got someplace to go?"

The boy does not respond, only stares down at the table as if still expecting more food to appear.

I reconsider, feeling Beth's eyes on my back, mean and acidic. "Tell you what. Go out the front door, then walk around back, in the alley. Hang out there, by the dumpster. I'll meet you in a couple minutes with something else to eat. Cool?"

The boy nods, stands, leaves.

"There, was that so hard?" Beth says, suddenly right behind me, breathing down my neck.

I sidestep away from her and head for the timeclock. "I'm going on my break."

***

The boy's waiting by the dumpster, just like I told him to. Arms at his sides, back stiff, face blank. The wind's picking up and I start shivering as soon as I step into the alley, but the boy doesn't seem the slightest bit bothered. The homeless, they get used to the cold. They learn to adapt. I met plenty of ex-hobos during my time in Centralia. A lot of them there on purpose, terrified of freezing to death out on the street, would rather commit a sloppy B&E than wonder whether or not they'd wake up the next morning. Chicago winters are a gamble nobody wins, except maybe Satan, and that motherfucker rigged the game from the get-go, anyway.

"Hungry," the boy says as I approach him, hoping like hell Beth doesn't get any wise ideas and peek her head out the back door. I hand him the brown paper bag I'd brought from my apartment. We're allowed to eat the food at the restaurant, but management makes us pay for it, and the discount's an embarrassment, so I just bring my own lunch. The boy rips the bag from my hands and tears it open, devouring the peanut butter sandwich within seconds. I light up a cigarette and take long, slow drags as he nibbles on the apple.

"Where'd you come from?"

No response.

"You all alone?"

"No."

"Who else is with you?"

The boy hesitates. "Friends."

"Friends your age or older?"

No response.

"Okay. Where are they, then?"

"Hiding."

"Hiding from me?"

He nods.

"Because they're afraid?"

Nods.

"Well. They don't need to be. I'm not gonna hurt them or nothing. But you all should be careful about the places you walk into. Almost got the cops called on you."

"No cops."

"Yeah, I know."

"Afraid. Afraid of the Bad Man."

"The bad man?"

Nods.

"You mean me?"

He shakes his head no.

"Then who?"

No response.

"Did someone hurt you, kid?"

"Hungry."

"Sorry, kid. That's all I got tonight."

"Tomorrow." It's not a question.

I shrug, weirdly uncomfortable with denying his request. "Yeah, sure. Just wait out here, though. Don't come in. Beth sees you again, she'll call the cops herself."

"Friends."

"Yeah. Bring your friends. Sure."

He points at me. "Friend?"

"Me?"

Nods.

"Yeah. Okay. My name's Owen. And I'm your friend."

The boy steps forward and hugs me and I wait until he leaves the alley before crying.

✳✳✳

My apartment door is ajar when I get home later that morning and I stop in the hallway thinking *fuck, not today,* but thoughts like those didn't help Becky, nothing helped her, so I clear my throat, making my presence more obvious, and the hands of my intruders reach through the door crack, waiting for me, always waiting for me, and grab my shirt and drag me inside the apartment. The door slams shut a second later and I'm flying, not an inch of me touching the floor, then all of me is slamming down—going *bang* against the hardwood and skidding forward— another victim of gravity, another idiot of stupid, terrible decisions.

I flop like a fish until I'm on my back. Standing above me: Kenneth and Mallory Noble, sixty-eight and sixty-three, faces dripping with tears, bodies trembling, determination fierce in their gaze.

The parents of Nancy Marie Noble Matilla.

Once upon a time, before I killed their daughter and grandchild, I'd been their son-in-law.

Kenneth stomps his boot in my face and my nose crunches and warm blood pours into my eyes, my mouth. It tastes like pennies. I drink it all in, telling myself I don't deserve to spit it out. Mallory raises a cane and slams it into my ribs and I curl into a ball as more blows strike. Everybody's sobbing, including me, but not because of the pain. As blood and snot choke my lungs I try to scream, "I'm sorry! I'm sorry!" but they can't hear me. It doesn't matter how loud I say it. They'll never hear me.

Fifteen minutes later, once they're both exhausted, we clean up the blood from the floor and I take a shower and bandage my new wounds. When I get out, they're sitting on the couch, three cups of coffee on the table in front of them. I sit on the floor, Indian-style, and sip at the cup closest to me. My body throbs. My nose is caved into my brain. My teeth ache. My innards moan. But it's okay. This is the way it's meant to be. This is the only way it *can* be.

They ask me if I'm okay and I tell them no and I ask them the same question and they echo my response.

The conversation evolves to other topics. How's work? Work is fine. How's your parole officer? A hardass. Are you doing okay on money? I'm doing fine. Will it ever stop hurting? No, it won't ever stop hurting.

I consider telling them about the boy I met last night and how much he reminded me of Bobby, but my body's not ready for another beating, not yet. We hug and say our goodbyes and I watch them leave down the hallway, toward the elevator. I don't bother locking the door as I turn and search for safety within the blankets on my air mattress.

Sleep does not find me for several hours.

***

Before heading out into the alley, I grab the trash bag I'd stashed under the sink earlier in my shift. The boy's waiting in the same spot as last night, next to the dumpster. A group of children similarly aged hide behind him, cowering in the shadows. They all stare at me as I approach, emotionless. The boy who looks like Bobby but isn't Bobby says, "Hungry," and I hold up the trash bag in my hand. He reaches out to take it but I pull away, lift the index finger on my other hand.

"Not yet. You want to eat, you gotta answer some questions first."

The boy's brow bends into a V. "Hungry."

The kids behind him all step forward, staring at me, and the boy shakes his head no and the kids return to the shadows.

"Hungry."

"What's your name? Tell me that, and you can have some of what's inside."

The boy hesitates, and for a moment I don't think he understands the question, then: "Nameless."

"Nameless?"

The boy nods.

I wave my free hand at the kids behind him. "And what about the rest of you? You all nameless, too?"

They don't budge. Continue watching my every movement. Cats hunting flies.

"Okay. Where are you from?" The question's for all of them, any of them.

"Nowhere," the boy who is not Bobby says.

"What does that mean?"

"Nowhere."

"You haven't always been in this alley. Where do you live?"

"Everywhere."

"What are you? Runaways?"

Nothing.

"What about the bad man? Who is he?"

They all flinch and look over their shoulders as if expecting to find the bad man waiting behind them.

"Bad Man is bad," the boy says. "Bad, bad, bad."

"But who is he? Why is he bad?"

The boy reaches for the bag again. "*Hungry.*"

I sigh and surrender the trash bag. The boy takes it and rushes behind the dumpster with the rest of his group. Camouflaged by shadows. Loud, wet chewing noises. A desperate feast of leftover pancakes and rolls. I shuffle my feet in the alley, shivering and lighting a cigarette, and try to remember the last time I've actually eaten. My stomach growls. Ignore the emptiness. Ignore the ache. Everything hurts just as it should.

I wait, hoping they'll come back out and talk to me a little more, but my break ends before they're done eating, so I flick my cigarette butt on the ground and head back inside the diner, wondering if I should do something more, if I should call somebody. Then Beth stomps toward me and shoves a plunger against my chest.

"Someone clogged the shitter."

***

Every night I feed the kids, their group seems to expand. I lose count at twenty. How the hell do they get here without being noticed? Twenty kids can't travel in a group around Chicago at 2:30 in the morning without drawing some kind of attention, yet they somehow manage to move around the city undetected. Sometimes people, they choose not to see things they don't want to be involved in. Sometimes it's easier to ignore a problem than to try solving it. The homeless are masters of stealth. Thinking about them makes people sad and angry, so they just don't think about them. It's easier that way. But I can't ignore these kids. I can't be that kind of person. I can't.

"I was thinking about maybe contacting a shelter," I tell them one night as they devour old hamburger patties behind the dumpster. "You know. A place you can all stay. It's too cold to be sleeping outside. Once the snow hits, you'll freeze to death. I'm surprised you haven't already."

The boy who is not Bobby steps out of the shadows and shakes his head. "No shelter."

"But where will you go?"

No response.

"You know, I can't just keep feeding you guys like this. I can't afford it. I . . . I can't get in trouble. I used to be in jail, and if someone sees me messing with you, they might send me back. Back to jail. And besides, don't you guys want to do something else besides just eat leftovers every night? You never talk to me. What do you do all day? Where do you go?"

Where do you hide? I almost ask.

And the boy cocks his head, expressing curiosity for the first time since we met. "Jail?"

I retreat back, embarrassed. "I don't want to talk about that."

He continues staring like that isn't a good enough answer.

"It was . . . it was a bad time in my life. I'm trying to do better. Like by helping you guys. But you gotta let me, first."

The boy's face goes blank again. I'm not going to win this. These kids are stubborn. They're used to living out here on their own. They don't want to change their lifestyles. They just want someone to feed them.

"Listen." I raise my hand like I'm going to place it on the boy's shoulder, then think better of it. "I won't be here tomorrow. It's my night off. So don't freak out when I don't show up, okay?"

"Hungry."

"I know. I'm sorry."

"Hungry."

"I'll be back in two nights, okay? So not tomorrow, and not the night after, but the night after that, I'll be back. You'll be . . . okay, right?"

Of course they won't be okay, but they're not going to die because I take two nights off from work. They survived long enough before finding me, and they'll survive long after I'm gone.

If the boy understands what I'm saying, his facial expression doesn't alter to show it. Sometimes when I talk to him, I get the feeling he doesn't exactly know English, only bits and pieces he's picked up over the years while living on the streets. But he doesn't seem to have an accent. When he speaks, his voice comes out in a monotone.

"Where will you guys go?" I ask, not expecting an answer.

But I get one, anyway:

"With you."

***

I tell them they're nuts, but they either don't understand or don't give a shit. I try to make them see things my way. How weird and suspicious it'd look, me, not only a grown-ass man but also an ex-con, being trailed by two dozen small children who are obviously homeless. People are going to have a lot of questions, I tell the boy who is not my son. They're going to intervene. Society just doesn't work like that.

And the boy says, "It fine."

I still don't agree to the idea, but there's no way for me to prevent them from following me on their tiny dirty feet as I walk to my apartment a little over a mile from the diner. It's seven in the morning and the sun hasn't quite decided to rise, which I get the feeling the children are grateful for. I've never seen them during the day and when I try to picture it in my head I get nauseated. I don't know why. But maybe I do, maybe I know exactly why.

This morning the city is surreal. Usually, walking home at this time, the sidewalks are crammed with other people, students and workers and joggers, everybody. But today the sidewalks are empty, as if reserved for me and the kids. And, while there's an odd car driving past now and then, the normal busy traffic does not seem to be present, and those who do drive our way don't even look in our direction. Like we're under some kind of cloaking spell, invisible to the public eye.

There are far too many of us to fit in the elevator, so we take the stairs up to my apartment. Again, we pass nobody. Once inside, I lock the doors and show them around. It isn't much, not by any stretch, and with them all in here there's barely any room to breathe, much less move around. Some of them cram together on the couch, and others sit on the floor, taking up all of the living room. I stand in the kitchen and they all stare at me, expecting something.

"Well, this is my home. You're all welcome to stay here as long as you wish. I know, there's not a lot of room, but it's all I got. Just . . . try not to make too much noise or draw attention. I don't think my lease allows for so many people to live here at once. But, uh, if you need to shower, feel free. I'll try to stop at Goodwill later and pick up some clothes that might fit some of you. Uh. There's not much food here, I'm sorry to say, but you can help yourselves to whatever you find."

The boy who is not my son points at a framed photograph of my actual son hanging from the living room wall. "Who?"

I ignore the question, pretending he hasn't spoken, but he continues pointing at it, waiting, so I swallow and try to remain calm. "That's my son. His name's Bobby."

"Where at?"

"He. Uh. He's dead. My son is dead."

"Dead?"

"Yeah."

The boy lowers his hand, doesn't say anything else.

My cell phone starts ringing, and all the kids flinch in unison. The caller ID says it's my parole officer. Fuck.

"Okay, guys, don't say anything, all right? I have to take this. Seriously. Don't make any noise." I don't know why I'm telling them this. I've never heard any of them even speak besides the one who originally showed up inside the diner. The rest of them, it'd be difficult to tell they existed if not for their odor.

Gonna have to buy some candles if they're staying here. Some Febreze and shit like that. Money I don't have.

I answer the phone. "Hello?"

"Owen. I was starting to think you weren't going to answer."

"Yeah, sorry. I just got home from work."

"And how is your job going?"

"Oh. You know. It's okay. It's a job."

"Beats a cell, huh?"

"Yeah . . . "

"Anyway, I was just calling to remind you of our appointment this morning. Wouldn't want you to be late."

"Appointment?"

"Don't tell me you've forgotten, Owen."

"What time was it at again?"

"Ten, Owen. The appointment's at ten. You *will* be here, correct?"

"Is there any way we can re—"

"No, Owen. That's now how this works."

"Okay. I'll be there at ten."

"Good. That's what I like to hear. See ya then."

I tell the boy who is not my son that I'm going to be gone for a couple hours, that they should just stay in my apartment and try to relax. I wish I had a TV for them to use. Instead, I show them my collection of paperbacks I've been slowly scavenging from Goodwill. I don't know if any of them can read, but if they can, they're in for one hell of a treat.

Before I leave, the boy who is not my son tells me they're hungry again.

"I know. I'll try to bring some food home on the way back, okay? You like Ramen?"

And the boy just stares, face blank. "Hungry."

Hungry, hungry. They're always so goddamn hungry.

I can't feed them all.

✷✷✷

The parole officer doesn't have much to say. It's the same conversation every time. How are you adjusting? Fine. How is your new job? Okay. Have you been in contact with family? Some. Where do you see yourself in five years? I don't know. Have you attended your required Alcoholics Anonymous meeting for the month? Not yet, but I will before the month ends. Have you had any alcohol since your release? No. Have you desired any? Yes. How often? Every second I'm awake. What stops you? The fear. The fear of what? Of hurting someone else. Of going back to jail. Of fucking up my second chance. Do you still think you deserve a second chance? No. Why not? I don't know. You don't know? No. Will you pee in this cup? Yeah, I'll pee in that cup.

***

On the way home, I stop at Goodwill and purchase a large assortment of children's clothing. There's not much money in my checking account and I'm holding my breath as I insert my debit card into the chip reader. Miraculously it goes through. I try my luck again at the Dollar General next door and buy a basket full of Ramen noodles. Again, it goes through. What the hell. Things are actually on my side this morning. Even my parole officer was mostly pleasant. These kids, it's like they're some sort of good luck charm. I ought to keep them around, see what happens. I already fucked up one child's life. Maybe this "second chance"—as my P.O. calls it—is a lot more significant than I realized. Maybe I was released from Centralia to help these kids, to save them. Feed them. Shelter them. Take care of them. Be the dad none of them ever had.

I walk into my apartment with a smile on my face, and I'm only two steps inside before the smile vanishes forever.

Kenneth and Mallory Noble.

Sitting on my couch.

Fuck, not now. Oh shit oh shit. NOT NOW!

The kids sitting on the floor around the couch all turn to me, faces stained red, as if asking, *What? What's wrong?*

I rush forward, stumbling for the right excuse. "Look, it's not what it looks like, okay?"

Still in denial about what I'm looking at, about what's happened while I was gone.

"You have to leave," I whisper, although I don't know who I'm saying this to. Kenneth and Mallory. The kids.

Myself. Someone, anyone. We all have to leave. Leave and never come back again.

I refuse to acknowledge reality until I'm up close, practically on top of them. Although Kenneth and Mallory are sitting and staring in my direction, they do not see me. Where eyeballs once rested, their sockets now remain black and empty, as if scraped clean and sucked dry. Their clothing is ripped to shreds and hundreds of tiny bite marks trail up and down their bodies. Their mouths hang open in a perpetual scream. Neither still possesses a tongue.

I back away, trembling. The kids don't move. The red on their faces. Of course I know what it is. And they know I know. They want me to know. The boy who is not my son stands from the floor and slowly approaches me, one hand out, fingers stained vermillion.

"Friend?"

✷✷✷

The next morning the bodies are gone. I don't know what the kids did with them and I don't want to know.

Nobody complains about being hungry.

Later, the boy who is not my son tells me about the Bad Man.

The Bad Man wants to hurt the kids. Wants to kill them. Has *already* killed some, will surely kill more. The Bad Man is evil. The kids try to hide but the Bad Man always finds them, no matter where they go, how far they run. The Bad Man travels in people's shadows. He's not human. He's everywhere and nowhere at once.

The boy who is not my son tells me about the Bad Man, then he tells me where the Bad Man lives.

"Help," he says. "Help. Help. Help."

✷✷✷

The Bad Man lives in a motel across the city. Come dusk, the boy leads the way, the other kids hanging back at my apartment. We take the train. No one seems to notice either of us. The boy already knows what room he's staying in. I ask the night clerk at the motel for an extra key, claiming to have lost mine at a bar. The clerk, annoyed I distracted him from whatever he's watching on his laptop, barely glances at me as he programs a new keycard and tosses it on the front desk.

"Have a good night," he mumbles, sitting back down.

No one's in the motel room when we slip inside, which is probably for the best. Gives me time to look around, get a feel for who this Bad Man really is. The room's a disaster. Empty fast food bags littered the floor. Discarded clothes here and there. Thick tomes with strange symbols on the covers. On the desk in the corner of the room, I find a large crossbow. It's loaded with an arrow, ready to go. *Why does he have this? Why does he have any of this?*

On the wall, above the motel desk, a corkboard hangs with dozens of photographs and drawings tacked within its borders. Printouts of maps laying out the streets of Chicago. Newspaper articles with headlines emphasizing grisly murders and strange disappearances. Photographs of random children. Photographs of murder scenes. Many, many pencil drawings of kids. Kids with black eyes and long fangs. Kids without faces. Kids with—

A noise outside the room. Footsteps. Heavy breathing.

I freeze. The boy who is not my son hides behind the bed. Someone inserts a keycard into the door lock. A click of acceptance. The handle turns. The door opens. A tall obese man in a fedora and trench coat stands in the opening. The brown paper bag falls from his grasp at the sight of me.

"What are you doing in my—" He pauses. "Did they send you?"

I don't respond.

"They did, didn't they? They sent you. They were too scared to do it themselves, weren't they? So they found someone else to do their dirty work." He laughs. His throat sounds clogged with phlegm.

"Who are you?" The words barely leave my lips.

"Who did they say I was?"

"The Bad Man."

Again, the laugh. "Well, they aren't wrong."

"You have to leave them alone. You have to go far away."

"I'm not going anywhere. Not after all the work I've done. Fuck that." He gestures to the corkboard, then stops. Sniffs. "One of them is here now, aren't they? I can smell the fucker. Where is it?"

As if on cue, the boy who is not my son stands from behind the bed, but this time when I look at him, he is no longer the boy who is not my son but is instead my son, my Bobby, my poor dead beautiful baby boy, and he is so perfect tears burst from my eyes at the sight of him.

The Bad Man grins. "Yeah, there you are, you motherfucker. I'll never forget that smell."

He reaches inside his trench coat, and I realize he's going for a weapon.

A weapon to injure my boy.

No.

I pick up the crossbow and aim it at the Bad Man and pull the trigger and an arrow shoots out and penetrates his gut. His hand falls from his trench coat, a pistol hitting the floor. The man groans and steps back, eyes wide and focused on me standing across the room, still holding the crossbow. I drop the killing device on the bed and move toward him. Fear and panic glow like electricity across his face. Both of his hands caress the arrow in his stomach but he doesn't pull it out, he doesn't dare.

I follow him out to the second-story landing, him still backpedaling until he bumps against the stair railing.

"You don't understand," he whispers, wincing and groaning. "You don't understand what they are."

But he's wrong. I understand exactly what they are.

"They're mine," I tell him, and push his chest with both hands. He stumbles back, reaching for air, and crashes down the stairs, rolling and flipping and screaming.

SCRAPS

By the time he reaches the bottom, he's silent again.

On the way back home, Bobby tells me he's hungry again, and I rub his hair and tell him he can have whatever he wants, anything at all, and he smiles and holds my hand and says, "Daddy?" and I smile back and nod and say yes, yes, yes.

BOY TAKES AFTER HIS MOTHER

MOMMY USED TO kill people before I was born, but I'm not supposed to talk about it. Especially not at school. Kids don't know how to shut their fuckin' mouths, she says. I say Mommy, I'm a kid, too, and she smiles and caresses my cheek and says I ain't like other kids, says I'm special as they come and don't I ever forget it.

She says the right person eavesdrops and the law will come tear us apart. Mommy says this is for my ears only and not anyone else's. Mommy says the world is full of evil waiting for its chance to pick our bones clean.

I don't want my bones picked clean. I like my bones just the way they are.

I asked Mommy why she used to kill people and she said there wasn't no single reason but a multitude of reasons that piled up over time until she couldn't stand it no longer, until her brain was like a tea kettle steaming out her ears, and the only thing she could do to cool it down was rage on human life.

Mommy says I'm not supposed to talk about her murderous past at school because no one will understand. They will just end up lighting their torches and sharpening their pitchforks and come breaking down our door. Mommy says if I tell anyone what she tells me, then I'll lose her forever.

I want us to stay together for the rest of time. Until the

sun crashes down and burns us all up like a big ol' marshmallow.

I believe her when she tells me this, truly and deeply from the bottom of my heart, but that don't stop my tongue from slipping during lunch one day. Bobby Quarles had just launched an assault of spitballs against my face and was laughing like I'd told him the funniest joke, and I couldn't take it no more. He'd been tormenting me since Mommy enrolled me in this stupid school. Some days, he'd sneak up behind me in the bathroom and pull my pants down. Some days, he'd wipe his booger on my neck in class. And some days, he got busy with spitballs.

Them spitballs, I can't stand 'em one lick.

Bobby, I tell him, you don't quit messin' with me and I'm liable to end your life, right here and now, swear to God. This kinda response only seems to make Bobby and his friends laugh harder, so I tell him if you think I'm joking, you have no idea what kind of Mommy I got, that I learned from the best, that if you want to slit someone's throat, you gotta make sure you dig in real good and deep, don't hold back any, slice that jugular open like the best piece of candy in the world's hiding inside.

Now everybody at the lunch table has got their eyes peeled on me, not moving, thinking who is this kid with these words, who is this alien with these threats.

But Bobby, he ain't buying it. You sound fuckin' weird, he says, you sound like a fuckin' weird faggot Momma's boy.

I tell Bobby that Mommy would wear his face as a mask if she caught him talking to me that way. Her last victim, my own daddy, he got much worse for just complaining about the quality of Mommy's cooking. How you think she'd react to these here spitballs, hmm?

Bobby's starting to take my words seriously now, I can tell by the sweat on his forehead, the fear in his scent, only he can't let anyone else know, but still his voice cracks and pops when he says, you're full of shit, your mom ain't killed nobody.

And I look him dead in his eyes and say, my mommy has killed over one hundred people in her lifetime, before retiring after cooking my daddy and feeding me his remains when I was just a little itty bitty baby. She'd started young, nearly the age I am now, with her own mommy. First it was the truck drivers, because truck drivers, they're like gnats or cockroaches, they're everywhere. They make for good practice killin', before moving onto bigger and better targets—targets like cops.

Your mommy ain't never killed no cop, Bobby says, but he don't know my mommy, now does he? Not like I know her.

Mommy, she's the biggest cop-killer in Texas, I tell him. Back home, there's a shoebox of bloody sheriff stars under my bed. She'd given it to me for my eleventh birthday, said I was a man now and I ought to know the truth about my own breed. Every night I look at those stars and dream of adding to the collection. I like the way they feel in my hands. I lose my mind sometimes imagining the other hands that have held these stars.

A new voice speaks up then, Cindy Lowe, the same girl who loudly stated I smelled like I'd shit my pants last week during math. Cindy, she says maybe someone should go get a teacher. Maybe someone should get help. This kid's clearing a freak, she says, this kid's an honest-to-god lunatic.

But Bobby shakes his head, asks what, you scared? You scared of this fuckin' faggot?

And Cindy hesitates before she denies it, says nah, she ain't scared, she ain't scared one bit.

But it's a lie and I know it and everybody knows it because the whole lunch table, they're terrified, terrified just like the world used to be afraid of Mommy.

I am Mommy's son, I am her good boy, I am her blood.

Blood, blood, blood.

You ever taste blood? I ask this to the whole table, but I'm looking directly at Bobby, and I can smell a whiff of pee, and I pray to God that it's Bobby's pee. I don't care about anybody else but Bobby. I want his pants to soak, to drown. Zero in on one target, don't stop until there's nothing left to destroy. Yes, Mommy. Yes. I know.

I tell Bobby that Mommy has a scrapbook in her nightstand drawer containing the obituaries of every man she's put to rest. I tell him that one time, when I was supposed to be asleep, I caught Mommy reading the scrapbook in bed, one hand under her sheets, moaning. My mommy, she won't hesitate to add you to her book. I'll add you there myself, you keep this shit up. No more spitballs, no more boogers, no more calling me dumb when I get an answer wrong, no more hiding sticky foods in my backpack, no more talking, no more breathing, no more anything.

Bobby says he don't have to listen to me, he don't have to listen to nobody. If my mommy killed so many people, she'd be in prison, he says, so you're full of it, you're completely full of it and none of us believe you.

If I was full of it, how would I know the gravesites of sixteen missing Dallas police officers? How would I know what the dirt feels like beneath my feet? When Mommy takes me on vacation, we don't go to Disneyland or Disneyworld or whatever the hell, we go to real places, we go to special places. My mommy, she takes me back in time, shows me what human beings are capable of, what they were designed to do.

Your mom's a fuckin' psycho is what she is.

Remember last month, when I didn't come to school? Nurse thought I had the flu, but really, Mommy just wanted to teach me how to skin an animal. That's why, the day before, we spent an hour in the pound, searching for just the right doggy. You start on animals, Mommy told me, then you move up to bigger game, move up to the things that matter.

Now Bobby's shaking, angry, afraid, a little mix of both. Can't tell if he's gonna run away or attack me, and I'm hoping, maybe even praying, he attacks me. He's done it enough times, let him do it once more, then I'll show Mommy I'm not afraid, I'll show her nobody's ever gonna push me around again.

The next time I go home with a bloody nose, it's not gonna be only my blood smeared on my face.

I asked Mommy once if I could be like her. If we could kill again. I ain't never seen Mommy smile that bright in my life 'til that day. I ain't never seen her so proud of her son. She rubbed my back and said she would love nothing more. But I wasn't ready. I still ain't, she says. Well, that's what she thinks. I'm Mommy's boy. I've been ready since I was a little baby but she just don't realize it yet. Soon she'll see. Soon she'll understand and rub my back again like that first day.

Bobby's still talking, saying I ain't shit, saying I'm a faggot and a liar and no girl's ever gonna fuck a boy like me, an ugly little faggot who makes up lies to scare people. Well I ain't scared, Bobby tells me, using the crowd's laughter to egg him on. Ain't nobody scared of a little shithead like you, so why don't you just go back to your momma and suck her titty and leave us all the hell alone.

But I'm no longer listening to what he's saying at this point. Maybe he's talking or maybe he's screaming now. Who's to say? The back of his head bounces against the floor and it's like we're on a trampoline instead of hard marble. When I reach for his face, I let Mommy's words flow through me, remember the way she said it was the easiest thing in the world, pulling a fella's eyeball out, just like scraping the guts out of a jack-o'-lantern, all you needed was the right kinda determination.

And determination is what I got, don't I, Mommy?

The souvenir in my pocket, I leave Bobby on the floor, shaking and crying for his own momma now, and calmly walk through the crowd of kids looking at me like I'm a crazy person, like I'm a monster, like I'm some kinda force of evil haunting their school.

I can't stop smiling.

I've dreamed of this day.

Mommy's already home when I open the door. Our bags are packed on the kitchen table. The school called her at work, told her everything that happened, and that I was missing and in big trouble.

The police want to talk to me. Everybody wants to talk to me. Especially Mommy, she wants to talk to me more than anybody.

She holds out her hand and I drop the souvenir in her palm and she looks at it for a good long time before leaning down and kissing my cheek and telling me what a good boy I am, what a good, smart young man I have become.

She gives me back the eyeball and tells me it's good luck to eat the first one. I stick it in my mouth and chew and it's rubbery and disgusting and it's the best thing I've ever tasted, better than Mommy's spaghetti, better than her hamburgers, better than the cheesiest pizza I've ever had. I swallow it and it slides down my throat and into my stomach and I pray it never leaves my body, that it stays inside me for the rest of my days, my little good luck charm. Before we leave, I collect my box of sheriff stars. I fantasize about filling up my own box with eyes. I wonder if people still see out of them once they're disconnected from their heads. I wonder if Bobby's seeing the inside of my stomach right now. I wonder if he's enjoying the view.

And as we rush out the door, into the car, I ask Mommy if she's proud of me, and she rubs my back and tells me she has never been prouder.

Oh, Mommy.

You're the best Mommy a boy could ask for.

I love you so much.

EVERY BREATH IS A CHOICE

SOMETIMES TOM PULLS his tie so tight he can't breathe, and he refuses to let go, even when the world around him begins to dissolve and his vision introduces black dots like cigarette burns on a film reel. He tells himself he'll keep pulling until the oxygen has fled his lungs, until his heart's thrown in the towel and collapsed, and sometimes he even gets close. He can feel the reaper's hand on his shoulder and he knows any second now it'll all be over, but he can't quite make it, something always makes him let go of the tie. Thoughts of Diana, maybe. Fantasies that she'll move back into the house, the house they shared for ten years.

Ten years.

You can't forget time. You can't block a decade from your memory. They'd had good days. They'd been in love. But only he seems to remember that now. Diana's memory's topsy-turvy. Diana only remembers David. Tom remembers David, too, although he tries his best to forget.

Tom straightens his tie and goes to work. On the train, he stares out the window and fantasizes about being anybody else in this city but himself. He wonders if any of them have had to make the type of choices he's made. If any of them understand true pain. True horror. Then he fantasizes about bashing his head into the window, over and over, until the glass shatters and impales his skull.

"Tom, you look unhealthy," his coworkers say when he's roaming around the office.

"Tom, when was the last time you slept?"

"Tom, are you eating okay?"

"Tom, you look like shit."

And Tom says the same thing each time, smiling sadly, staring into a cup of cold coffee:

"Sorry.

"Sorry.

"Sorry.

"Sorry."

Always apologizing, but none of them know what for. Tom knows. Diana knows. Somewhere, David knows, too. And that's all that matters. He's sorry. So fucking sorry he can't stand it anymore. In his cubicle, he hides and calls Diana. The ring lasts as long as a penny falling into hell. She won't talk to him anymore. Won't even acknowledge he exists. It doesn't stop him from calling her every day, every hour, every heartbeat, hoping she changes her mind, hoping she decides to love him again.

It's been five years since she moved out. Five years since Victor Waterman entered their lives, and five years since David left.

The last time Tom saw Victor, the judge was sentencing the monster to life imprisonment, with no chance for parole. Tom sat in the stands, listening to the audience around him applaud, listening to Victor scream obscenities, and realized it wasn't enough. It would never be enough.

During his lunch break, Tom stands on the edge of the roof, staring at the traffic moving below like ants. He debates stepping forward and seeing if his body flies or falls. A part of him is convinced he'll just float, stagnant. This is all a dream. He's been asleep for the last five years and this is what it'll take to finally wake.

He takes out his cell phone again and calls Diana. Straight to voicemail. He speaks into the recording, tells her their lives aren't over, there's still time to make things work. Tells her he's still the man she fell in love with.

Although sometimes he has trouble deciding which is stronger, his love for Diana or his hate for Victor.

Maybe they're the same thing.

The first time Tom saw Victor was a Saturday. The fact that it's a Saturday sticks out clearly, because Tom never worked on Saturdays. But that week, Stuart Jackson called in sick at the office, so Tom wasn't given a choice. He had to cancel his plans to take David to the park, even though he'd specifically *promised* him they'd play basketball that afternoon. Tom hated breaking promises to his son. Hated that look of disappointment, of distrust. It's one of the few faces Tom can remember of his son these days. He tries to remember what his smile looked like, but every time he thinks about it, all he sees is a distorted orb, a universe of blood where his mouth should be, a sea of tears and screams begging for help, for his daddy to save him.

That's what daddies are for, after all. Saving their sons. Making sure no harm comes their way.

Bad daddy, bad daddy, bad, bad, bad.

The first time he saw Victor, the monster had been stepping out of Tom's bathroom. Diana was on the ground with blood leaking down her thighs and David was tied to the radiator across the room. Both their mouths were duct-taped. Victor exited the bathroom, walked into the bedroom and caught Tom standing there, staring at the scene, not understanding any of it. Then Victor reached on top of Tom's nightstand, picked up a gun that Tom had never seen before, and pointed it at Diana.

After Tom's lunch break is over, he returns to his cubicle. Coworkers are talking about last night's football game. They ask him if he watched it and he shakes his head. He doesn't even know who's in the playoffs this year, or, for that matter, who's won the last five Super Bowls. He has to be honest. None of it matters anymore. That's the thing nobody at this office can understand. Nobody here understands loss. Nobody here knows what Tom has gone through, what he's sacrificed. They're all still protected safely inside their little bubbles. Sometimes Tom imagines coming in with a knife and popping all of them, one by one. This is what life is, he would scream. This is what you've been missing.

He sits down in his chair. He stares at a computer screen. On his desk, there are photos of Diana and David. These photos are the only way he passes the time.

He wonders how Victor passes the time, if he's allowed photographs in his cell, or if he has to stare at his cock for entertainment.

When Victor walked out of the bathroom, fumbling for the pistol on the nightstand, his pants were still unzipped, cock hanging out like a python covered in blood. The sight of it froze Tom, making the realization of what was happening sink in.

Then Victor pressed the gun against Diana's skull, smiling, licking his lips, looking at Tom like he was nothing.

After work, Tom drives straight home. He sits in the living room, in the middle of the sofa, imagining Diana on one side and David on the other. He opens his arms, hoping he'll feel their bodies. He would cry if there were still tears left to produce, but his soul hollowed out long ago.

For dinner, he eats two slices of toast. He pours a pot of coffee down his throat because being asleep is worse than being awake. He stays up until three in the morning watching television, but not hearing what anyone's saying.

Tomorrow's getting closer and he can't avoid it. The five-year anniversary. He tries to push it away, like seaweed in the ocean, but it's too late, it's stuck to his skin, clinging to his flesh, eating at him.

Tomorrow, tomorrow.

Tomorrow.

Five years ago tomorrow, Tom stood in the bedroom, shaking, staring at his bloodied wife, his terrified son. "Please," he whispered, "please don't."

"Please don't what," the man named Victor said, although Tom did not know his name yet.

"Please don't hurt them."

"I think it's too late for that."

"No. No. No."

"Yes."

Tom had never met Victor before. No one in his family had ever seen him until that Saturday. Later, Victor would admit that it was simply the first house to let him inside. He'd tried others, giving them that classic "I've broken down and need to use your phone" line, but nobody was dumb enough to buy it.

In court, Victor turned to Tom and grinned before saying, "Nobody until her."

In court, Tom lost it. He wanted blood. But even blood-for-blood would not be enough to quench his hunger. Five years he's fantasized about getting revenge, about cutting Victor open and wearing his flesh, if just for a moment, only to feel what it was like to be a monster.

Monster, monster, monster.

On the fifth anniversary of David's death, Tom calls in from work. Instead of dialing Diana, he drives across the city to her parents' house, where she's been living for the last half decade. Her father, well into his seventies, gives Tom one look and tells him to get off his property.

"You're no longer welcome here," he says.

"I just want to see Diana."

"Well, she don't want to see you, so beat it."

"Just one minute. Please."

"I'm going to close the door now," her father says, "and if you're still out here when I reopen it, I'm gonna do what I should've done fifteen years ago before you ever married my daughter, and introduce you to my sawed-off."

He closes the door.

Tom returns to his car, crying, sobbing, clawing at the steering wheel as he drives away into the fog. He is always driving into fog.

All he wants is his family back.

"Who are you?" Tom asked Victor, unable to take his eyes off the gun, off Diana's face as she silently screamed through duct tape.

"Me?" Victor said. "I'm nobody. I'm unimportant."

"Then please don't do this."

"It's already done, friend."

"Why?"

"Maybe this is punishment."

Tom fell to his knees, digging his nails into the carpet. It was all he could do to prevent his body from flinging forward and causing the gun to go off. "Punishment for what? *Punishment for what?*"

The man with the gun paused for a moment and shrugged. "I don't know. Punishment for not looking after this sweet piece of ass? Punishment for being born? Not everything has a reason, you know. Not everything needs to make sense."

"What?"

"Look, it doesn't matter. What's done is done. Now what happens next, that's what we need to discuss."

Tom trembled. "You raped my wife."

Victor nodded.

"You fucking piece of shit."

"I am."

"I'll kill you."

"We'll see."

Victor raised the gun and shot Tom in the chest. He flew onto his back, skull bouncing against the floor. Diana screamed through the duct tape.

In the car, Tom listens to the local conspiracy theorist on the radio rant about black helicopters and 9/11 cover-ups. Years ago, he'd have laughed at the kind of lunacy. Now, on the other hand, it sort of makes sense. Maybe the government is hiding things from them. Maybe they know what makes a monster a monster. Maybe nothing is as it seems.

He pulls into a gas station for a pack of cigarettes. A boy who barely looks old enough to drive takes his money. The boy could be anybody's son. He could be Tom's David.

Except this boy behind the counter, he ain't dead.

It was after the letters began arriving that Tom realized their marriage was doomed. Maybe it'd been doomed as soon as that last breath left their son. But Tom had managed to stay delusional until the letters started coming in. The letters from Victor. He'd missed the first couple. Diana had been hiding them, burning them, whatever, before Tom had a chance to see them. But one day he came home early, happened to stop and get the mail. Normally it wasn't his business to open his wife's letters, but he decided to make it his business once she started receiving postage with a penitentiary as the sender's address.

The first few sentences in the letter threatened Diana harm if she continued to ignore his letters. The rest of the message consisted of him professing his love to her.

Victor. In love with Diana.

Tom's wife.

Victor.

Their son's executioner.

In his rage, he'd ignored the early comments in the letter pertaining to Diana ignoring Victor. Just the fact alone that she'd been hiding the letters from Tom had been enough to raise suspicion. He'd started breaking things, hitting the bottle hard, playing Russian roulette with him and David's cat.

Eventually, the cat lost.

Diana didn't sleep another night in that house. Still hasn't.

The letters continued to arrive. Tom read them all.

The motherfucker was head-over-heels.

Tom didn't know how Victor had found out he'd impregnated Diana. Maybe Diana told him, then freaked out, decided never to contact him again. But it didn't matter. The damage was done. Victor knew he now had a son.

EVERY BREATH IS A CHOICE

Take one out of the world, bring another in.

Tom told her he didn't even want to know the kid's name.

"That doesn't belong to me," he'd said.

"He should've taken you instead," she'd said back.

"That wasn't an option."

Tom drives to the preschool, parks where he has a clear view of the playground. He lights up a cigarette, sits and waits. Eventually, the kiddos pile out of the building and embrace the slides and swings like reunited lovers. He watches them, wondering which one is the spawn of his wife and his wife's monster.

They all look the same.

They all look like David.

They all look like corpses.

Eventually he finds the boy. He doesn't know his name, but he's seen photographs on the few occasions he was crazy enough to push past Diana's father and enter the house. Tom gets out of the car and approaches the fence. He raises his camera and snaps a few pictures, then returns to the car and drives away.

He has work to do.

The last night Tom and Diana and David were together as a happy family was the Friday before Victor introduced himself to their lives. They'd gotten a pizza and rented a movie from Blockbuster. David was thrilled because the next day they were going to play basketball at the park. Basketball was his favorite thing in the world. Pizza was his second favorite. Tom remembered clearly how David was insistent he take off all the toppings from his slice, even the cheese. It didn't matter that David could eat a pound of cheese by itself—just not on pizza.

"No toppings, Daddy. That's disgusting."

That night, Tom and Diana made love for the last time.

He remembered holding her afterward, the blinds still open, moonlight showering their naked bodies. The world had felt perfect then.

He thinks about this night now and it is so far away.

He reaches out and only touches air. It is just him now. Him and Victor.

"Please don't hurt her," Tom had pleaded, his chest bloody and pulsating from the gunshot. "Please, God."

Victor couldn't stop grinning, like they were playing some fucked-up game and he was winning. He pushed the gun deeper into Diana's skull. "I gotta admit, of all the fine lookin' bitches in this world, I think I may have struck gold."

"Please."

"Just think, man. Fuckin' anybody could have opened up, invited me inside. It could've been *anybody*. And that anybody just so happened to be your wife."

"No. No. No."

"You must have the world's shittiest luck." Victor laughed. "And me? I must have the best luck. *The best.*"

"What do you want?" Tom said. "Dear God, what do you want?"

"I already got what I wanted, man. But shit. I guess a man's not a man once he stops prospecting, don't you say?"

Tom was silent. His body shook like an avalanche of sweat and tears and urine.

Victor grabbed Diana's hair and dragged her over to the radiator, leaving her next to David. David continued to cry through his duct tape. Victor took turns waving the gun in front of Diana and David.

The power of a firearm.

The magic of insanity.

The delusion of safety.

"I'll tell you what," Victor said, staring at Tom with wide, gleeful eyes. "Since we're having so much fun, I'll be nice. To let you in on a little secret, I was planning on killing both your girl and your kid here after I was finished with my business. I hadn't expected anyone to show up and interrupt us. But that's okay. You didn't know."

"Please."

"But, *but* given that you've been *such* a good sport about all this, I figure, hey, why not throw you a bone?"

Tom was past the point of wanting to kill this intruder. He wanted to spill the blood of God and the rest of the universe. Fuck this whole existence.

"So here's what I'm gonna do," Victor said, still waving the gun back and forth. "I'm gonna tell you right off the bat. I can't leave here with at least killing *somebody*. That'd be cheating, and I'm a fair player. But I don't have to kill you all." He giggled. "You see what I'm saying? Not everybody here has to die today."

"What do you want me to do?" Tom's chest was on fire and he wondered how long it'd take until his heart surrendered. "Please, what . . . what do you *want?*"

Victor took a while to answer. He just stared at Tom, smiling, in on a joke without a punch line.

Then he said, "I want you to choose."

And even though Tom immediately knew what he meant, he still said, "Wh-what?"

Victor pistol-whipped Diana and she fell on her stomach. Then he pointed the gun at David, Tom's boy, his own flesh and blood.

"I said, I want you to fucking choose. It's pretty simple, you know? Who do you want to live? Who do you love more? Your wife, or your son?"

"Fuck you." Tom tried to stand, but his body was numb, useless. The volcano of blood pumping out of his chest had paralyzed him.

Victor laughed. "Look, dude, I don't have to be nice. I can just kill them both and leave. But I'm trying to do you a favor here, letting you pick one to keep. So come on. Don't make me regret this."

"No. Please. *No.*"

Victor shrugged. "All right, whatever. No skin off my back. The both of them it is." He aimed the gun at Diana.

Tom screamed. Blood poured out of his mouth.

Victor paused, looked at him. "Have we come to a decision?"

After Victor was gone and Tom had managed to untie Diana, she started slapping him across the face and screaming, crying, calling him the worst names imaginable.

"Why didn't you pick me? *Why didn't you pick me?*"

All he could say was, "I love you, I'm sorry, I'm so sorry, I love you, I love you . . . "

Tom doesn't know if it's Victor's way of fucking him over even in prison that he's listed Tom's name under the allowed visitors, and he doesn't care. He hadn't even considered the possibility of not being allowed to see him. He'd driven the three hours to the prison in a daze. He'd driven out here before countless times, but he'd never had enough balls to actually get out of his car and walk inside.

Not until today.

Five years.

Fuck.

He sits behind the glass and waits a century. Eventually, Victor walks out of his hiding spot and joins him on the other side of the glass. He's lost a lot of weight since the last time Tom had seen him.

They sit in silence for many minutes, a wall of glass separating them. Tom can't bring himself to talk. After all this time, all the hours of practicing what he'd say, and he can't bring himself to even open his mouth.

Victor picks up the phone on his end and begins speaking. Tom doesn't know what he's saying, and he doesn't care. Today isn't about excuses or apologies. Today is about punishment.

Tom reaches into his pocket and pulls out two photographs, then presses them against the glass. As Victor leans forward for a closer look, Tom picks up his own phone and nestles it against his head.

He waits a good long while, allowing Victor time to stare at the photographs, one of Diana, the other of her new son. The son Victor had given her. He looks away from the photographs and stares Tom in the eyes.

"No, man. No. You can't do this. Please. Oh, fuck. Please."

Tom says one word. The only word that matters anymore:

"Choose."

MUNCHAUSEN

THE HOUSE DIDN'T look scary. From the outside, it resembled every other residence on the street. Bland. Forgettable. Another off-balance bungalow in desperate need of repainting. According to Lori's research, Habitat for Humanity had built this house nearly fifteen years ago, along with the rest of the neighborhood. It amazed her how quickly the owner, Andrea Thompson, had let it go to shit. The front lawn hadn't been mowed in several weeks, if not months. Dozens of tiles were missing from the roof. Tall, wild bushes concealed a picture window next to the front door, bushes that probably had never been trimmed in their entire existence. A wheelchair ramp infected with cracks and various colored stains led up to the porch. Most of the houses on this street had their share of chairs and toys and bikes discarded aimlessly throughout their yards, but this particular house presented no signs of outside activity. No signs of children ever having lived here. The house looked terrible but it didn't stand out from any other neglected home often found in areas commonly referred to as "the bad side of town". No, it wasn't the house that scared Lori. It was what she expected to find *inside* the house.

She rang the doorbell three times before she realized it was broken. She curled her hand into a fist and banged it against the wooden frame, the plastic bag containing a two-liter of Mountain Dew dangling from her thin wrist subsequently slapping against the door. In the other hand, she balanced a large stuffed crust pepperoni pizza. She waited half a minute before knocking again, afraid of coming off too anxious or impatient, even though the pizza was hot and uncomfortable and the bag of Mountain Dew continued to gnaw into her wrist. She didn't want to scare anybody away. She didn't want to appear anything less than friendly, anything less than *trustworthy*. For this interview to work, Andrea Thompson and Lori would have to become friends.

In addition to the pizza and pop, Lori had also brought a backpack, which she wore over her shoulders as she waited for someone to answer the door. The backpack's contents included the following: a voice recorder (fully charged), a yellow legal pad, a number of pens and markers, a first aid kit, a bag of zip ties, a taser (fully loaded), and a Glock 26 (also fully loaded). The taser her father had given her the year she accepted her first newspaper gig in the city. The handgun she'd bought the day after Andrea Thompson agreed to be interviewed.

Somewhere inside the house, the harsh smoker voice of a woman: "She's here! She's here!" It was whispered by someone not aware of her own volume, a kind of muffled shout.

Lori tensed as heavy footsteps neared and the front door swung open, revealing Andrea Thompson in all her glory. A tall, massively obese woman in a bright, polka-dotted house dress. Brown curly hair held up by blue and green ribbons. She smiled the same smile Lori had studied in countless photographs online. The smile disgusted her.

"You must be the reporter!"

"Yes, ma'am, I'm Lori Wright, we spoke on the phone. It's a pleasure to finally meet you, Ms. Thompson."

Andrea moved forward as if to hug Lori, but took the pizza instead. Lori switched the bag of Mountain Dew to her newly freed hand. Another minute or two and she would have needed to have her hand amputated at the wrist. Andrea stared at the pizza box in her grasp as if she held a long-sought-after treasure.

"You got the stuffed crust, right?"

Lori nodded. "Yes, ma'am, just like you asked for."

Andrea smiled again and gestured over her shoulder. "Please, come in, come in."

Lori followed the woman into the house, closing the door behind her. The front door had half a dozen different locking mechanisms installed into it. She considered snapping a photo of them on her phone but decided against it. There would be time for that later.

"You coming, dear?" Andrea called from another room.

"Yes, ma'am."

✳✳✳

They conducted the interview in the living room. Andrea sitting in her La-Z-Boy on one side of the coffee table, and Lori on the loveseat across from her. Andrea laid the pizza out on the table and flipped the lid open. The smell of melted cheese made Lori nauseated. Food did not sound appealing today, especially food drenched in grease. Lori came here with a job to do, nothing more, nothing less.

She glanced around the room and lost count of the photographs framed against the walls and along various tables. Most of them of Andrea's daughter, but a decent portion also contained Andrea herself. The majority of the photographs were taken at fundraisers and Disney trips. Andrea's daughter, wheelchair-bound, next to Goofy, grinning wide and revealing only her gums, not a tooth in sight. Andrea and her daughter—just a baby, then—outside their house, the day Habitat for Humanity presented it to them. Unsurprisingly, Lori saw no photographic evidence that the child had a father.

"So," Lori made another show of looking around the room, "where is Maggie, anyway? I was hoping she'd be joining us."

"Oh, she'll be out here in a little bit, don't you worry, dear. She's resting right now, is all. Once we're finished with lunch, I'll go check on how she's doing. Not like she can eat pizza through her feeding tube, anyway. Would just be cruel to have this in front of her."

"Okay, sounds good." Lori resisted asking who she was shouting at before answering the door, if Maggie was indeed asleep. She unzipped her bag and fetched the recorder and legal pad out. "I'm going to start the recording now, is that okay, Ms. Thompson?"

Lori kept waiting for the woman to wave and say, *Please, call me Andrea,* but it never came.

"Yes. Go ahead. Turn on your little fancy machine. As long as you don't mind recording the sound of me eating, of course."

"That's no problem at all, ma'am."

As soon as Lori turned on the recorder and set it on the table, Andrea seemed to increase the sound of her chewing, no longer even bothering to close her mouth as hot cheese and breading smacked against her nicotine-stained teeth. The combination of sound and sight sent waves of sickness through Lori's stomach. *Please don't vomit,* she told herself. *Please don't vomit.*

She cleared her throat and tried to focus on anything in the room besides the woman's mouth. "Lori Wright interviewing Andrea Thompson. The day is September second, twenty-thirteen. The time is . . . one-sixteen P.M. Location: Thirty-Five Old Lion Road. Percy, Indiana."

Andrea smiled mid-chew. "Aren't you professional! Ain't that the cutest thing."

"How's the pizza?" What Lori really meant: *I hope you fucking choke.*

Andrea nodded, seemingly thrilled by the topic. "Oh, my lord, it's truly something special. Stuffed crust is *my favorite.*"

"I remember from our previous phone call. I'm glad you're enjoying it. Are you ready to begin, Ms. Thompson?"

"I suppose we ought to or we never will."

"Excellent." Lori glanced down at her legal pad, full of questions she'd compiled back at her motel room the previous day. "You aren't originally from Indiana, is that correct, Ms. Thompson?"

Andrea tossed a half-eaten slice of pizza in the box and wiped her mouth with a napkin. The sauce on her chin looked like blood.

✲✲✲

THOMPSON: No. I was born in Pennsylvania.

WRIGHT: Harrisburg?

THOMPSON: You've done your research, girl.

WRIGHT: It's my job, ma'am.

THOMPSON: If you already know where I'm from, then why ask?

WRIGHT: Oh, just for clarification purposes. Making sure all my facts are actually facts. I wouldn't want to misrepresent you or Maggie in the article. How long did you live in Harrisburg, Ms. Thompson?

THOMPSON: Hmm. Well, let's see. I guess I moved shortly after I turned twenty-one.

WRIGHT: So that would have been . . . around nineteen-ninety-two?

THOMPSON: Yeah, that sounds right.

WRIGHT: Why did you move?

THOMPSON: Oh, you know, there just wasn't much for me back home anymore. My mom had been dead for a couple years. I didn't much care for my dad's new wife. God, she was a real bitch, let me tell you. And you can print that, I don't care. She knows how I feel about her. May the Lord forgive my language but it's the truth. I swear it.

WRIGHT: You're referring to Elizabeth Thompson?

THOMPSON: Yeah. *Liz* is what she goes by. I never understood what my dad saw in that . . . well, you know.

WRIGHT: And your mother's name was . . . Suzanna, correct?

THOMPSON: Yeah.

WRIGHT: How did she pass away, exactly? The reports I found weren't exactly clear . . .

THOMPSON: I thought this article was supposed to be about Maggie.

WRIGHT: Yes, ma'am, it absolutely is.

THOMPSON: Then what does any of this matter? Maggie never even met my mom. And as for . . . *Liz,* well, I believe she made it pretty clear how she felt about my baby girl.

WRIGHT: What did she do?

THOMPSON: When Maggie was first diagnosed, I called my dad and asked for help paying some of the medical bills. He said he needed to discuss it with his bitch wife first. And he did. And when he called me back the next day, he said they wouldn't be sending me any money. Can you believe that? Here I am with a very sick baby and they can't even send me a couple hundred dollars. And it wasn't like they didn't have it. I *know* they did. My dad owns his own *bait shop* for crying out loud. I'm sorry. Whenever I think about them, I start getting real mad.

WRIGHT: It's okay.

THOMPSON: Thanks, dear.

WRIGHT: What was special about Indiana?

THOMPSON: Oh, nothing much. It wasn't Pennsylvania, which seemed good enough to me.

WRIGHT: Did you have any money saved up when you moved? Where did you go? How did you make ends meet?

THOMPSON: What does this have to do with Maggie?

WRIGHT: The article's about both of you, Ms. Thompson. As I mentioned on the phone, remember? If we're going to tell Maggie's journey, then we must also tell her mother's journey. The readers will want to hear about the challenges you've faced, the obstacles you've overcome.

THOMPSON: I guess that makes sense.

WRIGHT: So, you came to Indiana, and . . . ?

THOMPSON: I met a man pretty quickly. Jacob. Maggie's

father. I was living in a motel as a maid at the time. Jacob was living in his parents' basement. A few weeks after we got together, I moved into the basement too, and soon got a job as a nurse's aide.

WRIGHT: How old was Jacob?

THOMPSON: Does that matter?

WRIGHT: My research shows he was . . . seventeen?

THOMPSON: So?

WRIGHT: What did his parents think about you moving in?

THOMPSON: Oh, they didn't seem to mind me too much. They were very busy people, both with full-time jobs.

WRIGHT: When did you become pregnant with Maggie?

THOMPSON: Not long after I moved in with him.

WRIGHT: When is Maggie's birthday, again?

THOMPSON: December twenty-first.

WRIGHT: And she's sixteen now, correct? Or will she be sixteen this December?

THOMPSON: She'll be seventeen in December.

WRIGHT: Are you surprised that she's managed to make it this far? She's had quite the battle.

THOMPSON: I thank the Lord every day He gives her on this Earth. Each morning is a true blessing.

WRIGHT: How long did you and Jacob stay together?

THOMPSON: He left before Maggie's first birthday. We had just rented our first apartment together, too. In my name, of course. He'd made sure of that.

WRIGHT: Did he give a reason?

THOMPSON: I don't think that's important for the article.

WRIGHT: Has Jacob had any contact with Maggie since?

THOMPSON: He used to visit her once in a while. But he got himself a new wife and family a couple years back and they moved down to Florida.

WRIGHT: Do Maggie and her father ever talk on the phone?

THOMPSON: Maggie doesn't do so well with telephones.

WRIGHT: What do you mean?

THOMPSON: Her brain . . . it's many years behind her actual age. Certain things she has trouble understanding, like talking on the phone.

WRIGHT: What else?

THOMPSON: Oh, you know. Tying her shoes. Getting dressed. Basic motor functions don't come very easily.

WRIGHT: Ms. Thompson, just for the record, can you state what illnesses your daughter has?

THOMPSON: Oh, sure. But where to begin? My Maggie, bless her heart, she's had it rougher than just about anyone in this world. Maggie . . . well, she was born premature, and with an extra chromosome, but of course we didn't find that out until Maggie was a little older. When she was just three months, we had to get her a breathing machine to battle sleep apnea. But if all she ever had was sleep apnea, my God, I'd consider us incredibly lucky. But no. The sleep apnea was only the beginning. From there . . . there was the muscular dystrophy and the leukemia, which, you know, opens up a whole 'nother can of worms. Chemo is a very serious matter, young lady. A single germ could kill my Maggie. And I haven't even gotten into the seizures. Oh, Lord.

WRIGHT: Wow. It's truly terrifying and heartbreaking that so much has happened to Maggie.

THOMPSON: She's my little warrior.

WRIGHT: Do you think maybe I could see her now?

THOMPSON: Well, I suppose that would be okay.

***

Andrea told Lori to remain on the loveseat while she fetched Maggie. As soon as the big woman was out of sight, Lori shot up and snooped around the living room. The framed pictures got more depressing the closer she looked. Every time she saw Maggie's wide, toothless smile she had to bite back the urge to break Andrea's nose. She wiggled open drawers but found nothing incriminating. The living room was innocent. Maybe a compartment existed somewhere in the house with a smoking gun, but Lori doubted she'd manage to locate it before Andrea returned. She sat back down on the loveseat and waited, and ten minutes later Andrea came back with Maggie in her wheelchair.

The girl looked exhausted, like she hadn't slept in days. She wore comically large black-rimmed glasses and a thick robe around her body. Her head was shaved to the scalp. When she spoke, her voice came out high-pitched, childlike.

"Hi, I'm Maggie!"

Lori waved at her. "Hello, Maggie. My name is Lori. I'm very excited to meet you."

Andrea pushed Maggie next to the recliner and sat down. She took one of the girl's hands in her own and held it, just as Lori expected the woman would. A mother showing affection for her daughter. A dog protecting its food.

"How are you feeling today, Maggie?" Lori smiled at the girl, the only alternative to crying.

"I'm feeling great, thanks!"

"Do you know why I'm here?"

"You're going to write a story about me!"

"That's correct. Very good." She glanced at Andrea in the recliner. "Do you mind if I ask some more questions? To Maggie, this time?"

Andrea stared at Lori like a predator preparing to pounce. "Not at all, dear. Go right ahead."

Lori smiled at Maggie again. "And are you okay with that, Maggie? Can I ask you some questions?"

The girl nodded, excited.

✳✳✳

WRIGHT: How many times have you been to Disneyland, Maggie?

MAGGIE: At least a billion!

WRIGHT: Wow, that much, huh? You must love it there.

MAGGIE: My favorite thing is the parade and the fireworks at night! They're the best.

WRIGHT: You know, believe it or not, Maggie, but I've never been to Disneyland.

MAGGIE: Oh my gosh! You gotta go. You gotta.

WRIGHT: Maybe one day I will. You'll have to tell me the best places to go, huh?

MAGGIE: Definitely.

WRIGHT: What other cool places have you gone to? The Make-a-Wish Foundation must treat you very well.

MAGGIE: Yeah, they like to give me and my momma vacations because I'm so sick all the time.

THOMPSON: They've sent us to Disney many times, once they paid for a Hollywood tour. Like, where they shoot movies and such.

MAGGIE: Yeah! I saw Harry Potter!

WRIGHT: Do you like Harry Potter, Maggie?

MAGGIE: When I am a grownup, I want to marry him.

THOMPSON: Now, Maggie, we've talked about this—

WRIGHT: Have you ever had a boyfriend, Maggie?

THOMPSON: Now, what kind of cruel question is that? You see the state she's in.

MAGGIE: Momma says I can't have boyfriends until I'm better.

WRIGHT: And do you know what's wrong with you, Maggie?

THOMPSON: I already done told you what was wrong with her.

WRIGHT: Maggie? What do you know about your illnesses?

MAGGIE: Well, I—

THOMPSON: I told you already. She got leukemia. She's on chemo. Her muscles don't work like they supposed to work. Did you really make me bring her out here so you could ask her questions that'd make her feel bad?

MAGGIE: It's okay, Momma, I—

THOMPSON: Hush now, baby.

WRIGHT: I apologize, ma'am. I didn't mean to offend. I was just trying to get a direct quote, for the article. But I understand your concerns, and I'm sorry.

THOMPSON: Just think before you talk, is all I'm asking.

WRIGHT: Maggie, how old are you?

MAGGIE: I'm—

THOMPSON: She's sixteen. Again, you already asked me that.

WRIGHT: That's right. Sixteen, going on seventeen, right?

MAGGIE: Yup. My birthday's in December!

WRIGHT: Wow. Seventeen sure is a big age. Any plans?

MAGGIE: Oh, I don't know. What are we doing, Momma?

THOMPSON: We have plenty of time to decide. Whatever you want to do, baby girl.

WRIGHT: What would you like to do, Maggie, if you could do anything in the world?

MAGGIE: I want to go to London and visit Harry Potter!

THOMPSON: Maggie!

WRIGHT: You really like Harry Potter, huh? You ever read the books?

MAGGIE: Over and over again! They're my favorite!

WRIGHT: That's great. I love the books, too.

MAGGIE: Momma, see? She likes Harry Potter, too.

THOMPSON: Yes. I heard.

WRIGHT: Ms. Thompson, I did have another question for you, if you don't mind.

THOMPSON: What?

WRIGHT: Well . . . some of my notes are confusing me. Of course, I've never been the best at math, so it's most likely a mistake on my end, but maybe you can help.

MAGGIE: Math sucks!

WRIGHT: Absolutely.

THOMPSON: Well? What are you talking about?

WRIGHT: When were you born, Ms. Thompson?

THOMPSON: What?

WRIGHT: What year were you born?

THOMPSON: Why on Earth would you need to know that?

WRIGHT: For the article. Just so I have my facts straight. You understand.

THOMPSON: Nineteen-seventy-two.

WRIGHT: And you moved to Indiana when you were twenty-one, correct?

THOMPSON: What?

WRIGHT: Earlier. You said you moved to Indiana after your twenty-first birthday.

THOMPSON: Well, if that's what I said.

WRIGHT: Is it accurate?

THOMPSON: I guess so. Yes. Why?

WRIGHT: Well, where my math is a little fuzzy, Ms. Thompson, is you told me you became pregnant with little Maggie here the same year you moved to Indiana, which means you would have given birth to her when you were twenty-two.

THOMPSON: Okay. So?

WRIGHT: So . . . if you were born in nineteen-seventy-two, and you gave birth to Maggie when you were only twenty-two, then that means Maggie was born in nineteen-ninety-three. Which means she couldn't possibly be sixteen, as you've mentioned multiple times now. She'd be almost twenty.

THOMPSON: I think I would know how old my own daughter is.

WRIGHT: I'm not claiming you don't know, not at all. I'm just asking for you to help me make sense of the math. It's not adding up.

THOMPSON: You know, it's starting to get kind of late. Maybe we should go ahead and wrap up this interview.

WRIGHT: I'm sorry if I offended you, Ms. Thompson. It was not my intent. We can talk about something else, if that's okay. I have other questions. Please.

THOMPSON: Just a few more, then you gotta get going.

WRIGHT: Thank you, Ms. Thompson. I really appreciate it.

THOMPSON: Go on then.

WRIGHT: I was curious about what kind of medications Maggie's required to take every day.

THOMPSON: Girl, if I started listing those off, we'd still be here come midnight.

WRIGHT: Maybe just the more critical ones.

THOMPSON: I don't want to get into any of that.

WRIGHT: Okay, fair enough. We can figure that out later.

THOMPSON: I don't think so.

WRIGHT: Oh, and speaking of medications, I almost forgot. Do you by any chance remember taking Maggie to a neurologist in Chicago named Lawrence Winzcnread?

THOMPSON: What? Uh. Maybe? We've seen so many doctors. It's hard to keep track of them all. You know, my head's starting to hurt. I'm kind of feeling dizzy.

WRIGHT: This would have been about two years ago.

THOMPSON: I don't remember. Sorry.

WRIGHT: It's okay. He still remembers. In fact, Lawrence Winzenread is the man who recommended I interview you in the first place.

THOMPSON: What are you talking about? Oh, Lord, I don't feel good.

MAGGIE: Momma, what's wrong?

***

Andrea released her grip on Maggie's hand and slumped back in the recliner. Still awake, but drowsy, unaware of her surroundings. Maggie gasped and stared at her mother, then swung her head back to Lori.

"What happened to my momma?"

"I think she's taking a little nap."

"What's wrong with her?"

"I don't know, Maggie." Lori leaned forward and closed the pizza box and stashed it under the coffee table. "Maybe she's just tired."

"No. Something's wrong."

"It's okay, Maggie. Your momma's had a long day. We'll just hang out here until she wakes up again, how about that?"

The girl looked unsure, but too afraid to argue. "Well, okay . . . "

"And since we're both here, would you be okay with finishing our conversation? So I can write my story about you."

"Okay."

"Excellent!" Lori smiled at the girl, hoping it convinced her that everything was okay, that they were all friends here. "Now, Maggie, maybe you remember the doctor I was talking about. Big, tall man, kinda looked like Severus Snape but with gray hair?"

"Hmm. No. I don't know."

"One day, at your appointment, your momma used the bathroom, and he leaned down real close to you and asked you to stand up. And you did. You stood up from your wheelchair. You stood up like you didn't even need a wheelchair. But as soon as you heard your momma coming back, you sat right back down and started crying and begging him not to tell anybody. Do you remember that, Maggie?"

Andrea groaned in the recliner, but remained helpless to the drugs Lori had spiked in the pizza.

Maggie shook her head. "I don't want to talk about that."

"Maggie, do you promise to be honest with me?"

"My momma . . . "

"Maggie, I need to ask you a question, okay? It's very important."

"Okay . . . "

"Can you walk?"

Maggie looked at her lap.

"Maggie, please. I need you to tell me the truth, okay? Can you walk? Do you really need the wheelchair?"

"My bones . . . they don't work like they're supposed to. Ask my momma, she'll tell you. I can't . . . "

Lori grabbed the voice recorder from the table and clicked STOP, then reached inside her bag and pulled out the Glock. She pointed it at Andrea. "Maggie, I need you to look at me."

Maggie lifted her head and screamed when she spotted the gun.

"Maggie, if you don't stand up right now, I'm going to shoot your momma. Do you understand me?"

"Yes."

Lori clicked the recorder back on and waited.

Maggie stood from the wheelchair. Her legs did not wobble. They kept her balance without any sign of difficulty.

Lori held the recorder close to her mouth as she spoke. "I would like the record to state that Maggie Thompson has just risen from her wheelchair without any assistance. Maggie, is what I say the truth?"

"Yes." The girl's voice lost its childlike sound.

"Can you please state what you're doing?"

"I'm standing."

"By yourself?"

"Yes."

"Please say it. For the recorder."

"I'm standing by myself."

"Great, thank you. Okay, you can sit back down, if you want. I have just a couple more questions, if that's all right."

Maggie returned to her wheelchair and wiped her nose with a tissue.

Andrea remained motionless.

✱✱✱

WRIGHT: Have you always been able to walk, Maggie?

MAGGIE: Yes.

WRIGHT: Is your mother aware that you're not actually handicapped?

MAGGIE: Yes.

WRIGHT: Then why do you pretend to need a wheelchair?

WRIGHT: I always have.

WRIGHT: Yes, but haven't you ever wondered why?

MAGGIE: Momma says it's what's best.

WRIGHT: Best for who?

MAGGIE: Me and Momma.

WRIGHT: How is it best for you to move around in a wheelchair?

MAGGIE: Because if I could walk, then Momma says the Wish people would stop letting us go to Disney.

WRIGHT: Do you know there are other kids out there who really do need wheelchairs? Who really can't walk?

MAGGIE: Yes.

WRIGHT: Do you think it's fair for you to lie about being handicapped so you can go to Disney while kids who really are handicapped don't always get the chance?

MAGGIE: I don't know.

WRIGHT: Yes you do. Do you really have leukemia, Maggie?

MAGGIE: I don't know.

WRIGHT: Yes, you do.

MAGGIE: *I don't know.*

WRIGHT: Maggie, this is what I think. I think you've never been sick, not in the ways your momma has said you've been sick. I think she's been faking your illnesses so people would feel bad for you and give her money. I think she enjoys looking like a hero. I think she's severely abused you in ways I can't even begin to imagine. I also think you're almost twenty years old and you're too old to be playing stupid about all of this.

MAGGIE: She's my momma.

WRIGHT: Do you know what Munchausen syndrome by proxy is, Maggie?

MAGGIE: What?

WRIGHT: Maggie, think about this. What happens once your momma's dead?

MAGGIE: Don't you dare.

WRIGHT: I'm not going to do anything to her, Maggie, calm down, she's just asleep. But eventually, something is going to happen to her, and once she's gone, where does that leave you? Nobody's going to take care of you. You're going to be by yourself. Are you prepared for that, Maggie? Because I don't think you are. I don't think you're even close to ready for reality. But I can help you if you come with me. We'll go down to the police station right now, and we'll tell them what's been going on, that your momma's been abusing you, that she's been giving you medications you don't really need, that she's been lying to doctors and forging medical diagnoses, that she's held you prisoner your entire life. You tell them all that, and you'll finally start to live like a real, normal girl should live. I promise you that, Maggie. I've been researching you for a while now and I want to help you so bad, I really do. Please . . . let me help you.

✳✳✳

"What's going to happen to Momma?"

Maggie stood over the recliner, staring down at Andrea.

"I don't know, Maggie. Hopefully she gets the help she needs, too." Lori touched the girl on the shoulder and she flinched. "It's okay, Maggie. You don't have to be afraid of me. I'm not going to hurt you."

"I'm scared."

Lori pointed at Maggie's hand. "She was holding your hand the entire time we talked. Does she do that when you talk to other people, too?"

Maggie nodded. "In case I start to say something wrong, she can squeeze it and let me know."

"Yeah. That's what I was thinking." Lori set the pistol on the coffee table next to the voice recorder and searched through her backpack.

"Am I really twenty?"

She paused, a handful of zipties in her grasp. "You didn't know that?"

Maggie shrugged. "Momma lied to me more than any other soul."

"Yeah. In December, you'll be twenty."

"Wow."

Lori took the zipties over to the recliner.

"What are you gonna do with those?"

"We're gonna tie her up so she can't go anywhere while we're at the police station."

"Will they hurt her?"

"Not too much."

"Okay."

Lori confined the woman's thick wrists together and then kneeled to her ankles, but her legs were too swollen for the zipties to wrap around. She stood and turned, meaning to grab a few more zipties from her backpack and combine them into a longer restraint, but froze in her tracks at the sight of Maggie standing across the coffee table holding Lori's gun.

The girl's whole body was shaking as she aimed it at her.

Lori held up her hands, palms out. "Please, Maggie, don't."

"I'm sorry, ma'am, but it's the way it's gotta be."

"Please. Maggie, I was just trying to help you. I know you don't understand it now, but this is for your own good. I promise. Okay? Your mother isn't healthy for you. She doesn't love you. Can't you see that?"

Maggie shook her head, sobbing. "I understand. I understand more than anybody."

She pulled the trigger over and over until the pistol started expelling dry-clicks.

Lori opened her eyes, expecting to find herself caught in some mysterious afterlife. Instead, she remained standing in the living room, Maggie still across from her. The pistol was now on the floor.

Maggie cried hard and loud and fell to her knees as if in prayer.

Lori turned around. Bullet holes littered the wall behind her. But not all of the bullets had connected with plaster.

One of them had bit into Andrea Thompson's face.

"Oh, shit."

Lori's own legs gave out and she collapsed into Maggie's wheelchair. She sat and watched the dead woman in the recliner awhile, listening to Maggie sob, and tried to convince herself that she'd done some good today, that she hadn't made a mistake by coming here.

Ten minutes later, she called 9-1-1.

ABDUCTION (REPRISE)

SOFIA STARED AT their cup of coffee for one, two, three seconds before asking their mother what she was talking about. The two of them were in her kitchen. The same house Sofia had grown up in. Once a week they came over for coffee. Usually their mom did most of the talking and they spent the whole time daydreaming. Not really thinking about anything, just drifting. Their mom loved to gossip—about coworkers, people she'd encountered at the grocery store, Sofia's childhood friends. Sometimes she said something that got their attention, but most of the time Sofia simply nodded and went, "Uh-huh," every couple minutes. It was their routine. They'd been doing it for years.

Except Sofia's mom had just said something that they couldn't ignore.

"Did you just say I was *kidnapped*?" Sofia asked, ninety-nine percent sure they'd simply misheard her.

"No," their mom said, then leaned forward the way she did whenever she was holding on to some juicy news, "I said you were *almost* kidnapped."

"What do you mean?" They didn't understand what she was saying. If they'd been kidnapped—or *almost* kidnapped—surely they would have known about this by now. It wouldn't be something they suddenly discovered at the goddamn age of thirty-two. "You're not making any sense."

"Well, hold on," their mom said. "Don't start overreacting . . . "

"I'm not overreacting. You're always accusing me of overreacting."

"Sometimes you can act a bit hysterical, is all I'm saying."

"Mom, you just said I was almost kidnapped. How do you *want* me to react?"

Their mom laughed. It came out as a nervous giggle. "Are you sure I never told you about this before? I could have sworn we'd already had this conversation."

"I think I would remember something like this."

"Hmm." She shrugged. "Well, it's not that big of a deal. It was a long time ago."

"What *happened*?" They gripped the coffee mug with both hands, squeezing so tight they feared the cup would shatter, but something prevented them from loosening their grip.

"You were just a baby," their mom said, sipping from her own coffee. "I don't even think you could crawl yet, you were that little."

"Was Dad alive still?"

"Mm-hmm, the cancer didn't get him until you were a couple years older. But he wasn't *with us* with us at the time."

"Where were we?"

"Sam's Club. Doing a little grocery shopping. Your dad liked to stay in the car, listen to the radio, do his crosswords. So, it was just us two girls."

"Mom—"

She held up her hand, already realizing her mistake. "I know, I'm sorry, it was an accident. Cut me a break, okay? This isn't an easy thing to talk about. Some memories are more painful than others, you know?"

They bit their tongue and didn't respond. Waited for their mother to figure out how she wanted to tell the story. Usually she blabbered at the rate of machinegun fire, so for her to be at a loss for words, Sofia wasn't quite sure what this meant—except that it was something far more serious than the typical mundane gossip that normally occupied this kitchen table.

"Okay," their mom finally said, "so, as I said, we were at Sam's doing a little shopping. I was pushing you around in the cart with your car seat in the basket. Making funny faces at you, trying to get you to laugh. You know. The stuff moms do with their dau—with their babies."

"But something happened."

"Something happened. Yeah." She took another sip to gather her thoughts, then wiped her lips with the back of her hand. "There was this woman."

"A woman?"

"Yeah. Maybe a couple years older than I was. I don't know. All the details are hard to remember, but yeah, she was there. This woman."

"What was she doing?"

"Well, at first I didn't suspect anything weird. We passed each other in one of the aisles, maybe one of us bumped into the other, whatever, and it led to a brief exchange. Nothing unpleasant. Just a quick 'pardon me' or 'oh, I'm sorry.' You've been to grocery stores before. You know what I'm talking about."

Sofia nodded and gritted their teeth and resisted every urge inside them to scream at their mom to get to the point already. She always took her sweet time like this. Especially when she knew Sofia was actually paying attention to what she had to say.

"So, yeah, the woman, she eventually notices you in the cart, and her whole face lights up. You'd think she had never seen a baby before."

"What did she do?"

"Oh, you know, just started showering you with all these compliments. Things like you were the cutest thing she'd ever laid eyes upon. That I was the luckiest mother in the world to have a baby so beautiful—which is nice to hear, don't get me wrong, but after a while, it starts becoming a bit . . . much. I told her thanks, that we appreciated it, and went on our way—except, when we turned into the next aisle, there she was again."

"What did you say?"

"The same conversation from the last aisle. Complimenting you. Asking all these questions."

"What kind of questions?"

"Oh, I don't know, like what your name was, how old you were, typical baby questions. Then I made the mistake of taking my eyes off you—just for a moment—to grab something from one of the shelves. I can't even remember what it was now. But when I turned back to the cart, the car seat was empty."

"She took me?"

Their mom laughed. "I looked down the aisle, and there she was, hugging you to her chest and speed-walking away from me."

"What did you do?"

"What do you think I did?" their mom asked. "I screamed, 'Hey, that's my baby!' I chased her. She ran. I screamed louder. People noticed. Someone stopped her. I forget who. Maybe security? Does Sam's have security? Anyway. She didn't make it out the door."

"Was I . . . was I *hurt*, or . . . ?"

She shook her head. "You were perfectly fine. Crying and a little shook up, but there wasn't a scratch on you."

Sofia still couldn't believe what they were hearing. It didn't matter how young they might've been when this happened. The fact that it *had* happened and they couldn't remember a single detail was what frightened them the most. That an incident so traumatic had been forgotten with time. Maybe they weren't old enough to have formed memories by then, but still. It felt wrong. Like something was *taken* from them.

"What happened then?" Sofia asked. "Was she arrested?"

She nodded as she finished off her cup of coffee. "Of course she was arrested. The cops came and everything. I had to make a statement. The whole time, your dad was out in the parking lot, *completely* oblivious to everything going on. We get back out to the car and he's like, 'Jeez, what took you so long?' Took him forever to believe me. Only when the paper came out and he saw the story—"

"It was in the *newspaper*?"

She looked at them funny. "What, you think a woman tries kidnapping a baby at Sam's Club and it *doesn't* make the local paper?"

"Do you still have it?"

"Have what? The paper?"

"Yeah," they said, hopeful, "the one about me."

"Why? You don't believe me, either?" Their mom chuckled, then lit a cigarette. "I swear, sometimes you're just like your dad."

"I just want to see it."

"I wouldn't even know where to look." She gestured at the kitchen. "It could be anywhere. It could be nowhere. This was over thirty years ago. I've never been much for scrapbooking."

"Do you know what happened to her?" Sofia asked.

"To who?"

"The woman."

"What do you mean?"

"After she was arrested. Did she go to prison? Was she released? What happened?"

But all their mom could do was shrug again. "I don't know."

"How don't you know?"

"Nobody ever contacted us about it. There was no follow-up. I didn't have to testify or anything. It just kind of disappeared."

"You didn't reach out and ask about it?"

"Why would I do that?" their mom said.

"I don't know. Weren't you at least . . . curious?"

"Sofia, that woman was crazy. I wanted nothing to do with her. After what happened at Sam's, I never wanted to see or talk to her again. As far as I'm concerned, she's dead."

✷

But she wasn't dead, Sofia discovered later that night, back at their studio apartment. Every light was off except the glow of their laptop screen on the mattress, surrounded by takeout Thai food and a thermos of ice water. They'd started eating in bed again after Tyler moved out a couple months back. There was no point in pretending to be tidy when there was no one else around to impress. They hated eating at the table. Or on the couch. In bed was perfect. Even if it had grossed Tyler out. But he was gone. Now there was no one left to disgust.

On the laptop, Sofia obtained a trial subscription to newspapers dot com. The service offered archives of practically every newspaper in existence. It took two seconds to locate their town's local paper. It took far longer to find the specific issue about their abduction.

First, they narrowed the date down to the first two years of their life. Then they tied their own name into the search. Nothing popped up. Which made sense, they supposed. It would've been unethical journalism to print a baby's name in a news story of this nature. Next, they tried their mom's name. Still nothing. Maybe it was policy to keep victims anonymous. That was fine. They weren't after the victims, anyway.

Sofia typed "kidnap" and hit SEARCH. A few TV listings for Lifetime movies, but that was about it.

She tried "abduct" next.

And there it was, in big bold text: **WOMAN ATTEMPTS TO ABDUCT CHILD AT SAM'S CLUB**.

The story, for the most part, fit exactly what their mom had told them earlier that morning. Except the newspaper listed the woman's name.

Frances Adams. Age thirty-four.

Which would have put the woman in her mid-to-late-sixties by now—because yes, she was still alive. Sofia found the woman's Facebook account and everything. It was active. Frances posted every day if not every other day. Usually just sharing memes, *Far Side* cartoons, stuff like that. Not a lot of text-based posts. Not a lot of personal photos, either. None, in fact. Her avatar was just some cute cat pic, something she probably didn't even take herself. Her friends list was set on private, but nobody seemed to interact with any of her statuses, as far as Sofia could tell. Maybe there were other posts—ones with text, ones with more personal information—that were also limited by privacy settings.

Sofia clicked the friend request button before they even realized what they were doing.

Then they sat there, eating the rest of their Thai food, waiting for an update.

According to Frances's profile, she still lived in the same town. Which they thought was crazy. Surely, after getting busted trying to *kidnap a child*, someone would decide to pack up and leave, go somewhere where nobody knew their name. Yet, that didn't seem to be the case here. The woman had chosen to stay.

Sofia wondered if they were the only baby Frances had tried to take. They wondered if there were others. And, if so, if their mothers had also stopped her like Sofia's mother had stopped her. Or if Frances had ever gotten away with it. And, if so, what she'd done with the baby afterward. What had been her plan? If she'd managed to sneak away with Sofia, what would this woman have done with them? Something sexual? Something violent? *Murder*? Was she looking to *profit* from the crime? Sell them on the black market somewhere?

So many questions, and no answers. At least not yet. Frances was still alive, and she wasn't in prison. Had never *been* in prison, Sofia didn't think.

After the initial news story about the arrest, there had been no follow-ups. Her name was never mentioned again in the local paper—or *any* paper, for that matter. There were other Frances Adamses, of course. But none like the one who still lived in Sofia's hometown. None like the one who had tried to kidnap a baby thirty-odd years ago.

✶✶✶

Frances accepted their friend request the next morning. It was the first thing Sofia checked upon waking up. They hadn't even bothered to throw away the Thai food container before going to sleep. It was empty, anyway, so what did it matter? It was too cold to attract things like ants. Come the summer, it'd be a different story, but that was still months away.

Not only had she accepted their request, but she'd also sent them a private message: *Hello. Do I know you?*

Sofia stared at the message for half the morning before getting up and taking a shower. They brewed a pot of coffee and paced around the kitchen as a bagel toasted. The laptop remained on the bed, still open, the Facebook message burning a hole in their screen. They couldn't look at that right now. They never expected Frances to reach out like that. Sofia had been hoping, at the most, she'd accept their request, then they could quietly lurk on her profile, maybe comb through her friends. What kind of maniac just messages someone like that?

A maniac who kidnaps people, of course.

Sofia had no idea how to respond. They only found out the woman existed barely twenty-four hours ago. And now there was a Facebook chat in progress. Sofia had initiated it with the request, sure, but Frances had been the first one to speak.

Why?

Because she was lonely. This friend request was probably the first interesting thing to happen to her in weeks, if not months. She was an old woman now. Did she live alone, or was she married? Did her partner know about Frances's past life as a child abductor?

Assuming she'd moved past that life at all.

Sofia was making a lot of assumptions lately. It felt like

such a waste, considering the truth—the *real* truth—was waiting for them over on the bed. All they had to do was respond. Tell her who they were.

Tell her that they knew what she had done.

***

Sofia had driven past Frances's house many times throughout their life, although they'd never known it until now. Not until they pulled up in her driveway and turned the ignition off and really looked at the place. She lived between Sofia and their mom. Almost exactly in the middle. They wondered what their mom would have said had she known that—or maybe she *did* know and had simply chosen to omit that part of the story when telling them yesterday. They wouldn't have blamed her. The fact that their almost-kidnapper lived so close was more than a little spooky.

No. They didn't think their mom had known this much. Otherwise, she would have moved a long time ago. They knew their mom. There was no way she would've been okay with living so close to the woman who tried to steal her baby.

Frances already had the front door open when they approached the porch. She stood on the opposite side of the screen door, looking frail and scared. Looking exactly how Sofia had imagined she would look the whole drive over here.

Sofia stopped on the porch and, for a moment, the two of them studied each other without saying a word, the only audible sound being the woman's wind chimes.

Then Frances smiled and said, "Ah, yes. I would recognize that beautiful face anywhere."

She invited them inside, and they accepted.

***

The house was small. Smaller than their mom's. Bigger than their studio apartment, but not by much. One look around confirmed their theory that she lived alone. This was not the home of multiple people.

She told them she had just finished brewing some tea, if they wanted any. They thought about it and nodded. Couldn't even remember the last time they'd had tea. All they ever drank was coffee, it felt like. But tea. Tea sounded amazing at that moment. It sounded perfect.

Frances prepared two cups and they sat in the living room. Frances on the recliner, Sofia on the loveseat. It took a couple sips to get used to the tea. The differences between tea and coffee were extreme. It wasn't the easiest drink to swap at the drop of a hat. But they were going to try. Maybe not forever, but for this moment? Absolutely. This afternoon, Sofia was a tea drinker.

Neither of them seemed to know what to say. There were a lot of awkward false starts at conversation. Back at their studio apartment, the Facebook chat hadn't birthed much further discussion, either. They had simply informed Frances who they were, what they'd found out, and asked if she would be interested in meeting sometime.

As fate would have it, they both had the afternoon free.

"I always wondered if this day would come," Frances said. She kept folding her hands in her lap and readjusting her legs. Too nervous to pick a position. Sofia could relate. They were both entering territory neither of them had explored before. At least, they assumed Frances hadn't. Maybe this wasn't the first time someone she tried to kidnap showed up at her door thirty years later. Something told them there hadn't been others, though, that Sofia had been unique in that regard.

"Am I the only one?" they asked, figuring there was only one way to find out for sure.

"The only one?"

"The only baby you . . . you tried to take."

"Oh." She leaned back in the recliner, avoiding eye contact. "I suppose so, yeah. There had been others, before and after—but mostly before—where I *almost* went through with it, but something always held me back.

"Why me?" Sofia asked. It was the one question they'd

been repeating in their head over and over since talking to their mom about it. What made them so special? Out of all the babies in the world—in this *town*—why had Frances gone after Sofia?

"It's a good question," she said. "Certainly something I've asked myself on a number of occasions."

"You don't know?"

"It's not that I don't know. It's that . . . I don't know how to describe it. I don't know the right words."

"Maybe try, anyway? I think you owe me that."

"Okay. Yeah. You're right." She set her cup of tea down on the table between them and stared off at the wall, mouth hanging open a little, clearly trying to figure something out. Then she focused directly on Sofia and said, "When I saw you in that store, in your little car seat, I felt something. Something I'd never felt before."

"What did you feel?"

"Like I said. You weren't the first one I considered . . . you know, bringing home with me. But you were the only one I did more than consider. I tried. I tried my hardest, and I failed."

"But *why*?"

At some point during the conversation, Frances had started crying. Sofia wiped their own eyes and discovered they had joined her. They couldn't remember the last time they'd cried like this. It felt so good.

"When I looked at all those other babies," Frances said, "they felt like someone else's child. Like they already had a mother, a father. But when I saw you, and you saw me, and you smiled . . . I knew . . . it was different. It was like I had finally found something I lost a long time ago, something I thought I would never find again. Something that would finally make me complete."

"I read the news story," Sofia said. "It said you'd miscarried. That's why you tried to . . . "

"That's true. I miscarried. More than once, actually. Until my husband decided I was no good, that I was ruined goods. By the time you and I crossed paths, he was long gone. I thought I'd live alone forever. That nobody would ever want to be my family. Until I saw you. Suddenly life felt like it could be okay again. If only I could take you home. If only I could raise you, nurture you, protect you." Frances paused, then cocked her head. "I've dreamt about that smile for thirty years."

Sofia realized she was talking about them.

They were *smiling*.

Because, yes, everything this woman was saying . . . it didn't sound insane, or criminal . . . in fact, they understood exactly what she meant. They'd felt a similar way most of their life. Look at what happened with Tyler. How they'd fucked that whole thing up, how they'd fucked up every relationship they'd ever been involved in.

"What have you been doing all these years?" Sofia asked. "Since . . . since it happened."

Now it was Frances's turn to smile. "My dear, I've been waiting for you."

∗∗∗

Sofia and Frances spent the rest of the afternoon talking and drinking tea. Then the next afternoon, and the one after that, too.

It became their new routine. Every day, they'd drive over to her house and they would talk about their lives.

Sofia would tell her about their childhood, about their other family, about their previous love interests, about their failed jobs, about their intense lack of interest in anything resembling a career.

Frances would tell them about the many jobs she'd had over the years, none of them lasting more than a dozen months. She'd tell them about how she never bothered dating once her husband left. How she sometimes parked in front of elementary schools and watched the children play at recess. How she liked to imagine one of them belonged to her. But it was too late for her. She was too old to be a mom. She'd blown her chance. At her age, it was more responsible to play make-believe.

ABDUCTION (REPRISE)

Meanwhile, Sofia would nod along to everything she was saying, never once drifting away from the conversation, latching on to every word Frances said.

After so long, they stopped visiting their real mom altogether.

***

At a certain point during their visits, Sofia started bringing little desserts to accompany their tea. Nothing they would personally bake, of course. They didn't know the first thing about that kind of stuff and had no desire to learn. But there was a bakery close to Frances's house that made the most delicious coffee cakes. Neither Sofia nor Frances could resist them.

It was on one of these trips to the bakery that Sofia found something in the parking lot. They'd just exited the building and was headed back to their car, cradling the box of coffee cake against their chest, when they heard it.

In the car next to theirs, something was crying.

In the back seat.

There was a baby.

Crying.

The car was otherwise empty. Where were the baby's parents? Perhaps in the very same bakery Sofia had just departed. They might've even been behind them in line. They could've been anybody.

No, not anybody.

Only a certain kind of someone would leave their baby alone like this.

Someone unfit to be a parent.

Someone who didn't deserve to have a child.

Sofia leaned forward and pressed their face against the window.

The baby noticed them.

The baby stopped crying.

The baby smiled.

Sofia smiled.

They both smiled at each other, together.

Somewhere deep in their stomach, Sofia felt a warmth they'd never experienced before.

They tried the door.

It was unlocked.

VIDEO NASTIES

JEREMY WATCHED THE TV screen, mesmerized.

***

[the man with a mask made of human skin holds the chainsaw high above his head, letting the engine roar like a crazed, starved animal before bringing it back down and slicing through the woman's skull; she screams as brains and bone fragments splatter the wall behind her]

***

[the blade enters the woman's skin, slowly, and it is so sharp it might as well be slicing through butter]

***

[at first it is just a drop of blood that appears, but then—very quickly—it is practically raining]

***

Jeremy and Eddie were at their Secret Spot, hanging out on the Couch, taking turns playing a handheld Gameboy. The Couch was an abandoned sofa they'd found in the woods one day, next to a railroad track. It stunk of mold and animal piss. No one else seemed to know about it, so they declared it their own Secret Spot, and used the Couch as a hideout to get away from all the bullshit of their regular lives.

Like most Saturday afternoons, they'd spent a majority of it at their Secret Spot, playing games and sharing liquor and cigarettes boosted from drugstores. It was Eddie's turn for the Gameboy, so Jeremy handed it over and got off the Couch to stretch his legs.

MAX BOOTH III

Multicolored leaves crunched beneath his feet. Sweat dripped down his forehead and into his eyes. It was too damn hot for October.

"I hate this town," Jeremy said. "All it does is piss me off."

"Yeah," Eddie said, eyes glued to the Gameboy screen, "it sucks."

"I hate the people here," Jeremy said. "I hate them all."

Eddie shrugged.

"There's never anything to do. Everyone is so goddamn boring. I'm tired of it."

"Yeah," Eddie muttered, "but what can we do about it?"

Jeremy thought about it long and hard, but came up with nothing. He grabbed another cigarette from their stash and sat back down on the Couch. It was useless.

"A bunch of fuckin' assholes," Jeremy said. "Every last one of 'em."

"We should just kill them all," Eddie said, and laughed.

At that, Jeremy did not respond. Instead, he sat on the Couch, smoking his cigarette, and remained quiet for a very long time.

A series of thoughts and ideas were running through his mind like mad. He would have been a liar if he'd claimed they hadn't crossed his mind in the past. Thoughts that made him excited. Thoughts that made his blood rush.

"Hey," Eddie said after a while, passing him the Gameboy, "it's your turn."

"No, that's okay," Jeremy said. "I'm done playing."

***

[screaming, he is lifted upside down and thrown onto the giant meat hook hanging from the ceiling and it enters his spine and exists his stomach, causing him to choke on his own blood and vomit]

***

The next morning was a Sunday. Jeremy was at Eddie's house by nine o'clock, knocking on his bedroom window. When Eddie finally woke up and opened the window,

Jeremy was standing there outside, practically prancing up and down.

"What the hell are you doing, man?" Eddie asked, rubbing his eyes. He nodded toward the backpack strapped over his friend's shoulders. "What's with the bag?"

Jeremy smiled. "Get dressed. Let's go to the mall."

"What are you talking about?"

"Just fucking get dressed, will ya?" Jeremy said. "We're gonna have some fun."

Eddie gave him a questionable look, then turned around and began scavenging clothes from his bedroom floor.

"Hurry the fuck up. We're wasting time here."

Eddie did as he was told.

***

The mall opened at ten. Jeremy insisted they walk there and not ask either of their parents for a ride.

So they walked, and by the time they reached the mall, it was just opening. They sat down in the food court. Eddie asked what they were doing, but Jeremy didn't answer; just kept looking around the mall, searching for something.

"I don't have any money," Eddie said. "Do you?"

"No, we're not buying anything," Jeremy said.

"Are we stealing?"

Jeremy was quiet for a moment, then nodded. "Yes."

"Oh," Eddie said. "That's why you have the backpack."

Jeremy looked at the bag on his lap and then at Eddie. "I want to fill this thing up before we leave here."

"With what?"

Jeremy sighed. "It doesn't matter."

***

The first store they entered was a candy shop. They ran in like lunatics, taking handfuls of gummy snacks and running back out. It was madness. Pure, blissful madness.

After the candy shop, they became more cautious. If they caused any more attention to themselves, they'd surely be kicked out of the mall before any real fun could be had.

But even that didn't last. The thrill of taking inanimate objects could only keep them going for so long. Two hours had passed, and the backpack was half full.

"I'm getting tired of this," Eddie said. "This is getting boring."

"Oh stop being a pussy," Jeremy said. They were sitting on a bench next to a water fountain, resting their legs. "There's other stuff we can do. There's loads."

Eddie rolled his eyes. "Like what?

It was then that they noticed a small child standing outside a shop all by himself. Just standing there, as if abandoned.

Jeremy smiled, looked at Eddie, then back at the baby.

***

"Let's get that kid lost."

***

[the doctor in the white coat carefully inserts his scalpel into his patient's eyeball and begins to dig it out of her socket; he flops it into his steel surgical tray and turns his attention to the other eye]

***

Later, in court, the prosecutor rolled in a portable television for the jury and played security footage of the Omni River Mall on the day of the crime. The video showed Jeremy Ohio and Eddie Bennett loitering in various shops, shoplifting miscellaneous merchandise.

The prosecutor fast-forwarded through two hours of footage until Ohio and Bennett approached a small child standing outside of a clothing store. They appeared to speak to the child for a few moments before taking him by the hand and leading him away from the area.

In court, Ohio and Bennett sat behind their defendant tables, silent and still.

***

The baby wouldn't stop crying. They didn't know how old he was, maybe two or three at the most. At first, he'd willingly come along with them. But now that they'd left the mall, all the fucking brat could say was, "Mommy! Mommy!" and cry his little stupid head off. They tried giving him some of the stolen candy but he just fought it away.

"Shut up, goddammit," Jeremy whispered, as they walked through the parking lot, "shut the fuck up." He took the back of his hand and swatted the baby across the face.

"Hey!" some woman shouted, getting out of her car. "What the hell do you think you're doing?"

Eddie started stammering, but Jeremy put a stop to it quickly. "We're just meeting our parents across the street, at that Starbucks."

"You just hit that kid."

"He was being a shit," Jeremy said.

Her jaw dropped. "Take me to your mother. This is unacceptable."

"Hey lady, mind your own business."

She started to protest more, but her cell phone rang and she gave up.

They continued moving, quickening their pace. The baby couldn't match their speed so he lifted and carried him. He already had a bump on his head from where Jeremy had smacked him.

A few minutes later, a guy passing by pulled his car over and stuck his head out the window.

"Are you boys all right? Where are your parents?"

"Everything's okay," Jeremy said. "This is our little brother. He's cranky, needs to hurry up and get home so he can nap."

"What happened to his head?" the man asked.

Jeremy shrugged. "Tripped."

The man nodded. "I understand that one. Good luck, kid."

"Thanks."

He drove off.

"Where are we going?" Eddie asked, nervous and excited sounding.

"We're just . . . going for a walk."

★★★

[the turtle attempts to flee but it is fruitless and it is caught and dragged back to shore by the men who decapitate the turtle and remove its arms and legs and shell, celebrating its death in the form of a feast]

★★★

The baby kept trying to run away from them and they kept having to grab him and drag him out of the street.

"We should just let him get hit," Eddie said.

Jeremy smiled. "Imagine all the blood."

Instead, they continued to lead him down the street, until they came across a canal at the bottom of a ditch.

"What if we pushed him in?" Jeremy asked.

"He'd drown," Eddie said. "You think he'd float or sink?"

"One way to find out," Jeremy said. "You want to do it?"

Eddie seemed to contemplate this, then shook his head. "No. Let's just leave him here. Maybe he'll fall in by himself. Come on. Let's go."

"You don't want to keep him?" Jeremy asked, sadly.

"We can do other things, without him. He's just a dumb old baby."

Jeremy stared at the baby a while and sighed. "He is a dumb old baby. He's wasted our whole day."

He dug his hands underneath the child's armpits and picked him up. "Haven't you, you fucking brat?"

"Momma!" the baby cried.

Jeremy had enough of that. He turned the baby upside down and released his grip. They watched as he sunk straight through the air like a stone, landing directly on his head.

The screaming that followed from the baby was loud and terrifying enough to send both Jeremy and Eddie running away as quickly as possible.

"Stop!" Jeremy shouted. "We have to go back."

Eddie gave him a horrified look, trying to catch his breath. "*Why?*"

"We just . . . we just *do.*"

VIDEO NASTIES

***

[everybody is screaming as loud as their lungs will allow but it is no use, what has been done cannot be undone; the bodies—or what is left of the bodies—form that of mountains in the madman's basement, their intestines and claw marks blemishing the walls]

***

"Is that boy all right? What happened?"

"I don't know, we just found him down at the bottom of that ditch, crying."

"Oh, my God, that's awful. You boys need to take him to the police station right away. It's just down the street there. Be fast."

"Okay, sir, thank you."

"Hey, kids. Hey! Where the hell are you going? The police station is the other way. Hey, goddammit! Kids, you're going the wrong way."

***

[the rape survivor confronts her monster by sliding her hand up and down his shaft, stimulating him to near orgasm, and it is only when he is about to come that the survivor smiles a wicked smile and brings out the knife and severs the man's cock and tosses it aside, standing up and walking away and listening to him bleed out]

***

"Mommy, why are those boys kicking that other boy? They're hurting him!"

"That's none of our business, honey. Come on back inside."

"But, Mommy . . . "

"Stop being nosy. Inside. *Now*."

***

Twenty-seven eyewitnesses.

Twenty-seven citizens that could have prevented a tragedy.

Twenty-seven heads that turned the other way.

***

They took the baby to their Secret Spot. There was simply no place else.

"What are we gonna do with him?" Eddie asked.

The baby was sitting on the Couch, sobbing.

"I don't know," Jeremy said. "What do you want to do?"

They watched the baby on the Couch cry and cry and cry for his momma. They were a long way from the mall now. Eddie tried to think but the baby was too loud, he couldn't concentrate on a damn thing.

"I want to make him stop crying," he finally said.

"Okay," Jeremy said. "Then let's make him stop."

There was a pile of bricks nearby. Jeremy picked one of them up, aimed and threw it. Eddie laughed and got himself a brick, too.

The baby's cries only became louder and louder.

✱✱✱

[the meth-head points the gun at the woman in the dirt and tells her to piss her pants or he swears to fucking God he'll blow her little girlfriend's brains out and make her lick up the mess, he isn't fucking kidding around here and she knows this and closes her eyes and focuses as hard as she can and lets her urine soak the crotch of her blue jeans]

✱✱✱

Jeremy emptied his backpack on the Couch. Stolen candy, firecrackers, batteries, and random toys came spilling out.

He dug a lighter out of his pocket while Eddie held open the baby's diaper.

Jeremy lit one of the firecrackers.

Then he lit another.

✱✱✱

"Fucking baby."

✱✱✱

The corpse of two-year-old Graham Frederickson was discovered three days later on a set of train tracks just outside town.

VIDEO NASTIES

A group of high school kids had driven into the woods with the intent of getting high and having sex. Instead, they found what they at first believed to be a doll cut in two.

It was not a doll.

***

Sixty-two injuries.

Most to the face and head.

According to the reports, the baby had still been alive when Ohio and Bennett left him on the train tracks, buried under a mountain of bricks.

Sixty-two.

***

Police collected the security footage from the mall and printed out a screenshot of the two boys responsible for leading two-year-old Graham Frederickson out of Omni River Mall. Their photos were broadcasted on every local channel.

Jeremy's mother was the first one to turn them in.

"I should have strangled that little ungrateful shit back when he was still attached to the umbilical cord," she later said.

***

[the killer stabs the woman's stomach repeatedly knowing full well that she is with child and that he is doing the devil's work and that the baby belongs not only to her but also to him]

***

"Did you kill Graham Frederickson?"

"It was Jeremy. He did it. He made me watch. I tried to stop him . . . "

***

[the boy's teeth begin falling out one by one and he can't stop them no matter how hard he tries, they go drip drip drip into the sink and soon he is without teeth altogether and after that goes the flesh upon his face and after that, everything else]

***

"Eddie went nuts. I couldn't save the baby. I tried. I really tried. But I couldn't. Eddie killed him. I'm so sorry. I'm so, so sorry."

***

"In this day and age, in this time of ultimate distress, we hear of these tragedies, these crimes that are so horrific they provoke such anger and disbelief in equal proportions. Let me tell you something, the world has not always been like this. These are awful, horrible times. These crimes, these are the ugly manifestations of a society that has become unworthy to even be called a society."

***

"Your honor, with all due respect, we have gone through at least two hundred films rented by the Ohio and Bennett families. Believe me, there were many scenes in these movies that you nor myself would ever wish to see, but in all honesty, there was nothing—no scene, or plot, or dialogue, not a thing—where you could pause it and say that—that, right there—influenced a child to go out and commit murder."

***

"Society needs to condemn a little more, and understand a little less."

***

"Frankly, your honor, that is complete bullshit."

***

At eleven years old, Jeremy Ohio and Edward Bennett were both sentenced to a minimum of ten years imprisonment.

They both left the courtroom in tears.

Outside, people rioted. Not due to the confinement of children, but for the sentence not being longer than what it already was.

They wanted their heads.

They wanted more blood.

They wanted it all.

***

[the two boys lead the baby into the forest and show him their Secret Spot and nothing is ever the same again]

LIST OF FAMILICIDES IN THE UNITED STATES (BY DECADE)

Article	Talk

Read	Edit	New Section	View History

This is a list of notable <u>familicides</u> that occurred in the <u>United States</u>. A familicide is defined here as a type of murder or <u>murder-suicide</u> in which a perpetrator kills multiple close family members in quick succession, most often children, relatives, spouse, siblings, or parents[1].

1900s, 1910s, 1920s, 1930s, 1940s, 1950s, 1960s, 1970s, 1980s, 1990s, 2000s, 2010s, 2020s

Perpetrator: <u>Brady Martin</u>
Date: Jan 19, 1901
Location: <u>Chicago, IL</u>
Killed: 4 (including himself)
Notes: Played 355 games as a <u>catcher</u> for the <u>White Sox Stockings</u>. Martin was antisocial and suffered from <u>paranoia</u> and hallucinations. On January 18th, he was physically removed from a game after threatening an <u>umpire</u> with violence. The next day, he murdered his wife and two children with an axe, then used a straight razor to slice his own throat.

Perpetrator: <u>Paul Michael Anderson</u>
Date: Aug 18, 1909
Location: <u>Hobart, IN</u>
Killed: 3 (including himself)

Notes: Anderson was a writer for <u>magazines</u>. He'd written several <u>novels</u>, but never managed to get any published. This led to financial difficulties within the household. On the night of August 18, Anderson tied his wife and daughter together in the family room before drenching them and himself in gasoline and setting the house on fire.

<u>*1900s*</u>, <u>*1910s*</u>, <u>*1920s*</u>, <u>*1930s*</u>, <u>*1940s*</u>, *1950s*, <u>*1960s*</u>, <u>*1970s*</u>, <u>*1980s*</u>, <u>*1990s*</u>, <u>*2000s*</u>, <u>*2010s*</u>, <u>*2020s*</u>

Perpetrator: <u>Geoff Donaldson</u>
Date: Feb 17, 1951
Location: <u>Crown Point, IN</u>
Killed: 3
Notes: Donaldson's pregnant wife and two young daughters were found repeatedly bludgeoned and stabbed in their Crown Point home. Donaldson had alerted authorities to the incident at 3:30 A.M., claiming someone had broken into their home and knocked him unconscious. Nine years later, Donaldson was convicted of the crimes and given three consecutive life sentences. He committed suicide in prison.

Perpetrator: <u>Jonathan Leer</u>
Date: Nov 9, 1953
Location: <u>Joliet, IL</u>
Killed: 5
Notes: Murdered his mother, wife, and their three children and evaded police for 18 years under a new identity. During the trail, Leer confessed that he'd been burdened with financial distress, leaving him with only two choices: accept <u>welfare</u> from the state, or kill his entire family. He was sentenced to five consecutive terms of life imprisonment.

LIST OF FAMILICIDES IN THE UNITES STATES

Perpetrator: Jim Roberts
Date: April 10, 1955
Location: Whiting, IN
Killed: 11
Notes: Occurred on Easter Sunday. Roberts, 17 at the time, sealed every exit in the house before proceeding to execute every member of his family with a shotgun. He turned himself into police later that night. He passed away in a state psychiatric hospital from cirrhosis of the liver at the age of 75.

1900s, 1910s, 1920s, 1930s, 1940s, 1950s, 1960s, 1970s, 1980s, 1990s, 2000s, 2010s, 2020s

Perpetrator: Daniel Bradley
Date: Feb 18, 2001
Location: East Chicago, IN
Killed: 4
Notes: Bradley was 13 when he murdered his parents, brother, and sister with an axe. Police discovered him alone in the house with the corpses after neighbors sent in for a wellness check. Bradley explained to interrogating that he had killed his family because he was sick of doing chores.

Perpetrator: Seth Nicholson
Date: Jan 7, 2002
Location: Rockford, IL
Killed: 7 (including himself and a dog)
Notes: Convinced his wife was preparing to leave him, Nicholson murdered all six of their children (ranging from ages 3-12) in their sleep, including the family dog. His wife, Brenda Nicholson, was a nurse and working the night shift during the incident. Afterward, Nicholson confronted his wife at the hospital and informed her of what he'd done. He then proceeded to stab himself in the heart.

Perpetrator: Andrew Chapman
Date: Aug 25, 2004
Location: Portage, IN
Killed: 4 (including himself)
Notes: Strangled wife and two children in their sleep, then hung himself in the kitchen. Holes were found hammered into the walls throughout the house and filled with spoiled animal meat. No known motive.

Perpetrator: Isaac Billings
Date: July 4, 2009
Location: Gary, IN
Killed: 3 (including himself)
Notes: On his 16th birthday, Isaac Billings murdered his mother and father in a hotel room, then committed suicide by leaping off a nearby casino's parking garage. It is not clear why the Billings family were staying at the hotel, or what motive Isaac may have had for these acts of violence.

Article	Talk

Read	Edit	New Section	View History

List of familicides in the United States (by decade): Revision history

View logs for this page (**view filter log**)

External tools: Find addition/removal (Alternate) ~ Find edits by user (Alternate) ~ Page statistics ~ Pageviews ~ Fix dead links

For any version listed below, click on its date to view it. For more help, see Help:Page history and Help:Edit summary.

(cur) = difference from current version, (prev) = difference from preceding version, **m** = minor edit, → = section edit, ← = automatic edit summary

LIST OF FAMILICIDES IN THE UNITES STATES

Compare selected revisions

- (<u>cur</u> | <u>prev</u>) 09:47 June 9, 2022 <u>feline_instinct</u> (<u>talk</u> | <u>contribs</u>) . . (124,095 bytes) (+55) *(Cleaned up source links, fixed more punctuation / grammar.)* (<u>undo</u>) *(<u>Tags</u>: Mobile edit, Mobile web edit)*

- (cur | <u>prev</u>) 09:35 June 9, 2022 <u>feline_instinct</u> (<u>talk</u> | <u>contribs</u>) . . (122,329 bytes) (−226) *(Removed "It was reported that, prior to the suicide, Billings removed every tooth from both of his parents and swallowed them whole." from the ISAAC BILLINGS entry; not an essential detail for the list summary. Information is found on subject's main page.)* (<u>undo</u>) *(<u>Tags</u>: Mobile edit, Mobile web edit)*

- (<u>cur</u> | <u>prev</u>) 09:17 June 9, 2022 <u>feline_instinct</u> (<u>talk</u> | <u>contribs</u>) . . (122,555 bytes) (-244) *(Removed "Autopsy revealed Chapman's liver was most likely on the verge of total failure, and he'd been suffering from cirrhosis for quite some time prior to the murders." from the ANDREW CHAPMAN entry; not relevant to the crime. Biographical information already exists on subject's main page.)* (<u>undo</u>) *(Tags: Mobile edit, Mobile web edit)*

- (<u>cur</u> | <u>prev</u>) 09:08 June 9, 2022 <u>feline_instinct</u> (<u>talk</u> | <u>contribs</u>) . . (122,311 bytes) (−724) *(Removed unconfirmed details about subject handing his wife "a plastic bag containing every one of their children's teeth" at her place of employment from the SETH NICHOLSON entry. Previous edit never provided a reliable source.)* (<u>undo</u>) *(<u>Tags</u>: Mobile edit, Mobile web edit)*

- (<u>cur</u> | <u>prev</u>) 09:02 June 9, 2022 <u>feline_instinct</u> (<u>talk</u> | <u>contribs</u>) . . (123,035 bytes) (+28) *(Fixed punctuation / grammar.)* (<u>undo</u>) *(<u>Tags</u>: Mobile edit, Mobile web edit)*

- (cur | prev) 08:53 June 9, 2022 feline_instinct (talk | contribs) . . (123,107 bytes) (-345) *(Removed "Every wall in the home had been graffitied with drawings of yellow monsters with long teeth. from DANIEL BRADLEY entry; not relevant to the crime. Every kid draws monster. That doesn't make them a murderer.)* (undo) *(Tags: Mobile edit, Mobile web edit)*

- (cur | prev) 08:45 June 9, 2022 feline_instinct (talk | contribs) . . (122,972 bytes) (−312) *(Removed "When questioned by authorities, Roberts claimed he was forced to commit the murders by a yellow demon with sharp teeth." from the JIM ROBERTS entry; no reliable source cited.)* (undo) *(Tags: Mobile edit, Mobile web edit)*

- (cur | prev) 08:39 June 9, 2022 feline_instinct (talk | contribs) . . (123,061 bytes) (+102) *(Cleaned up some external links.)* (undo) *(Tags: Mobile edit, Mobile web edit)*

- (cur | prev) 08:25 June 9, 2022 feline_instinct (talk | contribs) . . (122,859 bytes) (-251) *(Removed "When arrested, it was discovered that every single one of Leer's teeth had been removed and replaced with dentures." from the JONATHAN LEER entry; not relevant or interesting enough to note in list summary; it is not uncommon for people to lose their teeth as they age.)* (undo) *(Tags: Mobile edit, Mobile web edit)*

- (cur | prev) 08:22 June 9, 2022 feline_instinct (talk | contribs) . . (222,808 bytes) (-412) *(From the GEOFF DONALDSON entry, I removed the "someone with yellow eyes" detail about the man Donaldson claimed broke into their home, and also the "swallowing every one of his own teeth" detail about Donaldson's suicide*

LIST OF FAMILICIDES IN THE UNITES STATES

in prison; in both cases, these edits were not correctly cited—but even if they were, I am doubtful of their relevancy in the list summary. Entries here should be concise, leaving extraneous details for each subject's individual pages.) (<u>undo</u>) *(<u>Tags</u>: Mobile edit, Mobile web edit)*

- (<u>cur</u> | <u>prev</u>) 08:15 June 9, 2022 <u>feline_instinct</u> (<u>talk</u> | <u>contribs</u>) . . (122,796 bytes) -207) *(Removed "In his study, investigators discovered the charred remains of his most recent manuscript. Only the title—'The Jaundiced Man'—remained undamaged." from the end of the PAUL MICHAEL ANDERSON entry; not essential information for a list summary, plus it's already mentioned on the subject's main page.)* (<u>undo</u>) *(<u>Tags</u>: Mobile edit, Mobile web edit)*

- (<u>cur</u> | <u>prev</u>) 08:12 June 9, 2022 <u>feline_instinct</u> (<u>talk</u> | <u>contribs</u>) . . (121,219 bytes) (-190) *(Removed "He would often claim to teammates that a 'man with yellow skin' was stalking him." from the BRADY MARTIN entry; Martin suffered a long list of symptoms related to probable schizophrenia and I'm unsure why specifying this particular delusion is more important than the rest; everything is already laid out on the subject's main page, anyway, so there's no point in adding extra space to a list summary.)* (<u>undo</u>) *(<u>Tags</u>: Mobile edit, Mobile web edit)*

- (<u>cur</u> | <u>prev</u>) 08:07, June 9, 2022 <u>feline_instinct</u> (<u>talk</u> | <u>contribs</u>) . . (191,109 bytes) (-274) *(Removed unsourced and potentially biased material in article introduction about "The Jaundiced Man connection". I will further elaborate on the talk page after fixing the rest of the previous editor's misguided revisions.)* (undo) *(<u>Tags</u>: Mobile edit, Mobile web edit)*

- (cur | prev) 22:20, June 1, 2022 ApocalypseParty (talk | contribs) . . (85,656 bytes) (+3,137) *(Added relevant information pertaining to The Jaundiced Man and his possible involvement with several familicides— specifically, with familicides that occurred in the 1900s, 1950s, and 2000s. Please query before deleting. My sources are sound.)* (undo)

- (cur | prev) 12:02, January 14, 2022 WikiCleanerBot (talk | contribs) . . (119,391 bytes) (0) *(Fix errors for CW Project.)* (undo) *(Tags: WPCleaner)*

(newest | oldest) View (newer 50 | older 50) (20 | 50 | 100 | 250 | 500)

Article	Talk

Read	Edit	New Section	View History

Talk:List of familicides in the United States (by decade)

This article was nominated for deletion on May 24, 2022. The result of the discussion was **keep**.

This article is within the scope of WikiProject Lists, an attempt to structure and organize all list pages on Wikipedia. If you wish to help, please visit the project page, where you can join the project and/or contribute to the discussion.

This article has been rated as **List-Class** on the project's quality scale.

This article has been rated as **Low-Importance** on the project's importance scale.

LIST OF FAMILICIDES IN THE UNITES STATES

19th century [edit]

Why does this list begin with the 20th century? Surely there are recorded familicides before the 1900s, right? — CHAINSAWENEMA (talk) 04:49, March 2, 2016 (UTC) [reply]

Mass shooter criteria [edit]

There are several mass shooters listed here who killed more than just their family. Should they still be included? For example, Charles Whitman murdered his wife and mother, but he also killed nearly 20 other random people afterward. Can that still be defined as a familicide, or has the crime evolved into something else with the additional homicides? —shirleyjacksonfangrrl (talk) 08:92, February 17, 2019 (UTC) [reply]

Feminist agenda? [edit]

Why is it almost every entry on this list, spanning over a century, features a white male as the perpetrator? I made numerous edits to the page with additional entries featuring blacks and mexicans but people keep deleting them because there aren't enough sources? I put sources on everything I edit. Just because they aren't citing the so-called "main-stream media" that means they don't count? I thought wikipedia was supposed to be unbiased. — OneSixTwentyOne (talk) 23:12, July 19, 2021 (UTC) [reply]

The Jaundiced Man connection [edit]

I discovered some bizarre and frankly troubling page edits made by ApocalypseParty (talk) on June 1, 2022. Check out the revision history for the specific entries, but the basic gist is ApocalypseParty has created a series of connections between several of the familicides implying they might be associated with each other—if that is not the implication ApocalypseParty is intending, then I am having trouble understanding any other alternatives. ApocalypseParty seems to believe someone known only as "The Jaundiced Man" might be responsible—or at least associated—with these crimes. In many cases, this Jaundiced Man appears to be a yellow demon with sharp teeth—or, maybe the demon feeds on others' teeth? It is unclear. Either way, it doesn't belong on the page. Several of the sources cited are also questionable, and in at least one instance I suspect the website was created solely for the purpose of pushing ApocalypseParty's yellow demon guy agenda. It doesn't matter, of course. These edits were either a prank, or they were made by someone with deeply troubling mental problems, and I am a little concerned for the user's health. I've tried reaching out to them via their separate talk page, but never received a response. If there is any possibility of a mod tracking down this user's IP address and contacting their local authorities for a wellness check, I would highly appreciate it. Something isn't right here.—feline_instinct (talk) 11:47 June 11, 2022 [reply]

Do you have a family feline_instinct (talk)? I don't. At least, not anymore. But I did. I used to have a wife. I used to have a kid. They're long gone now. A consequence of sticking my nose in unwanted places, I suppose. You do not know what you are talking about and that is very clear to everybody here. I asked not to delete my edits without consulting me first. Do not tell me what is and isn't relevant. I know what is relevant. Have you ever tasted a tooth? Have you ever swallowed one? One that didn't belong to you, I mean. It changes a person. I know this from first-hand experience. I've had to do many things while researching the Jaundiced Man. Some things I am less proud of than others. You ask about my sources. You claim these connections are fictitious. You suggest my mental health is in jeopardy. I understand all of this. I appreciate the concern. Unfortunately it's too late for that. I have gone too far. There is no taking back what has already occurred. The only thing I can do now is spread the word and hopefully warn somebody else who can actually do some good. And one of the ways I am attempting to do this is by connecting the clues for people. Clues people wouldn't otherwise see. So, yes, I understand some of these details are already on the subjects' main pages, but that isn't going to help anybody connect the pieces—don't you see? They need them all together, on the same list. By removing my edits, you are doing a disservice to not just yourself but the world. This information needs to be public. Do not delete them again. It will not be good for you. Do not think I won't be able to track you down. I know realities you couldn't even dream of existing. — ApocalypseParty (talk) 03:03 June 12, 2022 [reply]

STORY NOTES

Note: It is highly recommended that you only read these story notes after finishing the collection. Don't say I didn't warn you . . .

"INDIANA DEATH SONG"—Easily the hardest and most personal creative project I've ever finished. Longtime followers of my career undoubtedly know what I'm about to say already, but this novella is based largely on my own childhood. Specifically, ages 13-16. I have struggled for fifteen years trying to write this story. For the longest time, it was meant to be a full-length literary novel. Only when I discovered a route into *genre* did things finally start clicking into place—plus, the realization that it didn't have to be a novel, that it could simply exist as a novella. I recommend googling "Truman Show syndrome" when you get the chance, because it's a real thing that I experienced for several years in my youth. A *lot* of "Indiana Death Song" is true, but a lot of it is also fictional. I'll let you, the reader, speculate on what really happened.

"YOU ARE MY NEIGHBOR"—When I was younger, a friend and I developed an unexplainable habit of breaking my neighbor's garage window. The neighbor would get it fixed, then that very night we would toss a brick through it and run away, laughing like fools without any concept of karma. To this day, I still don't know why we did it. Maybe writing "You Are My Neighbor" was my own attempt at trying to figure it out. Also, kind of unrelated but not really—a couple years after we stopped shattering his window, my friend's older brother broke into the neighbor's house and discovered a goddamn *mountain lion* caged in the basement.

"BLOOD DUST"—I shamelessly adapted this story from the song "Wild Pack of Family Dogs" by Modest Mouse. Wait. My lawyer just told me to use the word "interpreted" instead. Okay, I shamelessly *interpreted* this story from the song "Wild Pack of Family Dogs" by Modest Mouse. *The Moon & Antarctica* is my favorite album of all time, and it's on constant repeat in our house and my car. Several years ago, for an entire summer, my partner's son Dylan (the inspiration for "Bobby" from *We Need to Do Something*) would sing "Wild Pack of Family Dogs" over and over, which made me really realize how bleak and weirdly hopeful the lyrics were. After so long I was left with no choice but to try riffing on the song's incredible imagery.

"FISH"—I lost my virginity to an older woman on her period. Sometimes it's as simple as that, folks.

"IN THE ATTIC OF THE UNIVERSE"—By far the oldest story of mine included in this collection, and I have no memory of writing it, but I think it was the first time someone paid me for my fiction, even if it was only . . . uh, five dollars. For that reason alone, it will always hold a special place in my heart. The title comes from an album by The Antlers, although I feel like their other album *Hospice* is far superior. Check it out sometime.

"DISINTEGRATION IS QUITE PAINLESS"—I grew up in Northwest Indiana, if the stories in this collection didn't already make that abundantly clear. This specific area of the state is the home of many dunes, despite not being near a desert or a beach—okay, it *is* near Lake Michigan, but *my town* wasn't near it. I'm not going to pretend to understand anything about geography here, so don't expect me to explain it.

When I was a kid, a girl in my neighborhood asked me if I was interested in checking out "the homeless cannibal who lives in the dunes". I confirmed I was very much interested without so much as a second of hesitation. As she led me across town toward these dunes, which were of course located deep in the woods in the middle of nowhere,

I couldn't help but suspect the homeless cannibal was something she'd made up, and her real motivation had something more to do with intimacy. I'd never been kissed before, and I was nervous as hell about the whole thing. As it turns out, I don't know what she had planned, because shortly after arriving at the dunes we both fell down a steep hill, followed by our bicycles crashing directly upon us. She started crying and we went our separate ways. In retrospect, the homeless cannibal was probably more likely than the two of us ever making out.

The story title comes from a Lovecraft quote. I haven't read a lot of Lovecraft and am not the biggest fan of his work, but I was invited to a "Lovecraftian anthology" called *Shadows Over Main Street*, so my process included googling cool Lovecraft quotes that I could maybe recycle into a title, and then create a short story from that. I think it worked out pretty well. The full quote, if you're interested, comes from a story called "From Beyond"— *"You think those floundering things wiped out the servants? Fool, they are harmless! But the servants are gone, aren't they? [. . .] Things are hunting me now—the things that devour and dissolve—but I know how to elude them. [. . .] My pets are not pretty, for they come out of places where aesthetic standards are—very different. Disintegration is quite painless, I assure you—but I want you to see them. I almost saw them, but I knew how to stop."*

I have not actually read "From Beyond", so my apologies in advance if it's one of his ultra-racist stories. Maybe they're all ultra-racist. I have not done my homework here and deserve any and all social media shaming that I receive.

"SCRAPS"—I worked eight years as a hotel night auditor, from 2012 to 2020. In that time I encountered a vast variety of people. Check out my work memoir / absurdist comedy novel *The Nightly Disease* for a deeper exploration of what it's like to work at a hotel. But what inspired "Scraps" specifically were these two kids—brother and sister, probably early teens at the oldest—who returned to the hotel every night for just over a week asking for food. They were shy and afraid and always wore the same dirty clothes. Because I am not a monster, I of course gave them plenty of fruit and peanut butter sandwiches and juice from the kitchen and let them hang out in the lobby for as long as they wished. Somehow my manager found out about this, and she was not pleased. She told me next time they showed up to call the cops, that I was essentially helping them *steal* from the hotel. I laughed and told her I would not do any such thing, and would—in fact—continue to feed them if they continued showing up. I then had two nights off from work. I never saw them again. I don't know if the part-time auditor got the cops involved, or what happened. I hope they're okay and doing better now, at least.

"BOY TAKES AFTER HIS MOTHER"—I originally wrote this for a Misfits tribute anthology, but it was rejected. I later sold it to *Unnerving Magazine*, although I'm still pissed about that initial rejection. The story is a *perfect* riff on "Mommy, Can I Go Out and Kill Tonight?" One fun and cool fact about myself is I tend to hold grudges for years and years. I am a healthy person.

"EVERY BREATH IS A CHOICE"—I don't recollect what inspired this story, or when I wrote it. It was published in a charity anthology last year (2022), but I know it was sitting around for several years before then. The decision our protagonist is forced to make is such a fucking mean thing to put a character through. I was thinking about this story the other day and wondered who I would choose in a similar scenario: my partner, Lori—or my dog, Frank. And, to be honest, I still don't know. I guess, because Lori is more likely to read this collection than my dog, I'm going to *say* I'm choosing Lori here. But also, as I type this, guess who is curled up on my lap? Not Lori, I'll tell you that much.

"MUNCHAUSEN"—This one is inspired by the real-life story of Dee Dee Blanchard and Gypsy Rose. I wrote it after watching the truly nuts HBO documentary *Mommy Dead and Dearest*.

"ABDUCTION (REPRISE)"—A couple years back, I was talking to my mom on the phone and she nonchalantly mentioned that someone once tried to kidnap me as a baby while she was shopping at Sam's Club. I found myself getting a little obsessed with this discovery. It's a weird thing to learn about yourself. I was left with two choices: track down the woman who tried to abduct me, or just write a story about it and move on. The latter proved less time-consuming.

"VIDEO NASTIES"—Another story inspired by real-life events, sadly. Look up the murder of James Bulger and prepare to be depressed for the rest of your life. I apologize in advance.

"LIST OF FAMILICIDES IN THE UNITED STATES (BY DECADE)"—Sometimes when I'm tired, I browse lists containing abnormal statistics on Wikipedia. Unsolved murders, yes, of course, but I prefer more *specific* weirdness. Like people who vanished without a trace, or children who have been convicted of murder. My favorite ones usually involve family annihilation of some type. I use the word "favorite" here not in an edgelord sort of way. I don't take any joy in reading these articles. But there's something endlessly fascinating about it all and sometimes I can't stop thinking about them. My brain craves things that are not good for me. I won't pretend to understand it.

STORY CREDITS

"You Are My Neighbor" appeared in *Miscreations: Gods, Monstrosities & Other Horrors,* February 2020; "Blood Dust" appeared in *Chiral Mad 3,* April 2016; "Fish" appeared in *Hazardous Encounters*, February 2014; "In the Attic of the Universe" appeared in *New Dawn Fades,* November 2011; "Disintegration is Quite Painless" appeared in *Shadows Over Main Street Volume 2,* October 2017; "Scraps" appeared in *Ashes and Entropy,* December 2018; "Boy Takes After His Mother" appeared in *Unnerving Magazine #4,* October 2017; "Every Breath is a Choice" appeared in *Blood Bank,* May 2022; "Munchausen" appeared in *The Pulp Horror Book of Phobias,* May 2019; "Video Nasties" appeared in *Jamais Vu #1,* January 2014; "Abduction (Reprise)", "List of familicides in the United States (by decade)", and "Indiana Death Song" are original to this collection.

ABOUT THE AUTHOR

Max Booth III grew up in Northwest Indiana and now lives in San Antonio, TX. He's the head ghoul at Ghoulish Books, the host of the *GHOULISH* podcast, and the co-founder of the Ghoulish Book Festival. Learn more about his work at www.TalesFromTheBooth.com.

CPSIA information can be obtained
at www.ICGtesting.com
Printed in the USA
LVHW091741150723
752491LV00036B/674

9 781954 899148